MY NAME IS LEON

a novel

Kit de Waal

Simon and Schuster

New York   London   Toronto   Sydney   New Delhi

Simon & Schuster
1230 Avenue of the Americas
New York, NY 10020

Copyright © 2016 by Kit de Waal
Originally published in Great Britain in 2016 by Penguin Random House UK

First Simon & Schuster hardcover edition July 2016

SIMON & SCHUSTER and colophon are registered trademarks
of Simon & Schuster, Inc.

For information about special discounts for bulk purchases,
please contact Simon & Schuster Special Sales at 1-866-506-1949
or business@simonandschuster.com.

The Simon & Schuster Speakers Bureau can bring authors to
your live event. For more information or to book an event contact
the Simon & Schuster Speakers Bureau at 1-866-248-3049 or
visit our website at www.simonspeakers.com.

Interior design by Lewelin Polanco

Manufactured in the United States of America

10 9 8 7 6 5 4 3 2 1

Library of Congress Cataloging-in-Publication Data

Names: De Waal, Kit, author.
Title: My name is Leon : a novel / by Kit de Waal.
Description: New York : Simon and Schuster, 2016.
Subjects: LCSH: Brothers—Fiction. | Ex-foster children—Fiction. | Racially
    mixed families—Fiction.
Classification: LCC PR6104.E2336 M9 2016 | DDC 823/.92—dc23 LC
record available at http://lccn.loc.gov/2016000754

ISBN 978-1-5011-1745-9
ISBN 978-1-5011-1747-3 (ebook)

FOR BETHANY AND LUKE

MY NAME IS LEON

1

No one has to tell Leon that this is a special moment. Everything else in the hospital seems to have gone quiet and disappeared. The nurse makes him wash his hands and sit up straight.

"Careful, now," she says. "He's very precious."

But Leon already knows. The nurse places the brand-new baby in his arms with its face toward Leon so that they can look at each other.

"You have a brother now," she says. "And you'll be able to look after him. What are you? Ten?"

"He's nearly nine," says Leon's mom, looking over. "Eight years and nine months. Nearly."

Leon's mom is talking to Tina about when the baby was coming out, about the hours and the minutes and the pain.

"Well," says the nurse, adjusting the baby's blanket, "you're nice and big for your age. A right little man."

She pats Leon on his head and brushes the side of his cheek with her finger. "He's a beauty, isn't he? Both of you are."

She smiles at Leon and he knows that she's kind and that she'll look after the baby when he isn't there. The baby has the smallest fingers Leon has ever seen. He looks like a doll with its eyes closed. He has silky white hair on the very top of his head and a tiny pair of lips that keep opening and closing. Through the holey blanket, Leon can feel baby warmth on his belly and his legs and then the baby begins to wriggle.

"I hope you're having a nice dream, baby," Leon whispers.

After a while, Leon's arm begins to hurt and just when it gets really bad the nurse comes along. She picks the baby up and tries to give him to Leon's mom.

"He'll need feeding soon," she says.

But Leon's mom has her handbag on her lap.

"Can I do it in a minute? Sorry, I was just going to the smoking room."

She moves off the bed carefully, holding on to Tina's arm, and shuffles away.

"Leon, you watch him, love," she says, hobbling off.

Leon watches the nurse watching his mother walk away but when she looks at Leon she's smiling again.

"I tell you what we'll do," she says, placing the baby in the crib next to the bed. "You stay here and have a little chat with your brother and tell him all about yourself. But when your mommy comes back it will be time for his feed and you'll have to get on home. All right, sweetheart?"

Leon nods. "Shall I wash my hands again?" he asks, showing her his palms.

"I think you'll be all right. You just stand here and if he starts crying, you come and fetch me. Okay?"

"Yes."

Leon makes a list in his head and then starts at the beginning.

"My name is Leon and my birthday is on the fifth of July, nineteen seventy-one. Your birthday is today. School's all right but you have to go nearly every day and Miss Sheldon won't let proper soccer balls in the playground. Nor bikes but I'm too tall for mine anyway. I've got two Easter eggs and there's toys inside one of them. I don't think you can have chocolate yet. The best program is *The Dukes of Hazzard* but there are baby programs as well. I don't watch them anymore. Mom says you can't sleep in my room till you're older, about three, she said. She's bought you a shopping basket with a cloth in it for your bed. She says it's the same basket Moses had but it looks new. My dad had a car with no roof and he took me for a drive in it once. But then he sold it."

Leon doesn't know what to say about the baby's dad because he has never seen him, so he talks about their mother.

"You can call her Carol if you like, when you can talk. You probably don't know but she's beautiful. Everyone's always saying it. I think you look like her. I don't. I look like my dad. Mom says he's colored but Dad says he's black but they're both wrong because he's dark brown and I'm light brown. I'll teach you your colors and your numbers because I'm the cleverest in my class. You have to use your fingers in the beginning."

Leon carefully feels the downy fluff on the baby's head.

"You've got blond hair and she's got blond hair. We've both got thin eyebrows and we've both got long fingers. Look."

Leon holds his hand up. And the baby opens his eyes. They are a dusty blue with a deep black center, like a big period. The baby blinks slowly and makes little kissing noises with his mouth.

"Sometimes she takes me to Auntie Tina up on the next landing. I can walk up to Auntie Tina's on my own but if you come, I'll have to carry you in the basket."

The baby won't be able to speak until it's much bigger so Leon just carries on.

"I won't drop you," he says. "I'm big for my age."

He watches the baby blowing him kisses and leans into the crib and touches the baby's lips with his fingertip.

His mom and Tina and the nurse come back all at the same time. Leon's mom comes straight over to the crib and puts her arm round Leon. She kisses his cheek and his forehead.

"Two boys," she says. "I've got two beautiful, beautiful boys."

Leon puts his arms round his mom's waist. She's still got a round belly like the baby was still in there and she smells different. Or maybe it's just the hospital. All the babyness made Leon's mom puffed out and red in the face and now she's near back to being herself again. Everything except the belly. He carefully touches his mother through her flowery nightie.

"Are there any more in there?" he says.

The nurse and Tina and his mom all laugh at the same time.

"That's men for you," says the nurse. "All charm."

But Leon's mom bends down and puts her face close to Leon.

"No more," she says. "Just me and you and him. Always."

Tina puts her coat on and leaves ten cigarettes on the bed for Carol to have later.

"Thanks, Tina," she says, "and thanks for having Leon again. Think I'll be out on Tuesday by the sound of it."

Carol shuffles up in the bed and the nurse puts the baby in her arms. He is making little breathing noises that sound like the beginning of a cry. Leon's mom begins to unfasten her cardigan.

"Isn't he lovely, Leon? You be good, all right?" and she kisses him again.

The whole of the baby's head fits into her hand.

"Come to Mommy," she whispers and cradles him against her chest.

Tina's flat is very different from Leon's but it's exactly the same as well. Both maisonettes have two bedrooms and a bathroom upstairs and a kitchen and living room downstairs.

Leon's house is on the ground floor of the first block by the divided highway and Tina's house is up on the next landing. The roadway has three rows of traffic on each side and the cars go so fast that they put a barrier up by the sidewalk. Now if Leon and Carol want to cross the road, they have to walk for ages to go to a crossing and press a button and wait until it starts to beep. The first time it was exciting but now it just makes it take longer to get to school in the morning.

Tina lets Leon sleep in the same bedroom as her baby. She always makes a bouncy, comfortable bed when Leon stays. She takes two cushions off the sofa and then wraps them in a blanket and puts a little baby's quilt over him. When he is lying down she throws some coats on top and covers everything over with a bedspread. It's like a nest or a den because no one would know he was there, like camouflage in the jungle. His bed looks like a pile of clothes in the corner but then "AAAGGGH," there is a monster underneath and it jumps up and kills you. Tina always leaves the light on in the hall but tells him he has to be very quiet because of her baby.

Her baby is big and wobbly and his name suits him. Bobby. Wobbly Bobby. His head is too big for his body and when Leon plays with him, he always gets some of Bobby's dribble on his hand. Bobby's Wobbly Dribble. Leon's brother won't be like Bobby and just suck on his plastic toys all day and get his bib soaking wet. He won't topple over on the sofa under the weight of his big head and just stay there till someone moves him. Leon always sits Bobby up but then Bobby thinks it's a game and keeps on doing it.

Bobby loves Leon. He can't talk and, anyway, he always has a pacifier in his mouth but as soon as Leon walks in the door, Bobby wobbles across the carpet and holds Leon's legs. Then he puts out his arms for Leon to pick him up. When Leon's brother is older they're going to play together, soldiers and Action Man. They're going to both have machine guns and run all over the house shooting at targets. Bobby can watch.

Tina's house always has a window open and smells of baby lotion. Tina looks a bit like a baby herself because she's got a round face with puffy cheeks and round eyes that bulge. She makes her hair different colors all the time but she's never happy with it and Carol keeps telling her to go blond.

Tina always says, "If I had your face, Carol, it wouldn't matter so much," and Leon thinks she's right.

Tina has a leather sofa that is cold and slippery on Leon's legs and a sheepskin rug in front of the gas fire and a massive TV. She doesn't let Leon call her "Tina," like he calls his mom "Carol." He has to call her "Auntie Tina" and he has to call Carol "Mom" because she says children have to have respect. And she doesn't let Leon eat in front of the TV. He has to sit at a wooden table in the kitchen where there isn't much room because she has a big fridge-freezer with ice cream in it. Bobby sits in his high chair smiling at Leon and Tina puts two scoops in Leon's bowl and one for Bobby. Leon's brother will probably only get half a scoop because he'll be the smallest.

Sometimes, Tina's boyfriend comes, but when he sees Leon he always says, "Again?" and Tina says, "I know."

2

The first day when Carol brings the baby home, Tina and Leon and Bobby are waiting by the door. Carol holds the basket carefully with both hands and walks in whispering, "He's just gone to sleep."

She puts the baby on the floor in the living room and Leon tiptoes over. The baby has grown and his face looks different. He's wearing a new outfit in pale blue with a matching hat and he has a yellow fluffy blanket over his legs. Tina and Bobby go home and Carol and Leon sit on the carpet and watch the baby. They watch the baby turn his head and open his lips. They watch the baby move one of his miniature hands and when the baby yawns they both open their mouths and yawn with him.

Carol tilts her head.

"Isn't he beautiful?" she says.

"Yes."

Leon and Carol lean back against the sofa and hold hands.

"Aren't we lucky?" she says.

All that day and the next day, the baby is like the television. Leon can't stop watching him and all his baby movements. He hardly cries and when he does it sounds like a little kitten or a puppy. He watches Carol change the baby on a special plastic mat that's got rocking horses on it. The baby has got a really small willy but big balls. Leon hopes the baby's willy will catch up. Babies' poo is a funny color—it's not brown, it's greeny yellow—and Carol has to wipe all the poo off with special new baby lotion. Carol and Leon bathe the baby together. Carol holds him in a few inches of water and Leon splashes his belly and his bum. The baby's got a special white towel all to himself and when he's wrapped in it, Leon thinks he looks like the Baby Jesus in his manger. Maybe that's why his mom bought him Moses's basket, because he's come from God.

The baby blinks slowly and stares at Leon like he's trying to work out who he is.

"I'm your brother," says Leon. "Big brother."

The baby doesn't say anything back.

"Big. Brother," says Leon. "My. Name. Is. Leon. I am eight and three-quarters. I am a boy."

The baby stretches himself out to say he understands.

Leon tells everybody at school about his new brother. His teacher says he can tell the class, so Leon stands up after assembly.

"I've got a new baby brother. He's really small and he sleeps nearly all the time. That's normal because he's concentrating on growing. My mom says all babies are different, some sleep and some cry. She said that when I was a baby I was as good as gold except when I was hungry. I'm the one in charge of my baby when Mom's not there. When the baby was born he had a funny-shaped head but now his head has gone round again."

Everyone claps and then Leon draws a picture and takes it

home. His mom puts it on the fridge with a magnet next to a photograph that Tina took at the hospital.

After a few weeks, Carol says Leon can't go to school because it's too wet and rainy. That means Leon can play all day and put the television on and make toast if he's hungry. Carol leaves him in charge when she goes to the phone booth and when she comes back she's out of breath and asks him if the baby's all right. Leon would never let anything happen to the baby, so she worries for nothing.

When Tina comes round she knocks on the door and then lets herself in with a key. She always, always says the same thing—"Cal? It's me, Tina. Only Tina"—and when Leon was little he thought that "Only Tina" was her name. She brings loads and loads of clothes from Bobby and a bagful of toys. Some of the toys are quite good, even though they are for little kids, and Leon hides the best ones in his room.

Tina and his mom are in the kitchen.

"You still look tired, Cal. Is the baby keeping you up?"

Tina sounds like the nurse at the hospital, a little bit bossy. Carol starts crying. She's always crying these days.

"It's not like last time. I just feel sort of down, you know. I'm all right, it's just things getting on top of me."

Tina is saying "Ssshh" all the time and then he can hear her making a cup of tea. Sometimes when Tina comes to Leon's house she does the washing up as well and makes him beans on toast.

"Get yourself to the doctor, Cal. Honest, you've got to."

"I will, I will."

"You've got Leon to think of as well as the baby."

"Leon's all right," Carol says with a sniff. "He's a good kid, just gets on with it. He loves the baby, he really does, but everything else goes over his head. All he thinks about is guns and cars."

"You eating?"

"Byron came round every day when Leon was a baby. He

used to do all the cooking. He was great with Leon as well. Gave me a bit of a break."

Leon can hear Tina running the faucet and moving the dishes into the sink.

"If it was me, Cal, I'd see the doctor."

"Then when he went inside and I got depressed, they wanted me to go to some bloody center twice a week. Me with a baby at home, feeling like shit. Feeling like this."

"I'll come with you if you like. Bobby's in day care every morning now. We could go first thing."

"Them pills gave me nightmares as well."

"You need something, Cal."

"I know."

Later, when Leon's in bed, Carol comes into his room.

"I've just got him off to sleep," she says and sits down. "Did he wake you up?"

"I can't sleep, Mom."

"Try," she says.

"I can't. Can I have a story?"

Carol says nothing for a few moments and he thinks she might say no or that she's too tired but she takes a deep breath and starts.

"This is a story my dad used to tell me."

"Is it scary?"

"Scary?" Carol shakes her head and smiles. "No, listen. Once upon a time there was a mother with two boys, one was a baby. The oldest boy was very noisy. He had a very loud voice and he used to shout and bang his drum and kick the door and sing at the top of his voice and the mother used to tell him off. 'Ssssh,' she would say, 'you'll wake the baby.' And the boy's teacher would say, 'Ssssh, we can't do our lessons.' And the minister at church would say, 'Ssssh. We're in a holy place.' And the boy felt lonely like nobody loved him. He decided to run away. But when he got to the edge of the village, he saw a big bad wolf coming to eat everyone up. He was too far away to run back and warn everyone, so he opened his mouth as wide as he could and he roared, 'THERE'S A WOLF COMING!' And he saved the whole village and his mother and his brother, and nobody ever told him to be quiet again."

"Is that the end?"

"Yes. They all lived happily ever after. Sleep time now. Snuggle in. School tomorrow, sweetheart," she says and strokes his forehead.

"Am I sick? I might be sick," he says.

"No, you're not sick. Definitely school tomorrow."

Carol says this every night but it's been five days since Leon went to school.

"If you don't go to school you won't learn anything, Leon. If you don't learn anything you can't get a good job and a nice house and lots of toys. You like toys, don't you? I saw you! I saw those toys you took up to your room! Eh? Eh?"

Carol starts scrabbling her fingers on his chest, making him laugh.

"And anyway, you get bored at home and drive me nuts."

"I can help with the baby," Leon says.

"Jake. His name is Jake."

"You said—"

"It's his dad's middle name. Well, I changed Jack to Jake because I like it better. Do you, Leon?"

She kisses him before she turns off the light but Leon doesn't kiss her back. She promised he could call the baby Bo from *The Dukes of Hazzard*. Bo's got a red car and blond hair. His real name is Beauregard Duke and he's the best one in the whole show. Jake-regard sounds stupid. Leon doesn't know anyone at school called Jake and no one on TV called Jake. There is a shop on the other side of the highway called "Jake's Bakes" where they sell pies and fries and when the baby goes to school he's going to get teased about it. Leon wonders if he can get his mom to change her mind. Jake is the worst name he's ever heard.

3

Leon has begun to notice the things that make his mom cry: when Jake makes a lot of noise; when she hasn't got any money; when she comes back from the phone booth; when Leon asks too many questions; and when she's staring at Jake.

It's the third night that Leon and Jake are both sleeping at Tina's. It keeps happening all the time. Carol takes them up to Tina's and then she leaves them there for a few days. Last week it was two nights and before that it was three nights and sometimes it feels like they're never going home. Jake's basket goes next to Leon's den bed. Leon watches Jake for a few minutes because he makes special whistling noises when he breathes out and he makes his little hands into fists like Muhammad Ali. Jake opens his eyes and doesn't even cry. His eyes have become bright, zingy blue but the middle is still perfectly black, like a drop of ink in the sea. Leon and Jake like to just look at each other for a while and then Leon sings a baby song or whispers something.

"Are you all right, Jake? Sleepy time, sleepy time. Close your eyes. You're all right, Jakey. It's all right. Sleepy time, Jakey."

It's peaceful and cozy in the bedroom with Jake and Wobbly Bobby and the heavy weight of the coats. He watches the smear of light on the wall, listens to the babies breathing, hears the sizzling tires on the wet road outside.

The next day Carol comes to collect them from Tina's. She sounds excited and happy and stays for ages in Tina's kitchen, so Leon creeps into the hall.

"I found him. Yeah, I went to his mate's house and I just kept knocking. I knew someone was in and I shouted through the letter box that I just wanted to give him a message. I kept on knocking and then he answered the door. Tony did. Just like that. I was really surprised. So was he. I told you he wasn't avoiding me. He just didn't realize I was due. I mean, I told him but he forgot. He said he was working away. And anyway, he's not very good with dates."

Tina isn't asking questions like she usually does. So Carol just carries on.

"He said he couldn't talk for long because he had to get home. He's still living with that cow but I don't know why he's still with her. Neither does he. I told him he could move in with us. I know he wants to see Jake but he's got to be careful cuz if she finds out she'll stop him seeing his little girl and he dotes on her. She's done it before, she just uses his daughter to keep him. I'd never do that."

Tina offers Carol a biscuit. Tina's biscuit tin is always crammed full. Sometimes if there are lots of broken ones, she lets Leon pick them all out and eat them.

"No, thanks. Anyway, he said he's moving out. She doesn't know and he's not letting on until he's got everything in place. At his age, he wants to settle down for good."

"His age?"

"He's thirty-nine. You'd never know it, though. He's not old or anything."

"He's nearly forty."

"Thirty-nine. Honest, he doesn't look it. He looks our age."

"Twenty-five?"

"Well, you know, early thirties, but anyway, yeah, he said it hasn't been right for years between them. You know me, Tina. I never meant to hurt anyone but he wasn't happy even before he met me. If he was, he wouldn't have given me a second look, would he? He told me once he's got family in Bristol and Wolver-hampton, so he's not sure where he's going but when he gets there, it's gonna be just me and him."

"And the kids," says Tina.

"Yeah, of course. That's what he means. Me, him, and the kids."

"What about his daughter?"

"She'll come as well."

"Right," says Tina after a while. "And he told you that?"

"We only had a few minutes but yeah."

Leon goes back into the living room to check on Jake in his basket. He's nearly four months old and he's getting too big for his basket. He keeps hitting himself on the side and trying to get out and then he gets angry and makes noises like a cat. Leon got told off for trying to help him stand up, so Leon just watches now and tells Jake about different things he thinks he should know, like who is the best soccer player. But he doesn't feel like telling Jake about living with a girl and a cow in Bristol because Jake would probably start to cry.

4

Leon eats his toast sitting on the carpet by the patio doors. It's supposed to be summertime but the sky is the same color as the garden slabs—dull and gray—like the road to school, the cut-through to the precinct, or the dirty lane between the tower blocks and maisonettes.

There's a bundle of wood in one corner of the yard like someone was once going to repair the fence but forgot. Instead, the people in the maisonette next door have mended the hole with barbed wire because of their dog and the argument they had with Leon's dad when he used to live with them. Leon's dad stood in the garden, pointed his finger, and said (and Leon can remember it word for word), "If that fucking beast gets into this yard and bites my kid, I'll rip its fucking heart out, all right, Phil?"

The dog is called Samson and it has no fur on its chest because of a fight. Instead, it has a bald circle of pink skin and Leon imagines its little dog heart beating underneath and his dad's hands grabbing Samson's front paws and tearing them apart until the dog howls.

Leon knows the sound of a howling dog and when he sees Samson in next-door's garden, he stands and they look at each other through the rusty barbed-wire hole.

But today Samson isn't in his yard and Leon sits with his old Action Man and his new Action Man on the back step. Carol bought the new Action Man for Leon's birthday at the beginning of July and Tina bought the Action Man outfit. His dad sent him a card with some money in it, so Leon bought a better outfit with jackboots and a gun. When it's Christmas Leon wants two more Action Men with army uniforms. That will make four altogether and if he keeps going he will have a whole Action Man army.

Leon hears the doorbell and a man's voice. He picks up his new Action Man and they both crawl on their elbows, along the carpet, behind the sofa, and look through the gap in the door. A man is in the doorway letting cold air rush in. He's chunky and tall, wearing a long, black leather coat with a suit on underneath like he's the bad guy from James Bond. And from the way he has his hands in his pockets, he might also have a gun.

If he has got a gun and he tries to shoot, Leon will kick the door off the hinges and attack him before he can pull the trigger. Leon knows the moves people make before they shoot, like in westerns when they put their hands out to the side. Or, if Tina is in, Leon could rush past the man and ask her to come and help. Or call the police. Leon wishes he didn't always need the toilet when he gets excited or frightened. He bunches his trousers at the front and squeezes his crotch into the carpet to stop the pee coming out. The man speaks slowly with his head to one side like his mom is a baby or she's a bit slow.

"Don't make this into something it ain't, Carol."

Carol's crying and saying "Tony" all the time but the man isn't listening.

"I'm married. Good as. I didn't want another kid and I don't want another girlfriend. I don't want someone calling the house all the time and I don't want someone visiting my friends and making a fuss."

Carol's making gulping noises.

"Didn't I say that already?" the man says, still with his head to one side and still with his hand on the invisible gun.

"Don't pass messages to all my friends, either. It's pissing me off. Just leave it, Carol."

Carol starts speaking a few times but she can't get her breath, so her words come out lumpy and wrong.

"You haven't even laid eyes on him yet, Tony. What am I supposed to do? What am I supposed to think when you can't even be bothered to buy him a rattle?"

"Come off it, love. You saying this is about money?"

Carol's head shakes from side to side.

"No," he continues, "this is about the crap you've been telling yourself to cover a couple of months screwing in the back of my car, isn't it?"

Carol says nothing.

"I don't know what it is about you, Carol. Even with snot on your face you're a beautiful chick but you've got a brain like a rusty motor."

The man takes one of his hands out of his pocket and taps the side of his head.

"Yeah, rusty. As in not working. No inspection sticker. Breaking down. Not getting you from A to B. Worse than that, it's making A. Terrible. Fucking. Racket."

Leon and Carol both hear it at the same time. They hear the

man's voice go from soft to hard. Leon can tell Carol hears it because she jerks her head like he's slapped her. Leon stands up and
holds his Action Man in both hands.

"Listen, I'm not a bastard. All right? But start behaving yourself, for fuck's sake. No more of these bloody phone calls. Here."

The man puts his hand inside his jacket pocket.

"Take this for the kid and get on with your life. Get yourself
a nice boy that sells vacuums or used tires. Someone that finishes
work at five thirty and takes you to bingo. All right? It's not me,
love. It's just not me."

He tries to give something to Carol but instead she runs into
the living room, straight past Leon, picks Jake out of his basket,
and dashes back to the front door.

"He's yours, Tony, and you don't even care. Can't you even
come in, for pity's sake? Spend some time with him."

The man takes a step to the side and, as he does, he sees
Leon. He winks and makes two of his fingers into the barrel of a
gun that he points at Action Man and goes, "Poof." Leon smiles.
Then the man puts his head to the side again.

"Stop it, Carol," he says. "There's nothing more to be said."

He takes a step back and closes the door. Carol turns around
and screams at Leon.

"What are you doing listening? If you hadn't been sneaking
around he would have come in and spent two minutes with his
only son. Why are you so fucking nosy, Leon? Eh? You're always
creeping around, listening to things. Go to bed and stay there!"

Leon tiptoes upstairs into the bathroom and tries to be quiet
by peeing on the side of the bowl. He doesn't flush and he doesn't
wash his hands. He tries to count all the triangles on the wallpaper in his room but there are too many. He divides them up
into dark blue and light blue triangles and makes a pattern in
the shape of a tank by squeezing his eyes together and looking

through his eyelashes. Carol used to say sorry when she shouted at him but she forgets all the time these days, so tomorrow he will take twenty pence out of her purse. Twenty pence will buy him a Twix on his way back from school and he will throw the paper on the ground because he doesn't care.

Leon feels bad about smiling at the man who made Carol cry but if he comes back maybe they can both have pretend guns and shoot each other. Then again, he hopes that Jake won't grow up to be like his dad and say dangerous things in a quiet voice. Leon only smiled because it was polite. If the man comes back, Leon won't smile a second time. He will be on his guard and he'll protect Carol and Jake and then he won't get shouted at.

The next day his mom gets up early in the morning and says everything is going to be different. She says she's really sorry and she's going to try harder, so she makes a massive breakfast with pancakes and syrup like she saw in a recipe book. It doesn't taste nice and she starts crying when Leon doesn't eat it all. She mashes one up with some milk for Jake but as soon as she puts it in his mouth he's sick all over his top. She makes Leon promise to go to school so he can be smart and not have a life like she has.

"I want better for my boys," she says when Leon's hugging her on the settee. "I want you both to have lovely lives and lots of beautiful things. I want you to live in a nice house with a proper garden and want you to always love each other. I don't want any arguments. I'm so tired of arguments. And I want you to get out of this shithole. Get right out of it, far as you can. Don't look back. So you have to learn things and get an education. Don't be like me or your dad. You're so clever, Leon. Promise me something, sweetheart?"

"Yes, Mom."

"Look after him and look after yourself. Get something more out of life."

"Okay, Mom."

"Both of you. Do it for both of you."

She squeezes Leon so tight he has to push her away a little bit because he can't breathe.

"I'm going up now, love. Look after Jake for me."

Some days Leon doesn't go to school at all, just stays at home with Jake while their mom sleeps. But when he does go, Leon has to wake his mom up before he leaves to remind her about Jake. Sometimes she tells him to go away and he spends the whole day thinking about Jake's dinner or Jake's naptime. But other times, like when he's playing soccer or something, he forgets all about what's happening at home. Like when there was a new boy at school and the teacher told Leon to look after him at lunchtime. The new boy was much smaller than Leon and he looked scared. Leon told him where everything was and then they had to line up for their lunch. The new boy was called Adam and he had long hair. He said his dad was a teacher at another school. He said he had a dog.

"What sort of dog?" said Leon. "Is it an Alsatian or a Dobermann?"

"It's a poodle," he said. "It's my mom's. She calls it Candy."

"Oh," said Leon. "A poodle."

"Yeah, but I've trained it to bite people."

"Really?"

"Yeah. I could bring it into school and get it to bite everyone in the class."

"Could you?"

"Yeah. If I wanted."

They spent the whole afternoon telling each other about training dogs and how sharp dog's teeth were and which dog was the best. Poodles didn't come into the equation.

On the way home, Leon began to think about asking Carol for a dog that he could train. He could train it to bite Jake's dad.

He could train it to bite the old lady on the next floor who kept looking at him and shaking her head. He could train it to bite Tina's boyfriend and the mailman. Then when Jake got older they could get famous for training dogs. The best dog trainers in the world.

5

As soon as the summer holidays start, things get jangled up at home. Leon can go to bed whenever he wants and sometimes he can even go to sleep on the sofa because his mom doesn't notice. He can eat whatever he wants but if there's nothing in the fridge and nothing in the cupboard it doesn't really count. He has to look after Jake nearly every day and Carol keeps crying and going to the phone booth, leaving Leon in charge, and once when he picked Jake up, he wriggled so much that he fell on the carpet. He had stopped crying by the time Carol came back but it made Leon feel angry with her and he stole another twenty pence out of her purse. But he could have taken all the money because she doesn't know what's in there.

Early in the morning, just when it's getting light, Jake starts crying and Leon gets up with him. His diaper is always heavy and wet but as soon as Leon changes it, Jake starts smiling and laughing. Jake always wants the same thing for breakfast and now Leon has a good system. It took him a few weeks to get it just right but now he could tell anyone what to do to look after a baby in the mornings.

Change the diaper (remember to use the white cream or by the second morning the baby's bum is sore). Feed the baby but be careful going downstairs because babies move around in your arms and sometimes they're heavy; if you haven't made the breakfast bottle quickly enough, the baby will start crying again. Put six scoops of baby milk powder in the bottle and fill it with warm water from the kettle. You better taste it to see if it's not too hot. Sometimes if the baby is really hungry, you have to mix in some extra powder and a spoon of sugar. The worst thing is when the baby is sick. That makes a lot of mess and it can take forever to tidy up.

Even Carol doesn't know about the best routine for Jake and sometimes she forgets about him when he's in the high chair and Leon has to take him out. She goes to bed all the time, so Leon has to do everything. When he goes into her room, she's always hidden under the blankets with her pills next to the bed, some in a white bottle and then pink ones that you have to press out of a silver card. He pressed one out once. It looked like a piece of candy but after he licked it he threw it down the toilet.

Then, other times, Carol goes out and leaves him to watch the TV. She puts Jake in the stroller and takes him out for hours and when she comes back she's tired and Jake is crying. She leaves the stroller in the hall and just goes upstairs, talking to herself. Leon has to unfasten Jake's straps and take his baby suit off and feed him and sometimes all the things he has to do make Leon so tired and angry.

It seems like Jake's been crying for days. If he doesn't stop, Leon will have to go and get some money from Tina. If Tina isn't in then he will have to go to the lady next door who doesn't like him. He's already looked in Carol's purse but there isn't enough to buy some food for Jake, some diapers for Jake, and some candy for himself. There's no money at all, just some receipts, an old photograph, and an earring. Leon's tipped the whole purse upside down. He's looked between the cushions in the sofa and in the drawers in the kitchen and in the pockets of Carol's coat and everywhere else he can think of.

Jake isn't even wearing a diaper anymore because it smelled terrible and all the new ones are gone. He had to sit Jake on a towel in his basket and put some toys in with him but he can get out now and roll all over the place and looking after Jake is getting much too hard. And they're both hungry all the time these days. Jake has been crying all morning and Carol won't do anything.

Every morning, it's Leon who has to go and get Jake and pick him up and move him around a bit until he stops crying. The way his mom is behaving, you would think she was deaf.

Leon has shaken her and he has begged her and he has pulled at her arms but nothing happens. Even though she's awake she won't talk or eat and she won't get up. That was yesterday and the day before yesterday, and now, today, Leon has got to do something. He goes upstairs again into her bedroom. Pink light sifts through the thin curtains and the air feels heavy and quiet, like someone's holding their breath. One of Carol's hands lies on the sheet. Leon touches it with the tip of one finger. She doesn't move but her papery lips pucker over and over, like she's a goldfish in a bowl.

"Mom?"

Carol turns her head to the wall.

"I'm hungry, Mom."

He realizes that the whole room smells like Leon's diaper and that his mom has wet the bed again. He opens the window but only a little crack in case Carol gets cold.

If Leon can go to Tina and get some money then nobody needs to know that Carol is ill again. Leon can make her better if someone will give him some money. The last time things were like this he had to go and live with a lady and her husband and their cat and they kept taking him to church and making him sit still and it was horrible, so he will look after Carol and Jake, he will make her some tea and toast, and help her sit up and take her pills, and he will put a clean sheet on her bed and he will pretend. Jake starts crying downstairs, so Leon goes down and gives him a kiss.

"You stay here and play with your toys. Stop crying, Jake."

He leaves the door on the latch and goes upstairs to the next floor. He rings Tina's bell.

"All right, love?" she says.

"My mom said have you got any money?"

Tina looks along the landing and then over the railings.

"Where is she, Leon?"

"She's asleep but she wants me to go to the shop."

"Have you been to school today?"

"No, school ended last week. She said have you got a pound?"

Tina keeps looking at him and then she goes into her flat. She comes back with Wobbly Bobby and her handbag and closes the door.

"I'll pop down and see her."

Leon follows her and hopes his mom is awake and dressed and hopes that Jake has stopped crying. But when Tina walks through the door and he hears the sound she makes, he knows she will find everything out.

She walks into the kitchen and shakes her head.

"Christ," she says.

She walks into the sitting room and puts her hand to her mouth. She looks at how untidy Leon has been and how he has sat in front of the TV and eaten his cereal by putting his hand in the box. How he hasn't put Jake's diapers in the trash. How he should have opened the window like Tina does in her house and made everywhere smell of baby lotion. Leon sees what Tina sees. Why didn't he tidy up before he asked her for any money? Tina goes back into the hall.

"Carol? Carol?" she calls. She puts Bobby down in Jake's playpen and then runs up the stairs. Leon follows.

"Bloody hell!"

Tina starts shaking Carol and pulling her arm.

"Cal! Cal!"

She looks at Leon.

"Has she taken something? How long has she been like this? Cal?"

Suddenly Carol starts moaning.

"Leave me alone! Leave me alone!"

Tina starts making little slaps on Carol's face but she won't fight back or even open her eyes. Leon knows because he's been trying for days. Tina takes Leon's hand and backs out of the room. All the time, she's shaking her head and saying "Christ" or "God."

They go down the stairs together. Tina picks Jake out of his basket and wraps a towel round him. She picks Bobby up as well. She's carrying two babies and she's out of breath.

"Get my bag, Leon. Come with me."

They go to the phone booth at the end of the block and she makes Leon hold Jake while he stands outside. The door won't shut properly, so he hears everything.

"Ambulance, I think," she says. Then she waits for a minute and says his mom's address. Then she says they will need to get Social Services as well.

She puts the phone down and then says a number to herself over and over while she's dialing.

"Social Services?" she says.

Tina tries to squeeze the door shut but it won't close.

"There's two children that's been there for a couple of days at least. Yes. Yes. No, it's been going on a while. Yes. An ambulance is coming. Yes. On the next floor up, 164E, upstairs. I don't know, nine, and four or five months, something like that. Carol Rycroft. Yes. Leon and Jake. Jake's the baby. I don't know. No. Terrible. I don't know."

She listens for ages and then she says, "I'll take them to my house but they can't stay. No, sorry. Can't you send someone around? When? Christ. All right, just one night, then. I haven't got a phone. No. Yeah, 164E first floor, yeah. I'll be there."

When she comes out she's breathing like she's been running.

"Can you carry him, Leon?" she asks. "If we walk slow?"

Bobby is crying and Jake keeps wriggling but Leon keeps up with Tina, who doesn't walk slowly after all. When they get back to Tina's she puts Jake straight in the bath with Bobby and dresses him in Bobby's clothes. He's still crying but then she gives him a bottle and halfway through he falls asleep.

Tina keeps saying she's sorry and she has no choice. An ambulance lady comes to the door and Tina lets her in.

"We've got someone downstairs with Mom. You've got the children here with you?"

"They are both all right," she says, pointing to Jake, who is fast asleep, and then to Leon, who is next to her.

"He's nine and Jake is about four months old. I've fed the baby and I was just about to feed Leon. I think he's hungry, aren't you, love?"

Leon wipes his face.

"And a bit worried about your mom, eh?" says the ambulance lady. She squats down in front of Leon and squeezes his arm, then his other arm.

"You've been hungry for a little while, I bet."

Leon shakes his head. "No, I'm full."

When they start whispering about his mom, he wants to tell

them that she's kind and nice but they're not listening. The ambulance lady goes over to Jake and when she sees he's asleep she says she's going back downstairs.

After she leaves, Tina makes him beans on toast and he gets into the bath. He puts one of Tina's T-shirts on and he has some potato chips in front of the television. *The Dukes of Hazzard* is on but halfway through Jake starts crying again and Tina puts him on Leon's lap so he can give him a bottle.

"You're a good kid, Leon," she says. "You don't deserve this."

"Where's my mom?" he asks.

"She's been taken to the hospital, love. You could see she wasn't well. You should have come and told me. She was like this last week, wasn't she? I could see it in her face when she walked past me. How long's it been going on?"

Leon doesn't know.

"She's really bad this time, love. Worse than I've ever seen. I don't know what will happen."

But Leon does.

The social workers don't come until the next evening. There are two of them; one has black hair with white underneath like a zebra. They all stay in the kitchen for ages talking about his mom. He can hear Tina telling them everything.

". . . weeks and weeks, since before the baby was born if I think about it now. She was depressed the first time with Leon but I never knew her then. I think he's been in care a couple of times. She seemed all right before the baby but she's just, you know, not right. I mean, some of the things she does . . . and she dumps the kids at the drop of a hat. With me mostly. And she kept leaving Leon to look after the baby, you know, five minutes here and five minutes there. And he's been missing school."

No one says anything and then Tina starts all over again, saying the same things, saying bad things about Carol and pretending that Leon wasn't looking after Jake properly.

"She's just got worse without me paying attention," says Tina. "We had a bit of a row a few weeks back cuz she keeps borrowing money. She never pays it back, either. And I've had those two kids more times than I can count. They're lovely kids, but still. And I just said, you know, enough's enough. She had a right go at me. So I just backed off and I haven't kept a close eye. I used to but I've got my own family to think about. It all got out of hand when the baby's dad finished with her. Tony, I think he's called. Don't know his second name. She took it bad. I mean really bad."

"What about Leon's father? Is he around?"

"Him? Byron? Not him, he's taken off. Carol said he was supposed to go to court and he couldn't face it. But even when he was around he wasn't much use. He'd come and go as he pleased. He'd be with her for a couple of weeks and then he'd be off. Then he was inside for a bit and as soon as he was out they were arguing all the time. And drinking. Both of them drank. And anyway, when she got pregnant by Tony it all just came to a head."

Leon sees that Tina has left her handbag on the sofa. He leaves the door open but gets her purse and takes out fifty pence. He puts it in his trousers and puts everything back where it was. He tiptoes back to the door of the kitchen.

"Like I said, I've really tried. I've had them both here on and off for months and, you know, much as I want to help, it's just got to stop. I mean, she's had a breakdown, hasn't she?"

Leon opens the door wide. They all look at him. Social workers have two pretend faces, Pretend Happy and Pretend Sad. They're not supposed to get angry, so they make angry into sad. This time, they're pretending to care about him and Jake and his mom.

"I want to get my things," he says.

They all look at each other.

The Zebra takes him down to his flat. Tina has given her the key. She looks around the kitchen and opens the fridge. She opens

the back door and sees all the diapers that Leon has thrown outside. She walks slowly upstairs and helps him pack some clothes
for Jake and some clothes for himself but he can only take one
bag of toys.

"Whatever you can take in that backpack is okay," she says.
"We can come back for the rest another day."

Leon has to leave one of his Action Men because he has to
make some space for Jake's toys and everything won't fit into his
red pack. When the Zebra has filled a suitcase they go back to
Tina's. She picks Jake up and wraps him in a blanket. Tina tries
to give Leon a kiss.

"You'll be all right, Leon. I'm so sorry, love." She bends down
and he turns his face to the wall. He holds his backpack in front
of him. He can hear her sniffing and crying and he thinks of her
fifty pence in his pocket and the candy he will buy.

On the drive to where the foster lady lives, the Zebra talks all
the time but Leon is sitting in the back next to Jake with his pack
on his lap and he pretends he can't hear. Jake has fallen asleep in
a special baby car seat and Leon's glad he didn't hear Tina lying
and the Zebra going on and on asking him questions and trying
to make him say bad things about his mom.

6

In the morning, Leon opens his eyes and listens. He can't hear Jake crying. Then he remembers. He's in the foster lady's house. Last night when they arrived with the Zebra, the lady came to the door, took Jake, and kissed him even though she'd never met him before.

"Bless," she said.

The lady steered Leon toward a TV room and told him to sit down.

"You can watch what you like, love," she said but there was only the news on. He could hear the Zebra in the kitchen and even though half of him didn't want to, he had to listen. The Zebra was talking in a loud whisper.

". . . he's been the carer . . . baby and mother, yes, both of them . . . malnourished . . . failure to thrive . . . drug dependency . . . ambulance . . ."

All the time the lady was saying "Mmm" and "I see" and the Zebra kept going on and on.

". . . breakdown . . . emergency placement . . . court order . . . squalor . . . state of the place . . ."

And then right in the middle of a sentence, the lady told the Zebra to go home. He heard the front door open and heard her saying, "Yep, Judy, yeah, I've got it. Off you go. Yep, we can do all that tomorrow. All right, yes. Off you go. Bye."

The lady had given him a Jammie Dodger biscuit from a golden tin and asked him if he wanted another one, so Leon had three altogether with some hot chocolate and when he went to bed, he didn't even dream.

The smell of breakfast fills Leon's nose and cramps his belly. He doesn't want to make any noise because Jake is still asleep. He must be asleep because he's not crying. Leon is in a soft, warm bed and there are black-and-white soccer balls on his quilt. Wooden airplanes hang off the ceiling and turn in a cool breeze from the open window. Even the curtains have got a soccer-ball pattern on them. The wallpaper is made up of lots of soldiers in red army jackets with black rifles and, best of all, Jake isn't crying. The smell of food is so strong it pulls Leon downstairs. He can hear the lady singing a nursery song and Jake is laughing. He can hear plates and knives and forks clattering against each other. He tiptoes to the door of the kitchen and listens outside but the lady must have heard him.

"In you come, sleepyhead. Bacon sandwich with ketchup. All you can eat."

Leon sits at the yellow kitchen table and the lady puts a massive bacon sandwich on the plate and cuts it in half. Then she plonks the ketchup bottle down next to him and says, "Dig in, sweetheart."

Jake is wearing a bib with a dinosaur on it. He looks clean and fresh sitting in a high chair by the window and the lady goes over to him and starts pointing at things in the front garden.

"Bird," she says. "Bird. Lovely little bird."

She keeps talking to Jake and he's trying to talk back, so Leon can eat his sandwich in peace. It tastes like the best thing in the world with soft bread and lots of meat and the sauce that drips on to the plate and he's got an enormous glass of orange juice that tastes sweeter than Coke and he has a bite of the salty meat and a swig of the sweet orange juice and he keeps doing it until everything is gone.

Then the lady just puts another sandwich on his plate.

"Growing boy like you. Bet you can't eat all of that."

But Leon does, with another glass of orange juice, though during the second sandwich he pays attention to the lady and what she is saying. He is waiting for her to ask questions about his mom.

"Now, not everyone would be able to see the resemblance between you two," she says, folding her arms over her big chest, "but Maureen can." She smiles and points to her forehead. "That's me, Maureen, and I've got an eye for kids."

Leon licks the sauce off his fingers and looks around. Maureen's house smells of sweets and toast and when she stands near the kitchen window with the sun behind her, her fuzzy red hairstyle looks like a flaming halo. She's got arms like a boxer and a massive belly like Father Christmas. On the kitchen wall there is a giant wooden spoon and it says "Best Mom" and next to that there is a painting of Jesus with all his disciples and he's showing them the blood on his hands.

"So you're nine," says Maureen, taking his plate and filling his glass up with orange juice again.

Leon nods.

"And he's nearly five months."

Leon nods.

"And you're the quiet one."

"Yes."

"But he's the boss."

She smiles, so Leon smiles back.

"I get the picture," she says. "Bet he's had you up and down like a yo-yo. He'd be giving you orders if he could speak, wouldn't he?"

She goes over to Jake and gives him a plastic mixing spoon. Jake starts banging the tray on his high chair. Leon and Maureen put their hands over their ears.

"Have I made a mistake?" she says and Leon laughs.

"So what's his routine then?" she asks and she sits down opposite him at the yellow table. She picks up a pad and a pencil and writes "Jake" at the top of the page.

"You tell me what he likes and doesn't like, so I don't get it wrong."

"He gets up too early," says Leon.

She writes it down.

"And if I'm having something to eat and he wants it, he has to have a bit but only if it's good for him because sometimes it's chewing gum."

"No chewing gum." She writes it down.

"He likes *The Pink Panther* but he doesn't understand it. But I do, so I tell him what's going on."

"*Pink Panther* with Leon," she says and writes it down.

"When you put his top on, if it gets stuck he goes mad and starts crying and then you can't get it on him at all, so you have to wait until he's forgotten. But sometimes if you have to put him in the stroller, you can't wait, so you have to just . . ."

Leon doesn't know if he should tell her about the times when he loses his temper with Jake and shouts at him.

"You have to just tell him to be quiet?"

"Yes," says Leon.

"I get the picture," she says and she writes down "Pest."

Leon tells her everything. How if you want Jake to go to sleep you have to keep stroking his head or the side of his cheek. How

Jake puts everything in his mouth and you have to keep both your eyes on him all the time, so sometimes you can't even watch the TV. And how sometimes it's too hard.

Eventually, when Maureen has two pages of writing, she sits back in her chair.

"Thanks, love. You've been really helpful. I might ask you one or two things as we go along but I think I've got the basics. Now what I'd like you to do is leave me to see if I can manage with His Nibs while you go off and have a bath."

She takes Jake out of his high chair and kisses him again.

"What a pair of eyes!"

She turns Jake around so Leon can see his face.

"He wants to say thank you, Leon, love. Thank you for looking after me so well. That's what he'd say if he could speak."

They all go upstairs together and Maureen pours some blue stuff in the bath and the bubbles come right up to the top, so fluffy Leon can't even see the water. He sits in the bath listening to Jake shouting and laughing and Maureen telling him the names of all the things they can see.

7

Sometimes, even though everything is really nice at Maureen's house, Leon can't sleep. Him and Jake are in the same bedroom. Jake goes to bed first and then Leon goes to bed after a bit of TV with Maureen or after he's had a play with his toys. He always has a bath with bubbles and he always has a biscuit and then he has to brush his teeth. He's never hungry but just sometimes he can't sleep. Jake is in his cot, breathing soft and low, but Leon stares at the ceiling and the patterns of light on the wall. It gets later and later and eventually he hears Maureen come up to bed after the news. He tiptoes in.

"What's this?" she says. "Can't sleep?"

Leon nods.

"Five minutes," she says and pats the space beside her on the bed.

Leon snuggles next to her and asks her for a story.

"I don't think so," she says, "no good at stories, me. I don't see the point of half of them. All wolves and giants and things that don't exist. Memories are what I like. Things that really happened."

Leon says nothing and Maureen nudges him.

"Go on then. Tell your Auntie Maureen a story that really happened."

So Leon tells her the story about when his dad found out about Jake and never came back.

It was nighttime and his dad had put him into bed and tucked him in and just when he was having the best dream he kept hearing "Bitch."

Leon tried to stay in his dream but the words from downstairs kept getting in the way. He was dreaming about being a soldier. He had two medals for bravery and one for being the best shot. He was strong and tall, taller than his dad, and he was wearing a bandana and army pants with lots of pockets and a double strap of bullets across his chest. He was creeping through the jungle with his men with a rifle and a gun and a secret knife in his sock. If he had to use it, he knew what to do. A twig snapped and they all dropped to the ground. Someone shouted "Bitch" and "Fucking hell" and Leon knew that he wouldn't be able to move and his men would go on without him. This had happened before when he'd been in a good dream.

The words kept pushing in and Leon kept trying to move ahead and catch up with his men. He was in charge and he had to tell them to avoid the clearing where they could get picked off one by one. He had to tell them to use hand signals and keep quiet but all the time he could hear shouting rushing up from downstairs, sliding under the door and flying around the room like angry bats. "For fuck's sake, Carol!" That was the sort of thing that could get his troops killed and Leon couldn't decide whether to wake up or stay with his men. If he stayed with his men he would carry on hearing the words and eventually he would wet the bed. But if he woke up and went to the toilet he would have to hear what his dad was saying and the last time he got caught listening he was slapped on his legs.

Enemy soldiers were hiding in the jungle. It was their jungle, so they knew all the best places, under leaves and between rocks. One rushed out, "Ayyeeeeee!" and threw a grenade. When it landed, all Leon's men flew up in the air. They were all killed. And Leon was dead as well and he looked down on his khaki green uniform and his sweaty face from the jungle heat and at the trail of sticky blood that ran out of the corner of his mouth and he stepped over himself and got out of bed.

He crept out into the hallway and went to the toilet. He didn't flush it because then his dad would have heard him. He tiptoed back into his bedroom and half closed the door. Sometimes it used to be Carol doing all the shouting and sometimes it was his dad. Halfway through the argument, his dad started laughing and saying that his mom was a crazy woman. His dad always has to say things ten times like, "Crazy, crazy, crazy, crazy," and then he starts talking fast West Indian that no one else can understand.

Once when they were at Tina's house, Leon heard Carol say, "If it wasn't for Leon I would tell him to fuck off," and then she started crying. Leon wanted to tell Carol that he'd heard swearing lots of times and she could say "fuck off" if she wanted to.

But in the morning the sun was slicing through the curtains, the radio was on downstairs, and it wasn't a school day. Everything might be okay.

He got out of bed, opened his door, and listened. He could hear Carol singing, so he went downstairs. He kept listening all the time just in case his dad was in. He looked in the kitchen but there was no one there, so he pushed open the door to the living room.

The swishy blinds were closed and the room was full of smoke. His dad was gone and Carol was standing by the gas fire looking in the mirror, singing with her voice all broken up. Her blond hair was sticking up at the back where she had been lying on it and all her curls were flat. Everything was too loud, the music and her voice and the sharp feeling in the air. Carol's face was red on one side and her eyes were puffy and half-closed. It was like she'd said many times before: just because she's singing, it doesn't mean she's happy.

She waved her cigarette at him.

"Get some breakfast, Leon, and get dressed. I'm tired."

Leon can't remember what happened after that, so he has to stop telling Maureen his story. He's warm and comfortable on Maureen's bed and he feels like falling asleep.

"Up you get," she says and she leads him back to his own room. She strokes his forehead and pulls the blankets up over his ears.

"You'll have lovely dreams tonight, Leon, love. Sssh, lovely dreams. I promise."

8

It's impossible to choose a favorite dinner at Maureen's house. Everything has a funny name like Shepherd's Pie or Toad in the Hole or Spotted Dick and she always has a different sauce with every meal like mint sauce or apple sauce or bread sauce, but Leon doesn't like bread sauce because it reminds him of when he saw a cat being sick. And then apart from the dinners Maureen likes Leon to eat snacks. So if he's playing or watching TV she just comes into his room with a plastic plate with a sandwich and two biscuits or a cold sausage cut into pieces and a doughnut. And she always says, "There you go, pigeon. That'll keep you going."

But around Christmastime the snacks get out of control and Leon can't keep up with them. Even before Christmas, Maureen starts making mince pies and fruit cake and Christmas pudding and buys extra food on top of the food they already have, which is spilling out of the cupboards. And there's tins of biscuits and chocolates everywhere. Maureen doesn't even notice if there's one missing. On Christmas Eve, Maureen sits down in the kitchen opposite Leon while he's eating his dinner. She puts two slices of bread and butter next to him.

"Lancashire Hotpot," she says. "You'll need that for the gravy."

Leon doesn't say anything because he has his mouth full and Maureen likes him to have manners.

"Now, you know what day it is tomorrow?"

Leon nods.

"And you've written to Santa?"

Maureen thinks he is Jake's age and that he still believes in Santa Claus. Everyone knows that the parents buy the presents. Leon knows that Carol has disappeared because every time the social worker comes he hears her speaking to Maureen in the kitchen. She says things like "Still no word" or "We've heard nothing." And once she said, "Legally, it's abandonment," and Leon knows what that means. The social worker never talks about Leon's dad. She just said, "When they catch up with him he won't be seeing daylight for a long time. So that's him out of the picture." So Leon knows that he won't be getting anything for Christmas from his parents and tomorrow when he wakes up there will be nothing for him to unwrap. Leon puts his spoon on the table. He wipes his mouth with a paper towel and pushes his plate away.

"Eh? What's this? Don't like it?"

"I'm not hungry."

"Since when?"

"I don't have to eat it."

"No, you don't. And you don't have to be rude neither."

Leon says nothing. Maureen's dinner is sitting in his belly like a bag of sand and he's getting angry with her.

"You won't want any pudding then?"

"No."

"No?"

"No thank you."

"No thank you to trifle?"

"Yes."

"Yes you don't want trifle or yes you do want it?"

After a while, Leon uses the piece of paper towel to dab his eyes.

"Do I have to guess or do you want to tell me?"

"I don't care about my presents."

"Oh, I see."

"And you think I'm a baby. You think I believe in Father Christmas. And I don't. Everyone knows it's the mom and the dad that have to buy them. I'm not stupid."

Maureen pushes her chair back and lifts her eyebrows because she's surprised that he knows about Father Christmas. She hasn't told him he can get down from the table, so he has to sit and wait. Instead of speaking, she eats his bread and butter. When she's finished, she folds her arms over her belly and takes a deep breath.

"So," she says, "you've guessed about Father Christmas. I was wondering when that would happen. What should we do about Jake?"

"What do you mean?"

"Well, shall we tell him? Shall we tell him he hasn't got anything for Christmas?"

"He has!" says Leon. "I bought him something with my pocket money. I bought him the baby drums."

"Yes, you did. Even though I said you'd regret it. You still bought the baby drum kit and come Boxing Day you'll wish you hadn't. What else do you think he's got?"

"I don't know."

"What about me? Do you think I've bought something for Jake? And his social worker? Do you think she's bought Jake a present?"

Leon looks at her and nods.

"Right. Eat your dinner and tomorrow morning we'll see what's what."

In the morning, really early, he hears Maureen calling him, and Jake is trying to call him too.

"Yeeeyyii! Yeeeyyii!"

Leon runs downstairs to the living room. Maureen is holding Jake and Jake is holding a big present in silver wrapping paper.

"Say thank you, Leon."

"Thank you, Jake."

Leon sits on the floor and opens it but even before he gets the paper off he knows it's an Action Man, he just doesn't know which one.

"It's Sharpshooter! Look!"

Maureen turns Jake around to face her.

"Jake! You clever boy. How did you know?"

Then they open Jake's present from Maureen, which is Big Red Bear. Then it's Maureen's turn to open a present, so she chooses a big box with lots of stamps on that came by airmail. It's from one of her children and it's a book about cooking cakes.

"Lovely," she says and kisses it.

Then Leon opens a present from Maureen, which is a *Dukes of Hazzard* racing set, then another one for Jake from Gill next door, which is a baby piano that needs batteries and Maureen says she will never, ever buy them. Gill next door has bought Leon a sweater with a stripe around the chest. It's red and blue. Then Maureen has another cookbook from somebody else that she says is for slow cookers. Then Leon has a present from his social worker, which is some Meccano, and then another completely different Meccano set from "The Whole Team at High-field Family Services," and then, just when he thinks he has finished opening presents, Maureen pushes something out from behind the sofa.

"And that's your last one," she says.

It's an Action Man Cherilea Amphibious Jeep with a trailer. It's the exact one he saw on the commercial. The exact same one! When he jumps up to hug Maureen he nearly knocks her over.

"Steady, pigeon," she says but she hugs him back and kisses his cheek. "Merry Christmas, Leon, love."

9

Right below the ball of his skull, right where his knuckly back-bone pokes up toward his brain, Leon has a little dent. It's a groove that dips in between two hard parts and Maureen made it.

She must have made some kind of mark by now after six months of him living with her. It's where she pushes Leon with her thick fingers whenever he has to do something, to go some-where, to pick something up, to watch what he's doing. Go to bed. She never pushes him hard but it's always, always the same place, same spot, right on his neck. Leon's dad used to use funny words and he would have called that place his "neck-back" and then it would have been clear where it was. But Leon hasn't seen his dad for such a long time that he's nearly forgotten the things he used to say and the funny way he talked. Leon's dad used to say "Kyarell" instead of "Carol" and say "Soon come" every time he left the house. That's when Leon's mom used to get annoyed with him, because he never came soon and he never came back when he said he would. And now she's doing the same thing.

Leon's sitting back on the sofa with Jake asleep on his legs. Jake always gets hot and starts to sweat when he sleeps and beads of water on his forehead sparkle in the light from the television. His curly blond hair goes brown and two round pink spots appear on his creamy face.

Leon likes to watch Jake breathing. Jake breathes through his tiny perfect nostrils and lets the air out either side of his pacifier. Then, just as the pacifier is about to drop out, Jake, in his sleep, draws it back in, sucks on it three times, and starts all over again. Breathe in. Breathe out. Catch the pacifier. Suck three times. Breathe in. Breathe out.

But sometimes, if Jake's dreaming maybe, he mutters something or cries out and the pacifier falls onto his sleep suit and Leon has to be there to catch it and plop it back in for the three sucks before Jake notices and wakes up. Because if Jake wakes up before he's ready, nobody gets any peace. Least of all Leon, because Jake always messes up Leon's games and Maureen nearly always sides with Jake and that's that.

"Up you come, sweetheart."

Maureen carefully lifts the damp baby off Leon's bare legs and as soon as she has Jake in the crook of her arm she pushes Leon toward the stairs. Pushes him in his neck-back. Leon realizes then that all his toys have been put away and the cushions have been rearranged while he and his brother have been sitting on the sofa.

Someone is coming. Leon knows who it is. The air is different. And there have been phone calls. And Sally or whatever her name is has come and bounced Jake on her lap and said how precious he is and that he has to have a chance. Maybe Carol is coming back. Maybe she's gotten better. And Sally has given

Leon lots of sad smiles like he's sick or like he's fallen over and cut his knee. It's not Pretend Sad, either. And Maureen keeps shaking her head and saying it isn't right. Maureen has been quiet for days and keeps looking at him and saying, "I don't know, I honestly don't. It's a bad, bad world."

The air has been different since yesterday.

"Upstairs with you, Leon, love. Upstairs and give that face a good going-over and put a nice shirt on. Up you go. Quick as a flash. And wash your hands."

She fattens the cushions he's been sitting on and sits herself down in his spot, which is near the door, where she can get up quickly and let the new social worker in. He watches her from the staircase snuggling her nose against Jake and he knows what she's doing. She's smelling the baby smell of him. The baby life of him. His perfection.

Maureen's broad back obliterates the whole of Jake and be-cause she's just washed her orange hair it runs like wet snakes down the skin on her freckled back. It's hot in the house and Maureen's wearing a pink denim dress with no sleeves and one huge pocket at the front like she's a massive kangaroo. Leon comes down with a new face and a new shirt. He sits next to the social worker because every other social worker always says, "Come and sit next to me," and this will save everyone the bother.

"Remember me?" she says. "Salma? I came yesterday to talk about you and Jake. Remember, Leon?"

It was only yesterday and since then nothing has been the same so of course Leon remembers her. She has the sad smile back on her face and also the look of fear. Maureen also has a different face. Leon knows that if the social worker wasn't here, Maureen would have called up her sister and said, "Know what, Sylvia? They've pissed me right off again, they have.

Social Services? Waste of bloody space, if you ask me." But she never swears when the social workers are around. Neither does Leon.

Then Salma starts talking while Maureen bounces Jake on her lap. Maureen keeps shaking her head like she would like to say *no, no, no* but she doesn't say anything at all. Leon agrees with everything Salma says.

"Jake is still a very young baby."

"Yes," says Leon.

"He needs to be in a family."

"Yes," says Leon.

"Lots of families are looking for babies."

"Yes," says Leon.

"You love Jake, don't you, Leon?"

"Yes."

"Everyone knows how much you love your little brother. Even though you look very different, you can see you're brothers and that you love each other. Maureen's always telling me how you let him play with your toys and he will only sleep on your lap and no one else's. And that's lovely."

Leon nods.

"Wouldn't you like Jake to be in a family with a mom and dad of his own?"

"Yes."

"That's what we want as well. We want every child to have the best. You and Jake and all the other children who can't be looked after by their first family."

Salma takes one of Leon's hands out of his lap and he's glad he remembered to clean them.

"You're not a little boy now, Leon. You're nine. You're nine years old and so tall that you look about eleven or twelve, don't you? Yes. Or thirteen. A lot of people think you're older than you

are. And you're very sensible as well. You had a long time looking
after other people, didn't you, and that made you grow up very
fast. Oh, I know you still like your toys and your games, but still."

Salma looks at Leon's hand and puts it back where it was.
She then folds hers together and coughs. Leon sees her look at
Jake. Then she looks at Maureen and he wonders if she's asked a
question because no one speaks for quite some time.

So Leon says, "Yes."

"Leon, we've got a family that want to look after Jake. They
want to be Jake's new parents. Isn't that good, Leon? Jake is going
to have a new mommy and daddy."

"Yes."

"And soon, one day, a family will come along that will want
you for their little boy."

Leon nods.

"Do you understand, Leon? Jake is going to be adopted. That
means he's going to have a new forever family. But even though
he won't be living with you anymore you will still be able to get
letters from him and find out all about him."

Leon looks at Maureen before he speaks.

"Jake can't write."

Salma laughs very loud and Leon knows she's pretending.

"Of course he can't! He's only ten months old! No. His new
mommy and daddy will write the letter to you and probably even
send a photograph as well. See!"

She has his hand again.

"I know this is hard for you, Leon. Very hard. We wish things
were different but if Jake is going to have a chance . . ."

Maureen is up. "Thanks, Salma. He understands, don't you,
pigeon?"

Maureen taps his neck-back and inclines her head to the
kitchen.

"Curly Wurly?"

Leon gets up and goes into the kitchen. It isn't Saturday. It isn't Christmas and his room is very untidy, so why he's getting a Curly Wurly is a mystery. Then again, he has been very polite. He hasn't interrupted, answered back, or tried to be too clever by half. There are three other Curly Wurlys in the cupboard and, as he's the only one in the house who eats them, Leon smiles. Maybe every time Salma comes and he doesn't lose his temper he'll get a Curly Wurly. He eats it in the kitchen but, before he's finished, Maureen calls him back in to say goodbye to Salma while she changes Jake in the bathroom. Salma puts her hand on his shoulder and shows him her sad smile again.

"You're a good boy, Leon. I know this is hard and you're a good brother to Jake but we have to think of his future."

"Yes."

Later, when Jake's in bed and Leon's watching TV, Maureen asks him about what Salma said.

"She means it, you know, love. Did you understand that, Leon? Jake is going to be adopted."

"What's adopted?"

"Jake is going to have a new mom and dad."

"Why?"

"Because, love. Just because. Because he's a baby, a white baby. And you're not. Apparently. Because people are horrible and because life isn't fair, pigeon. Not fair at all. And if you ask me, it's plain wrong and—"

She stops suddenly and winks.

"Tell you what. Now His Nibs is finally asleep, let's you and me get the biscuit tin out."

She comes back with a massive mug of coffee and the Golden Tin, which everyone knows is never allowed in the front room but this is, after all, a day of sad social workers and spontaneous

Curly Wurlys, so Leon says nothing. As she squashes a cushion into the small of her back, Maureen lets out a sigh that to Leon sounds a little bit shaky and he can hear something in her throat when she speaks.

"You stay here with your Auntie Maureen, love. Eh? We're happy enough, aren't we? You stay here with me."

10

It's clear to Leon that Salma is mistaken and there aren't lots and lots of families looking for babies because February vacation comes and goes and Jake is still reigning over 43 Allcroft Avenue. Leon still has to share his toys and Jake still has to sleep on Leon's legs. The only thing that's changed is that Jake has two teeth coming at the bottom and where he keeps dribbling onto his chin it's sore with a rash. Leon has to dab it carefully, otherwise Jake cries for ages and no one gets any peace.

Then one day, Maureen comes to collect him from school on her own.

"Where's Jake?" he asks.

"Salma and a nice lady and her husband are looking after him for half an hour. Just you and me. Great, isn't it?"

Leon knows she's pretending. Maureen takes his hand when they cross the road and she hasn't done that for ages. She says that they are going the long way home, under the subway and through the park. She walks very slowly and keeps stopping to look at

houses and plants and asking Leon about school. Then she pro-
duces from her pocket a small pack of chewing gum.

"Here you are, love. Have these but spit them out before you
get home. I don't want gum on the carpet."

There's only Salma and Jake at home when they get back and
Leon sees Salma nod at Maureen as soon as they get through
the door. It was a nod that puts Maureen in a bad mood for the
rest of the day. The next day is Saturday, so Leon plays with Jake
as quietly as he can and they both watch baby programs on the
TV. By the afternoon he thinks Maureen's bad mood has worn
off, because while Jake is having his nap she calls him into the
kitchen and puts two chairs close together. She sits down on one
and makes him sit on the other.

"You know Jake's been having some visitors this week, don't
you? While you've been at school, he's had a nice man and a nice
lady spending some time with him, playing with him, and taking
him to the park."

Leon says nothing.

"Well, those people are coming for Jake today, love."

She brings his head down on to her shoulder and begins
rocking backward and forward. Leon feels a little bit sick from
the rocking and he thinks he must have put the wrong vest on
because all his clothes feel wrong all of a sudden. He's very uncomfortable sitting there too close to Maureen.

"We'll say goodbye to Jake and then you and me can have a
good old cry if we want."

She's very hot. Leon tries to sit up. He wants to ask her a
question and it's the same question that he's tried to ask Salma
three or four times but he knows that when he's asked the question and he gets the answer then everything is going to be worse.
And until he asks this question everything will stay the same.
But now, because the people are coming for Jake, Leon knows
he's running out of time. He manages to pull back so he can see

Maureen's face. It's all pink and blotchy and her chest is going up and down. She's started crying without him.

"Am I going with him?"

Maureen doesn't say anything right away but she swallows something down. Then when she does start talking she sounds funny and her bottom lip is wet and loose.

"No, pigeon. No. You're staying with your Auntie Maureen."

Almost as soon as she says that the bell rings and Maureen gets up. She puts her hand on Leon's shoulder and squeezes it hard.

Salma and two other people come in. They keep smiling at him and they are all talking at the same time, trying to see who can say the nicest things to him, and considering Jake is asleep upstairs they are all being much too loud. First of all, Maureen brings down the small blue-checked suitcase and gives it to the lady, who gives it to the man, who says he'll put it straight in the car. Then Maureen goes back upstairs and gets Jake, who's just waking up. If you let Jake sleep and sleep and sleep without being disturbed he wakes up in a great mood. He starts smiling before he even opens his eyes and the blue middle bit is all sparkly and bright and the black middle bit is dark and shiny. He starts waving and shouting and even when he had his rash he would be laughing about nothing at all. When Leon sees Jake he goes straight over to him and Jake leans out of Maureen's arms and pulls Leon's hair.

"Careful, Jake!" the lady says.

"He doesn't hurt," says Leon. "He always does it. He wants to play with me."

The lady doesn't look at Leon, she only looks at Jake, and her blue eyes are sparkly and bright as well because she's trying not to cry like Maureen.

Leon uncurls his brother's fist and kisses it. Jake's trying to get out of Maureen's arms and Leon knows that he's seen his yellow truck on the carpet. Suddenly, Leon's pants are too tight and he wants to pee and his legs feel bendy and he's very angry with Maureen. He picks up the yellow truck and gives it to Jake and tries to stand still. Something inside is telling him to run away or to hit the lady but Leon stands still. Everything goes quiet. Maureen hands Jake to the lady and Salma strokes Maureen on the back. The man keeps saying thank you and touching Jake on the top of his head. No one notices when Leon goes into the kitchen. No one notices when he takes the Golden Tin into the garden, throws the plain biscuits over the fence, and stuffs seven chocolate digestives into his pocket. When he goes back inside Salma and Maureen are standing at the door waving.

"Come and wave, love," says Maureen but Leon walks right past her and up the stairs and into his room. He takes the biscuits out of his pocket and slams them on his chest of drawers. He wants to eat them, all of them, one after another or even together all at the same time, but he doesn't seem to have any room in his throat or his chest or in his belly.

Leon begins to hum. He clamps his mouth shut but lets the noise squeeze out of his nostrils and between his lips. He hums the music to *The Dukes of Hazzard* and, while he does it, he pulls all the blankets off his bed. He hums the music to Jake's baby program and kicks the wardrobe door open and throws all his clothes onto the floor. The lady who took him is in for a surprise if she lets that pacifier drop out. Leon knows all the words to that baby program, so instead of humming he begins to sing. He sings as loud as he can. He shoves and shoves his mattress until it slides off the bed and onto the floor and sings until his throat feels gravelly and sore. He rips his clothes out of his bureau and flings them across the room, singing and singing. He piles a blanket over his head and sits on the mess he's made and he sings until he lets out every word and all the space comes back into his chest and his belly, until he isn't angry with Maureen, so that when she opens his door he doesn't want to hit her.

She doesn't say anything for a few moments and then she steps over his mattress and closes the curtains.

"Coming down for your tea, love?"

He knows she sees the biscuits that have fallen on the floor. If she tells him off he'll have to be angry with her again. But she picks her way through the mess, gathers them up, and puts them on his bedside cabinet next to a photo he's only just noticed. It's of him and Jake on a cream shag carpet before Jake had his rash. And Maureen has put Jake's Big Red Bear next to the picture frame.

"You need something to remember your brother by. Jake won't need Big Red Bear where he's going. He'll have lots more."

Maureen picks up Big Red Bear with its pale blue satin ribbon and tries to snuggle it next to Leon.

She pretends that Big Red Bear can speak and moves it from side to side.

"Time for tea," says Maureen, trying not to move her lips.

"I'm not hungry."

"Nor me," she replies.

Then Maureen kisses him on top of his head, which she has only done once before, when he had a nightmare about drowning. She touches him lightly on his neck-back.

"Come on," she says in her own voice. "We'll skip our tea today. Skip tea and go straight to ice cream. We'll tidy this up later."

Leon shuffles off the bed and follows Maureen downstairs.

II

At first Leon thinks he's in a dream about fighting a dragon. But then Maureen is shaking him and he can't seem to open his eyes.

"Leon! Leon!"

Somehow he is sitting next to her on the bed, and when he opens his eyes he can see from her face that something's wrong.

"You're grinding your teeth again, Leon! It's four o'clock in the bloody morning. Wake up!"

One side of his face hurts and it feels like he hasn't been asleep all night. He was fighting an evil monster that was picking up people with his claws and eating them. Blood dripped from the monster's lips and some of it splashed on Leon and then the monster saw him and started chasing him. Leon ran and ran and then when he couldn't run any more, he turned round and just when he was about to stab the monster and win, Maureen woke him up.

"Honestly, Leon. I wish you could hear yourself. I've never

heard nothing like it. Goes right through me. Leon! Don't go back to sleep! Leon!"

First of all she makes him take a pee even though he doesn't want to. She stands at the door and the bathroom floor is cold on his bare feet. She tells him to sit down to pee because he's too tired to stand, so it's really hard to concentrate on making the pee come out but she won't let him get off the toilet until he has done it. Halfway through he nearly falls off, so he has to hold on to the sink with one hand. Then the stairs feel wobbly under his legs and he's grateful when Maureen says he can sit on the kitchen chair and have a biscuit.

"Now where's this all come from, eh?" she says, filling her spotty mug with boiling water. "As if I didn't know."

Leon tries to rest his head on the table but she's having none of it. She makes him sit up straight like he's in school and drink his juice. He tries to eat his biscuit but it feels too heavy and it drops on to his lap and onto the floor. Leon is so tired and so angry with Maureen.

"Right," says Maureen, poking him in his neck-back. "I know you're upset but you and me are having a talk. Take this and wipe your face."

She hands him a tea towel for his tears. It smells of mashed potato.

"In there with you, on the sofa, and get the green blanket over you. Come on."

He does as he's told and puts the green blanket over his legs even though he isn't sick. Maureen sits down next to him and puts her coffee on the floor.

"Right, mister. You awake now? You listening?"

Leon nods.

"Answer me this. How many children have I fostered over the years? I know you know the answer because I saw you eavesdropping the other day when I was talking to the new neighbors. So, go on. How many?"

"Twenty-two," he says.

"Exactly. So I've fostered twenty-two children. How many children have I got of my own? Not counting stepchildren and we'll come to them in a moment."

"Robert and Ann."

"Twenty-two and two?"

"Twenty-four."

"How many kids have Robert and Ann got between them?"

Leon screws up his eyes so he can think.

"Three, Leon. Three. Now I don't see them as often as I'd like on account of the fact that they live abroad but we're going to count them because I did look after them when they were here. So, we were on twenty-four and we're adding three."

"Twenty-seven."

"Good. How many stepkids?"

"Two."

"Twenty-seven and two, Leon. I know you're half-asleep but pay attention because this is important."

"Twenty-nine."

"Twenty-nine. We're going to round it up to thirty, because that's you. You're number thirty. So, do you think I might know something about children, Leon?"

"Yes."

"Do you think there is anyone who knows more about children than me?"

"A teacher?"

"No, not a teacher because the teacher's job finishes at half past three and my job never ends. And my job never ends because I look after you even when you're not here because I think about you and I care for you and I love you. You and all the children that I've ever looked after. Do you understand, Leon?"

"Yes."

"Right. Now listen carefully because I want you to under-stand something and I don't say this to all the children because it's not always true but with you it is true, so you have to believe it. And when you believe it you will stop grinding your teeth and I might be able to get five minutes' sleep before sunrise. All right?"

"Yes."

"It will be all right."

Maureen wipes Leon's face with the corner of her dressing gown but because it's made of the same silky stuff as the cushions his face is still wet and begins to itch.

"You will be all right, Leon. You will be all right."

Leon uses the towel again because it's better for tears.

"And one day," she says, "you will see your brother again. He will find you or you will find him and you can tell him all about what you've been doing, about your soccer and your toys and your shows. You can ask him all the questions about what he's been doing because he's not as grown up as you, so he'll still be doing baby things, won't he? You'll be able to help him with his toys. It might not be for a long time, you might even be grown up and you won't be playing with toys anymore. But you will see Jake again. He hasn't gone forever."

She goes into the kitchen and gets him another biscuit but this time it's got chocolate on it and Leon realizes that he didn't hear her taking the lid off the Golden Tin, so Maureen has a secret hiding place.

"I'll keep saying it until you believe me, Leon. You will be all right and that, mister, is a promise. I know you miss him, pigeon, and that the future seems a long, long way away but I know what I'm talking about. Right, you can have one more sip of your juice then go and have another pee so you don't wet the bed."

On the way up the stairs, he thinks of a question but by the time he gets into bed he's forgotten it again. It was something about how long away the future was but he can't think of the exact words to say.

Maureen kisses him and just before she turns the light out he hears her talking to herself.

"I should have got him to brush his bloody teeth."

12

"All right, Salma, love. Come in."

Leon stands at the top of the stairs just out of sight. There's a little gap in the banisters where if he keeps his head dead still he can see who comes to the door. If he's in his room playing with his toys and he hears the bell, it's easy to slide off the bed and tread carefully on tiptoe along the brown carpet to the very top of the stairs. He crouches down and if they're not whispering, he can hear what they say. He's heard Maureen swearing lots of times, like when she called Margaret Thatcher a bloody cow because of the miners. And once she said Margaret Thatcher could kiss her ass and Leon laughed and got caught eavesdropping. Maureen says that if he keeps listening to people's private conversations his ears will shrivel into prunes and drop off. Leon always checks his ears at night just in case.

Maureen takes Salma straight into the kitchen. She'll make coffee for Salma and then they'll talk about him. He creeps down the stairs in his socks to the sitting room and sits quietly in front of the television. Salma's bag is on the sofa. Salma always has a handbag and another leather bag that she keeps her files in. The files are sticking out and her handbag has the zipper open. He can hear her with her sad voice.

"His last report card was a bit of a concern, I agree."

"Bit of a concern? He's got no friends. Spends his break on his own. Doesn't do his work. It's not like he's thick. He's grieving, if you ask me."

"I'm sure he'll settle down, Maureen. It's got to be a shock for him but we're confident we've done the right thing. It's not just about him. Separately, they've got a chance, but together . . ."

Maureen snorts. "Jake's got a chance, you mean. You've split them up and in my books that's a sin and I won't change my mind on that."

"What would you have done then, Maureen? Have neither of them adopted? Because that's the choice."

"I have no idea what I would do, Salma." Maureen is washing the dishes and making them clank together in the sink. "That's why I'm not a social worker. Anyway, how is he?"

Leon pulls the straps of Salma's handbag until it's right next to him. He eases his hand inside and feels for her purse. His eyes are on the door. His ears are in the kitchen.

"Good. New mom and dad are delighted, obviously. He's settling in well. Well as can be expected. It's early on but it looks like a good match."

Leon unzips the purse and he pokes two fingers in. He feels the cold metal of a coin with sharp corners. Fifty pence. He plucks it out, puts it in his other hand, clenches his fist around it. Zips up the purse and feels the cold sweat drip down his back. He pushes the bag with his elbow until it's back where she left it. He can hardly breathe.

Salma is still talking.

"Mom and dad have taken him to the park, introduced him

to the family, taken lots of photographs. They make a lovely family, Maureen. They've got a big garden."

"Big garden, eh?" says Maureen. "How lovely." She bangs the saucepan into the sink. "And what about this letter he's supposed to get? Hang on, let me just check on Leon, I want to talk to you about something, Salma."

The kitchen door opens quickly but Leon is prepared. He's standing by the television pressing the button to turn it on. He doesn't turn round.

"All right, love?" says Maureen. She goes back into the kitchen and the door clicks shut.

Leon dashes upstairs faster than a cheetah. He slips the fifty pence under his mattress. He'll move it later. He comes downstairs so quickly and so lightly that he's out of breath again. But he lands in his seat and leans on a cushion in twenty seconds. He can't hear anything from the kitchen but the droning of the two women. He shuffles over in his seat next to Salma's leather bag so he can be nearer the door but it's no good. Nothing. All Salma's files are sticking out of her bag, brown folders with white paper inside. These are the files that the social workers hold whenever he asks about his mum. They look through their files and check dates and addresses but they never let him see for himself. And he's a good reader. He flicks through the corners of the files. He sees his name and his birth date. He sees Jake's name and birth date. He sees his mom's name and her birth date. He squeezes his hand between the pages and pulls.

Due to Carol's itinerant lifestyle and mental health issues, it has been difficult to make a full and detailed assessment. Carol was given the opportunity to attend a weekly access visit to Leon and Jake to assess her commitment and capacity for caring for her children. She failed to attend these appointments without explanation. She has also failed to attend access visits arranged at the foster carer's house on four separate occasions, again without explanation. Carol Rycroft did attend the Family Center without appointment, where she stayed for twenty minutes speaking to the Duty Social Worker about her new life and plans for the future, which did not appear to include caring for Leon and Jake.

The most recent psychiatric assessment of Carol Rycroft undertaken by Dr. Ann Mulroney (attached) concluded that Carol Rycroft has an emotionally unstable personality disorder which presents in maladaptive behavior that has formed the background to her mental health problems. She presents with a range of behaviors including anxiety, restlessness, stupor, and transient mood swings into hypomania. She reports previous episodes of mild to medium clinical depression following the birth of her first child, Leon, who has consequently spent several short periods in various foster care short-term placements. She also reports that her mother and maternal grandmother both had psychiatric disorders but this could not be verified. She is unwilling or unable to provide any details of either child's biological father although limited information has been obtained from Tina Moore (see later).

Carol Rycroft's current condition is complicated by her dependence on prescription drugs and alcohol use. Her personality disorder is also manifest in Carol's high level of self-interest as opposed to the interests of her children. The Psychological Assessment concluded that Carol Rycroft is unlikely to be in a position to care for either child unless she is willing to undertake further psychological input for a period of no less than eighteen months.

He tucks the paper back where it was and opens the kitchen door. "When am I going to see my mom?"

Salma puts her face up close to Leon and smiles.

"Remember we talked about this, Leon? Remember we said—"

"Why do I have to wait all the time?"

"Well, it's because—"

"I'm hungry," he says.

Salma smiles again and rubs his shoulder like he's fallen over. "Course you are."

Salma goes back to sipping her coffee while Maureen takes the lid off the biscuit tin.

"Tea's in half an hour," she says.

Leon nibbles the biscuit and stares at them.

"What?" says Maureen, folding her arms. "You been listening at doors again? You'll hear something you won't like one of these days."

She touches his cheek.

"Not today, though. It's all good today. Go on, off with you. Half an hour of TV and I'll put the tea on. Sausage and mash. Now hop it."

She closes the door after him and he sits down by the papers that say horrible things about his mom. He knocks Salma's bag over with his elbow and when it falls on the floor everything spills out and he kicks it with his foot so that the papers get jumbled up. He stands over the mess and dribbles the soggy biscuit from his mouth onto the papers, a brown sticky mess with crumbs in it. Then he gathers them up and puts them back in Salma's bag.

13

When Leon wakes the next morning the house is very quiet. Outside, there is a car running its motor in the avenue and far, far off, he can hear a train on a track. Leon's never been on a train but he knows they can take you all over the country faster than a car. He saw an ad about it. One day, he's going to get on a train and find his mom.

He can hear the trilling of a bird in the tree next door. There are birds that trill and birds that coo and sometimes Leon would make bird noises for Jake and Jake would pull Leon's lips like he was trying to grab the sound before it came out. Jake was always touching something—if it wasn't Leon himself it was his cars and his toys, and when Jake was going to sleep, he would hold on to Leon's fingers. Sometimes, thinking about Jake makes Leon feel sick.

Even before he opens his eyes, he can tell that Maureen is still asleep because his room is above the kitchen and the first thing she does in the morning is make a cup of coffee. She calls it "witch's brew" and once she let Leon taste it and he agrees with her. She has to put three sugars in to make it taste nice.

But the reason Maureen is still in bed is that there is nothing to get up for. Jake used to wake them up every morning and, without Jake, Maureen has been staying in bed later and later. She says it's because of her chest but Leon knows what it really is. The empty sound in the house is louder than Jake crying for his bottle. It's louder than his laugh. Louder than his baby drums. And if Leon turns round and looks at Jake's cot in the corner of the room, he knows that he will get angry with Maureen, so he picks at a scratch in the wallpaper and puts the pieces in his mouth. They taste of fish sticks.

Leon goes downstairs and still Maureen is in her room. He makes some Weetabix and eats it in front of the TV with the sound down low. He has the room to himself and he can watch what he wants, he doesn't have to have the baby programs on and Jake isn't screaming or trying to pull his hair. He makes some more Weetabix and sprinkles it with masses of sugar. Then he eats three of Jake's special yogurts without bits in. Maureen comes down and tells him to clear up his mess but when he goes into the kitchen she grabs him and snuggles him until he wants to cry.

"Right, mister," she says as she tidies up, "what's me and you doing on a miserable Saturday?"

Leon shrugs.

"We got that *Dumbo* video for later," she says, "and I've got some shopping to do but that won't take long. Shame it's raining."

Maureen stands in the doorway with her special pink hearts mug of coffee.

"Tell you what, we'll go for a little bus ride," she says. "We'll go and see Sylvia. Haven't seen her for ages."

Maureen's sister lives very far away and they have to take two buses. The first one stops on a busy road where there are lots of shops and too many people. Maureen holds his hand tight and people will think that Maureen is his mom. She's fat and her hair is too orange and he doesn't want anyone to think that his mom isn't beautiful, so he tries to get his hand back and put it in his pocket.

Maureen keeps stopping to look in shopwindows and saying how expensive everything is. The only good shop has lots of toys in the window—*Clash of the Titans* figures with Charon and Calibos—but Maureen won't wait, because they have to find the second bus and that takes forever. They pass factories and shops and enormous houses that are broken down and boarded up. Eventually, they get off the bus and stand at the bottom of a steep hill. Maureen looks up to the very top, shakes her head, and takes a deep breath.

"Here goes," she says.

She starts slowly, stopping every few steps and holding on to gates and grasping at hedges because she can't breathe. She tells Leon to carry her shopping bag and she shuffles along the pavement with one hand on her chest and the other swinging in the air. She has the same face as when she cries and Leon hopes she won't start until she gets where they're going. They take ages to get to the top and walk down the path to the bungalow.

Sylvia gasps when she opens the door.

"What on earth? Maureen! Get in here."

She helps Maureen inside.

Maureen can't speak and tell anyone what's wrong, so Sylvia gets her a glass of water.

"What happened?" she says again, lodging a cigarette in the corner of her mouth and feeling Maureen's forehead. Leon has seen Sylvia once before, when she came for Christmas dinner. She smoked all the time and didn't say one word to Leon. She didn't even bring him or Jake a present. She doesn't look like Maureen. She's very skinny and she has dark purple hair that looks like it's leaked onto her skin. She has long nails that match her lipstick and black tights with little holes all over them. She's wearing the same shoes that Carol wore once when she went out at Christmas with Tina. But if you added Tina's age and Carol's age together they still wouldn't be as old as Sylvia. She turns suddenly to Leon and points the cigarette at him.

"Did you see what happened?"

Leon shakes his head and sits next to Maureen, who pats him on his back.

"It's all right, Leon, love," she whispers. "She's not blaming you."

"Have you had a turn, Mo?" Sylvia asks.

"Got a tight chest, that's all. Got a sort of wheezing rattle or something every time I try and do anything."

Maureen sips the water and makes an ugly face.

"Coffee, Sylvia, if you don't mind. Three sugars."

"It'll be that sugar that's got you wheezing, if you ask me."

Sylvia goes to the kitchen and Maureen winks at Leon.

"She's all right, is Sylvie. Once you've known her fifty years."

Leon plays on the floor with his Action Man while the horse racing is on the TV. Maureen and Sylvia spend the day laughing and sometimes Maureen can't breathe because she thinks the joke is so funny.

"Remember Janet? Janet Blythe? Curvature of the spine with that funny nose?" says Sylvia.

"Yeah."

"She's got married to Gordon."

"Gordon Gordon? We talking about the same Gordon?"

"Yeah, Gordon. Goldfish Gordon with the lips."

"No."

"Yes."

"No. I can't believe it."

"Imagine their kids."

"They're too old for kids, Sylvia."

"I know but imagine."

Then Sylvia makes an ugly face, pulling her lips down and shoving her bottom teeth out, and Maureen has to lie on the sofa and keeps saying "Don't. Don't."

Even though Leon takes his Action Man, it's very boring at Sylvia's house. All they do is talk about the olden days when they were young and about all Sylvia's boyfriends and different people they know and who is married and who is separated and who is playing around.

Sylvia takes a photo album out and tells Leon to sit between her and Maureen.

"Wait till you see our Mo in some of these," she says.

The album is heavy on his legs and he has to put his feet up on tiptoe to stop it falling to the floor.

Sylvia turns the pages while Maureen wheezes next to him.

"There she is."

Sylvia points to a black-and-white picture of two girls in tight polka-dot dresses and funny hair. He can't see their faces because it's all blurred.

"That's her. What do you think?"

Sylvia keeps nudging him but he doesn't know what to say because it doesn't look like Maureen. It just looks like an old film from the Second World War.

"Look at this one," Sylvia says, turning another page, and Maureen gasps.

"God, I haven't seen that before. Where did you find that? Where was it taken? Southend?"

"Not Southend, Mo. That was when we went to the beach with Percy and Bob."

"It's Southend, Sylv."

Sylvia takes the photograph out and points at the back.

"What does that say? Morton's Holiday Park, Hastings, June 1949."

"Bloody hell. I'm skinny there."

"And look at me!" Sylvia is laughing. "I look like a bloody tart with my tits out like that."

Maureen frowns at Sylvia and looks at Leon.

"She needs a swear box, doesn't she, Leon?"

But Sylvia is turning pages and paying no attention and this goes on for ages, taking the photographs out and reading the address on the back and talking about where they were taken and where they lived and who is thin and who is fat and who is still alive and who is dead and who was handsome and who's got no teeth now. It goes on and on until they tell Leon he can put the TV on and see if there's a soccer match to watch.

Then, when they think he isn't listening, they start whispering. Maureen talks about Carol and tells Sylvia all over again what she's already told her on the phone. She tells her about Jake leaving and how upset she was and how Leon was grinding his teeth and she tells Sylvia about Carol not coming for them and Sylvia smokes and nods and shakes her head, saying things like "You wouldn't believe it" or "Never" like she hasn't heard it before.

Leon asks if he can go to the toilet.

"It's down the hallway, love," says Maureen. In Sylvia's bungalow there are no stairs, just a long corridor with bedrooms and a bathroom. Leon opens all the doors one by one. One bedroom is decorated in pale blue with a frilly bedspread and matching curtains like a princess lives there. Sylvia's too old to be a princess but it smells of her fusty, old perfume. The other bedrooms have single beds with pink carpet, then right by the bathroom there is a tall cupboard with sheets and pillowcases and towels and cardboard boxes. On the way back from the toilet he passes a door that leads to the garden. The key's in the lock, so he turns it and goes outside, walking slowly, looking right and left. Some people have dogs in their garden.

But there's no dog, just a square patch of grass and a green plastic tub of yellow flowers. Sylvia's underwear is on the line and it's the same color as her bedspread.

Maureen and Sylvia are talking; they chirp like birds when they're together. He goes quietly up to the sitting-room window but he can't see anything through the net curtains.

"Social workers are a waste of space if you ask me, Mo."

"Some of them."

"I can't stand them. Had my fill of that bunch when I worked in that home. Going out and looking after people is one thing. Having them in your own house is another, Mo. You've got social workers in and out with all them bloody visits, checking up on you, trying to catch you out. They come in for coffee and spend half the day talking about themselves. If I want friends, I'll make my own. And I don't know why you're still bothering at your age."

"I'm good at it. Anyway, it's for the kids."

"That one will get adopted, won't he, what's his name again?"

"Leon. Not a chance. That's what they say."

"Well, all right, it's a shame for him, but you're still running yourself ragged, that's all I know."

Leon drops down by the window ledge and goes back inside. He locks the door and puts the key in his pocket. When he goes back into Sylvia's living room, they both shut up.

"Washed your hands?" says Maureen.

Leon nods.

Maureen struggles up onto her feet.

Sylvia hugs her and grips her shoulders.

"Promise me, Mo. The doctor."

"I will, Sylv."

"I know what you're like."

"No, I will, really. I haven't felt right for a few weeks."

"Promise me."

"Yes, I will. Tomorrow."

"Sunday?"

"Monday then."

"Swear it, because we've been here before and you forget all about it."

"I swear, yes. Leon will remind me, won't you, love?"

Leon nods and Sylvia pokes him in the back.

"You make bloody sure. If you don't and anything happens to her, you'll be sorry."

The next day, Maureen doesn't get up and she lets Leon make her witch's brew and toast. He is careful with the brew because he has to boil the kettle and stand on a chair to make sure it all goes into the mug. Then he makes the toast and puts apricot jam and butter on it and then puts it all on a tray. He carries it all the way upstairs and into her room. Maureen eases herself up in bed and smooths the blankets on her lap. She takes the tray off Leon and shakes her head.

"You are a star, you are, Leon. My best and lovely boy. Can't believe you made this all by yourself. Nine years old and we've already got a chef in the house."

She points everything out.

"Toast, jam, little plate, coffee in my special mug, and not a single drip on the tray. Good boy. You've got a job for life, you know that, don't you?"

Leon smiles and she takes his hand.

"It will be all right, love. You and me together. We'll be all right and you can stay with Auntie Maureen for the foreseeable as far as I'm concerned. You're not to worry."

"You have to go to the doctor," says Leon. "Tomorrow you have to go."

"Yes, yes. See how I'm feeling in the morning."

But Leon can hear the crackling sound that comes from her throat like a cough that won't come out. And her face is the same color as the sheets. He can tell when Maureen's trying to be happy and when she's worried and he knows now why Sylvia kept making her promise.

14

"Leon! Leon!"

Maureen has had her no-nonsense voice on all day. Even before Leon was properly awake she was using it, talking on the phone in her bedroom and saying bad things about his mother. Again. Leon heard her.

"She must have got a bloody surprise when she called Social Services. She had two when she took off. Now there's just the one and he's got quite a temper when he's roused. No wonder, life he's had. She's been sick apparently, so the social worker said. Sick, in and out of institutions. Yeah, yeah, somewhere up north, then Bristol and God knows where else. Well, I don't know, some sort of breakdown. I've said it before and I'll say it again, I'd have to be pretty sick to keep me from my kids, know what I mean?"

But Leon doesn't understand why Maureen should be talking about his mother all of a sudden. She's never even met her. Leon's the only one who really knows what Carol's like and even he hasn't seen her for a long, long time.

"Leon! Come down here, I said!"

He's nearly as tall as Maureen and looking her straight in the eye.

"Come on. Someone's coming to see you today."

"Who?"

Maureen prods him all the way to the kitchen and tells him to wash his hands while she watches.

"Properly, Leon. I'm standing right here."

She folds her arms and, as she does, Leon sees the softness creep back into her face.

"Come on, love. Don't take all day. You're having a visitor. I wasn't sure whether or not she'd come, so I haven't said anything until now. We've been here before, haven't we? Her saying she's coming and then not coming, eh? But she's on her way apparently, so look sharp."

Leon says nothing. Maureen often says nice things and nasty things both at the same time. She passes him the towel and while he dries his hands she puts her hand to his cheek.

"Your mom's been very ill, love. And it's been a long time, hasn't it? Nearly a year and that's forever at your age. So just take it slow with her, all right? She might be, well . . . different, you know? Not like you remember, all right?"

Leon feels sick but he can't tell Maureen because then she might say he can't see his mom.

"Want a Kit Kat?" she says.

He nods.

"Go for a pee first. You know what you're like if you get excited. Toilet first and then have a Kit Kat."

They wait together by the window. It's the sort of day where it never gets properly bright. It's not raining but the pavement is wet and looks like dirty metal in the misty light. Maureen is wheezing behind him, holding the net curtain out of the way.

"These need a good soak in the bath," she says. "We'll take them all down tomorrow. Wipe these sills as well. Want to earn some pocket money, Leon?"

Maureen always talks when he's trying to concentrate. Suddenly a sports car pulls into the road, slows down, and stops right outside Maureen's house.

"This is it," she says and she lets the curtain drop.

Leon shirks Maureen's hand from his shoulder. Inside the sports car are Carol and a man. The man is white, so he knows his dad hasn't come but it doesn't look like Jake's dad, either. Leon and Maureen both go and sit on the sofa. They're not speaking. Leon is waiting for the bell to ring and Maureen is waiting to tell him to answer the door. It takes ages. Why won't she come inside? Why hasn't she come for him? Maybe she will drive away and Leon will never see her again. Lots and lots of words, most of them bad, come into his mouth and Leon has to swallow them down as usual. She's not coming in and, anyway, he hates her. Leon gets up and starts towards the back door.

"Wait!" Maureen whispers.

He hears a car door slam, then another. He rushes to the front door and opens it and she's there, honestly, really, truly there, walking down the garden path toward him. The man's with her, a few steps behind, walking with his hands in his pockets. Carol is smiling but she's crying as well and Leon wants to run to her to make her better but before he can move she seems to crumple down on to her knees and the man catches her under her arms and helps her up.

"Thank you. I'm all right. I'm all right. I want to go on my own."

She puts her arms out and Leon walks slowly in case he

makes her collapse again. She wipes her sleeve across her face before she kisses him. She's trying to say something but nothing comes out. Leon is glad she's crying because now Maureen will know that she cares.

"Come in, love!" shouts Maureen from the doorway. "Come in and bring your friend."

The man shakes his head and starts walking back to his car.

"Be back in a bit, Carol, love. You all right?"

Carol waves him away and they all go inside and sit on the sofa. Carol kisses Leon again, much too hard, and Leon decides not to say anything just in case it comes out wrong or he starts to cry as well.

"How's my little boy?" Carol says but she isn't looking at him. She's trying to find her cigarettes. She always does this and Leon has to take the bag and look for her. He tries to take the bag off her but she snatches it away and he sees Maureen frown. He knows that later Maureen will be on the phone to her sister saying bad things about Carol, about her crying and smoking and coming with a man. So he sits close to his mom because he belongs to her and she belongs to him.

"I've got something in here for you," Carol says. "I've bought this for you."

It's a pencil-and-pen set in a wooden box. It looks like it belongs to a teacher or a professor.

"I didn't get a chance to wrap it, Leon, love. Do you like it?" Carol has her cigarette poised at her lips, her hand frozen like she can't continue until he says yes.

"Yes."

"Good." She squeezes the lighter and then blows the smoke out really hard.

When Carol starts speaking, Leon can see how she's changed. Her teeth and her fingers are yellowy brown like mustard and her cheeks go in like a skeleton. And she smells different. She keeps putting the cigarette in her mouth and leaving it a long, long time and then when she talks all the ash drops off the end and wisps of smoke curl around her words.

"You all right?" she asks and she nods to tell him what the answer should be.

Maureen brings in two cups of coffee.

"There you go, two sugars."

Carol takes the cup and Leon sees it shake in her hand.

"Can't control things these days," she says, trying to laugh. "Not as bad as I was though. Not by a long shot. I never knew nothing about nothing," she says. "I was so ill I couldn't tell you my own name."

Maureen shakes her head.

"They said I had that postpartum depression when I had my baby. My mom was the same when she had me and they hospitalized her. They gave you electric-shock treatment in them days."

Leon watches her trying to hold the cup with two hands and smoke her cigarette at the same time.

"Then I lost touch with Tony, that's Jake's dad. I thought he was the one, I really did. And, anyway, I just went to pieces. No one's fault. Took me months to get better. I was in the hospital for a bit and then they gave me a room in the Maybird Center."

"Maybird Center?" asks Maureen.

"There's two on-site social workers round the clock. It was so noisy I felt like I was going round the bend, so I moved out. Thought it was best for everyone if I stayed clear, you know, get myself straight, and I'm getting there. I am. But when I got in touch with the Social they said they'd given my baby away. Broke my heart."

They are all quiet.

"They took my baby," she says and starts to cry again so that her coffee shakes in the cup. "My baby."

Maureen puts her hand on Carol's and squeezes.

"Leon took it very badly too, Carol," says Maureen.

Leon wants to tell Maureen to mind her own business. She should leave him and his mom to be alone. Carol sniffs.

"I don't know what to do. It's one step forward and then I can't cope."

Maureen takes the cup out of Carol's hand and gives her a tissue to wipe her tears. Leon gets a biscuit.

"Leon's missed you, love. Haven't you, Leon?" Maureen says with a fake voice.

Leon says nothing.

"He's hoping you can get back on your feet. He's doing well at school but we've had one or two setbacks with meeting his targets, nothing serious but it's been hard on him. Hasn't it, Leon?"

"No."

Maureen shakes her head.

"Are you moving back here now then, Carol? Now you're a bit better?"

His mom isn't listening. She is staring at the dead eye of the television. She looks like she's reading the paper, because her lips are moving. Maureen and Leon look at each other because neither of them knows what to say. Eventually Carol finds her words.

"It was the best day of my life when I found Alan. That's who brought me. He's dead good to me. Runs his own business. Pool hall." She pats Leon twice on his jeans.

"Wants us all to go out to the seaside. We can go in his sports car. You love cars, don't you? He said he's going to take you on the bumper cars. Would you like that?"

Leon doesn't say anything. He doesn't want to share his mom

all the time. He doesn't want to share his mom with Maureen. He doesn't want to share his mom with Alan.

"Anyway," she continues, "I'm trying, that's the point. I'm aware of my issues and behaviors."

She speaks like she's just learned some new words.

"I'm addressing things. Trying. I've got to take it slow. I can only come when Alan can bring me in his car cuz I'm not very good on the bus. Makes me ill."

Leon sees Maureen raise an eyebrow and fold her arms.

"Makes us all ill, love," she says. "Anyway, would you like to see Leon's bedroom? He's been collecting soccer cards."

She motions to Leon to stand up.

"You lead the way for your mom, Leon."

Leon helps Carol up and takes her to his bedroom. It's funny having her in his room. She doesn't know where to sit.

"It's nice," she says. She looks at his posters on the wall and then she looks out of the window.

"I wonder what time it is," she says.

She looks at the soccer cards he's been collecting and sticking on his chart. She keeps saying "that's nice" and "lovely" and she's pleased it's so neat and tidy.

"You like everything in its proper place. You used to be good at organizing and making things nice. I do remember, you know, Leon. I remember you taking care of me."

She bends her head to his and their foreheads touch. She puts her hands on his cheeks and moves them slowly around his neck, drawing him in, but then suddenly she draws back and takes a deep breath.

"Is it warm in here or is it me?" she says.

She opens his wardrobe and stares at his clothes like she's counting them. She fiddles with the knob on the door and then notices the certificate he got from school for never missing a day for a whole term and she says she can't believe how big his feet have become.

"They're enormous, Leon. You're going to be tall like my dad. He was six feet four and—"

She catches sight of the picture of Jake on the white carpet and crumples down on his bedroom floor.

"Mom, Mom!" Leon shouts but she is rocking to and fro with her hand outstretched toward the photo. Leon runs downstairs to tell Maureen to come and help him get her up. They sit her on the bed and she starts crying again, saying, "Oooh, oh."

Maureen has a different voice when she tells her to calm down.

"You're frightening him, Carol. Pull yourself together."

Carol goes to light a cigarette.

"I don't allow smoking upstairs, neither."

Maureen helps Carol up and takes her arm.

"Come on, up you come. We'll go down together. Me and Leon will help you."

They sit her on the sofa.

"Can I have that photo of my baby?" she says. "It's his birthday next week. And I haven't got a photograph of him. No one's even given me a photograph."

Maureen makes a funny face like she's trying to find the right words to explain.

"Er, no, Carol. No, you cannot. That picture was taken by me for Leon. Paid for by me. He hasn't got much else, has he? He's not at home with you where he should be and he hasn't got his brother, which he's finding bloody hard if you don't mind me saying."

Maureen folds her arms like she's finished but she hasn't.

"And you say you're not well. That's also hard for a little nine-year-old. I know because he lives with me and I see it."

Carol stands up suddenly.

"He's falling behind at school. Hasn't made any friends, have you, Leon? And he's starting to get light-fingered. I'd be worried if he was mine."

Carol draws the net curtain back and peers through the glass.

"Alan'll be here in a minute. I better get ready."

She puts her coat on, puts her handbag in the crook of her arm, and opens the front door. Leon stands next to her and she takes his hand in hers. She squeezes his fingers and he can feel her love traveling all the way down from her heart into his. It's like special electricity, a secret. They watch for the sports car. His mother used to smell of shampoo and their old house. She used to smell like her bed and her sheets, she used to smell of different cigarettes. She used to smell of beans on toast and bath time. But all he can smell now is Maureen's air freshener, stronger than the smell of his mom and where they used to live.

Maureen comes and stands behind them. Leon can feel all the words she's keeping inside that she wants to say and all the things she feels about his mom. She only lets a few of them come out.

"You've got a lovely son in Leon, you know. He's as good as gold and he misses you."

Carol looks up and down the street and fidgets with her handbag like she needs another cigarette. She keeps squeezing Leon's hand but she looks the other way and he knows she's trying to speak with her fingers, telling Maureen to shut up and telling Leon that she's got good memories of when they were all together and that she still loves him and why did they have to take Jake away? Maureen speaks a bit louder.

"My house is always open to you if you want to visit him."

Carol steps out onto the garden path.

"Alan's looking after me, Leon, you're not to worry."

The sports car stops outside and, before she walks away, Carol puts their foreheads together and kisses him. Leon tears away, upstairs into his bedroom, takes the photograph of Jake quick as he can and runs after her.

"Mom! Wait!"

"You're a little angel," she says.

She holds the photograph against her heart and walks slowly away. Leon stands on the street and watches her get into the car. She says something to the man and he laughs, then the sports car turns the corner and is gone. Leon stands on the concrete step in Maureen's house at the curve of the avenue looking at the empty space where his mom was. He feels a dark star of pain in his throat and the last warmth of her touch on his fingers. When Leon goes inside, he turns the television on and sits on the sofa. Maureen tells him off for having the volume too loud.

"You're a good boy, Leon. A bloody good kid considering. You don't deserve this. I know it's not her fault, but Jesus Christ Almighty. It's not a fair world, I can tell you. And that photo was for you, not her."

She tries to give him a hug but he's very angry with Maureen for not liking his mother and not believing she's really ill. Leon saw with his own eyes how she fell apart when she saw Jake. And he knows what his mother knows. That someone else is holding Jake and kissing him. Someone else is looking into the perfect blue of his perfect eyes. Someone else is smelling him and touching the soft skin on the back of his hand.

Late that night, when Leon lies on his bed, he misses the photograph of Jake and he has to close his eyes to remember it. He holds on to Big Red Bear and thinks about all the things he didn't say to his mom. How long will it be for her to get better? When is she coming back for him? What happened to the rest of his toys at the old house? Will she come back? Where is she?

Where is Jake? What will he get for his birthday? What is wrong with her? Why doesn't she come back?

Then he says, under his breath, so Maureen won't hear, all the bad words he has stored up all day since his mother came and took the photograph and drove away without him.

15

It's the middle of the night when the ambulance comes. Maureen wakes him up, calling and calling and calling. Leon springs out of bed, turns the light on, and runs into her room. Her face is like cold porridge and her hair is wet, stuck to her head. She's half sitting up and she has an old man's voice.

"Nine-nine-nine," she says. "Nine-nine-nine now."

He stands by the front door like the operator tells him to and he's glad, because he doesn't want to see Maureen when she sounds like a dying man in the middle of the night. He wants to pee so badly his leg starts moving all on its own. The ambulance comes with the flashing lights and he lets them in, shows them the way to Maureen's bedroom. While they go in, he runs to the bathroom and does the longest pee of his life. He waits downstairs in his pajamas and they tell him he's a good boy and that he's done a brave thing and Leon decides he might be an ambulance man when he grows up. They sit him in the back of the ambulance and put a mask on Maureen's face. One of them speaks into a walkie-talkie; it crackles and hisses and Leon wishes he had one. Maureen holds her hand out for him but he's scared to touch her in case she dies. This might be the time that there's no one to look after him.

At the hospital, a woman police officer asks him all about Carol and Jake. He tries very hard not to cry. But when she gives him a little hug, it's like spilling a glass of soda, everything comes out in a rush and he can't stop the tears and the noise that comes out of his heart. The policewoman takes him into a room on his own and gives him a tissue. She tells him that Maureen isn't going to die.

"She's not going to die, Leon, sweetheart, but she can't talk, and right at this minute, you can't see her. That doesn't mean anything bad, you not seeing her. It means doctors and nurses are looking after her while I look after you."

"Yes," says Leon.

"And when she's better, they'll let you know because you're the brave one who saved her life. Now isn't that something to smile about, eh? You'll be able to tell everyone at school all about it, won't you? You'll be a hero. You are a hero. A brave hero and a clever boy. There it is, a little smile. It's the smallest smile I've ever seen. Is there another one in there? A bigger one? That's it, that's the one I was looking for."

Then everything gets a bit better because the policewoman takes him to the café and buys him a jelly doughnut and a hot chocolate. Someone else gives him a comic book and then he sits in the Panda car and presses the buttons that make the light come on. The policewoman shows him her walkie-talkie and lets him say, "Come in, come in," but no one answers. She says she's going to tell everyone at the police station how brave he's been. The policewoman is a bit like the nurse at the hospital when Jake was born: when she says something you believe her. They sit in a waiting room with a black-and-white film on the TV. There are four gangsters in an old-fashioned car chasing a man who's hanging off the back of a truck. The car is skidding all over the road and just when the gangsters are having a shoot-out, Sylvia bursts into the room. She crouches down by his chair and squeezes his arms.

"You saved her life, love. Good boy, good boy. Thank you."

She kisses him and he can smell her cigarettes and her special old lady smell that's worse than Maureen's. The stink makes him want to push her away. But she holds his hand and shakes it.

"You're a proper little man, you are."

Later on, the emergency social worker comes and soon there's a huddle of them standing together in the corner of the room. A doctor, the nice policewoman, the social worker, and Sylvia, all talking about him with their arms folded. One by one they look at him and shake their heads and even when he tries really hard he can only hear a few words.

". . . bronchial pneumonia with complications . . ."

". . . weeks rather than days . . ."

". . . appropriately accommodated . . . police checked . . ."

And Sylvia keeps saying, "I could, I could. I'm only part-time at the supermarket. I could. He's a good lad. He's saved her bloody life, he has. She always said he was a good kid, Mo did. I'll have him. Yes, I will. Bless him."

The social worker starts writing on some paper and says, "Short term, we're talking short term."

They all come toward him at the same time.

The social worker kneels down until her face is a few inches from Leon's. She has glasses that make her eyes look massive like she's an alien.

"Right," she says, "you're going back home to Maureen's, to your own bed with Sylvia and she will look after you tonight. She's been a registered carer before, so we're quite happy she knows what to do. You like Sylvia, don't you? Good, good. You've been very grown up, Leon, and everyone is really proud of you.

Maureen will be in the hospital for a little while and tomorrow we will work out what will happen to you long term. Obviously we will try to keep you at home. I think you've had a pretty rough time lately and we don't want to add to that, do we?"

She looks around at the others and they all nod. Sylvia lights a cigarette.

"So, we're doing our best, we want you to know that, all right? Good boy."

16

There are too many things that Leon doesn't like and he's made a list of them in his head.

Sylvia.

Sylvia's house.

Having to move to Sylvia's house even though they said he could stay at Maureen's house but they lied. Sylvia only stayed one night in Maureen's house; then she said she was sick of it and she was going back to her own house and he had to go with her.

The sheets on his new bed in Sylvia's house. They're pink.

The way Sylvia keeps going to visit Maureen in the daytime when he's at his new school.

His new school. Again.

Sylvia calling Maureen "Mo" all the time or "our Mo" to leave Leon out.

Nobody letting him talk about Jake. Maureen used to let him talk about Jake and she would join in.

No one remembering that he's got a brother.

Two girls in his new school who made him swear and get into trouble.

Sylvia's cereal.

The way on Saturdays Sylvia keeps telling him to go outside to play when all the best shows are on.

Her smell.

His mom not coming to get him.

All the toys he couldn't bring to Sylvia's house because of the mess they make.

No one talking about Jake's first birthday because they've forgotten about him but Leon hasn't.

His new social worker, because they keep changing and this one has bad breath and she keeps saying, "I'm new."

Bedtime at Sylvia's house because it's too early and he can't sleep when it's light outside.

Sylvia's laugh when her show's on.

People pretending all the time.

All the things he doesn't like keep coming one after another and eventually the Zebra turns up again. She says what the other social workers have said before, that living with Sylvia is only temporary and that when Maureen comes out of the hospital he can go back to live with her. For ages, he didn't take anything out of his backpack because he believed what they said but then it got to eight days and they said a bit longer and then a bit longer and then he had to go to a new school. So Leon came up with a good idea. If they could find his mom, then he could stay with her just until Maureen gets better. He could look after Carol because he's done it before and it will be even easier because it will just be the two of them now that Jake has gone. But when he tells the Zebra his good idea she just says no.

"We've talked about that already, Leon. Your mom moved to Bristol and she's living in a halfway house. She needs a lot of support. She's seeing doctors, taking some new medication, and talking to people about how she feels. She's trying to get back on her feet but it takes time. They don't allow children there and, anyway, Leon, we would have to make sure that your mom could look after you properly even if she wanted to."

Leon turns away while she is still speaking. The Zebra's got a new hairstyle. Now there are two white stripes at the sides as well as the back. She thinks she looks great but she doesn't. The Zebra's black suit is too tight and her white shirt is trying to bust open. But out of all the social workers he's ever had, she looks at him the most. And when he looks away, she stops speaking until he turns round.

Leon picks a scab on his finger because he can tell that he's going to cry. Or get angry. If he concentrates on something else, or makes a little pain on his finger, then it stops the tears. Or if it's anger that's coming, the best thing to do is pretend it's not happening or have some candy or find something to play with. Sometimes, he takes ten pence from Sylvia's purse.

"Why?" asks Leon.

"Why what?"

"Why can't I look after her? I did it before."

"Because that's not being a child, Leon. You're a young boy and your mom is an adult and she has to look after you. Not the other way around. When she can't look after you, we make sure there is somebody else that can. And right now that person is Sylvia."

Sylvia stands in the doorway, listening and smoking and tutting. Sometimes Sylvia is like a robot. Her arm puts the cigarette in her mouth and then takes it out and holds it in the air. Then the arm does the same thing over and over until the cigarette is finished. When she's not paying attention, the ash lands on her blouse and she doesn't even notice.

"Why can't I see Maureen?"

"I just said why. She's still not well, Leon. And she's got a virus. They turned me away when I went. No one's allowed in."

"I've told him ten times," Sylvia says, "and you've told him. It doesn't seem to go in."

The Zebra strokes Leon's arm.

"It's hard, isn't it, Leon?" she says. "But you know what? Come with me. Come on."

She gets up and opens the front door. Leon follows. She goes to the trunk of her car and lifts the lid. She leans in and pulls out a bike.

"Who do you think this is for?"

It isn't new but it is definitely a BMX. Leon stands out of the way while she puts it on the pavement. He looks at the Zebra because he isn't sure if it's true. That she really means it.

"Go on then," she says. "You can ride a bike, can't you?"

He jumps on and turns around and around in a circle.

"See!" he shouted. "My dad showed me."

"Lovely! You be careful now!"

But Leon doesn't want to be careful. He wants to ride as fast as a car. Faster than a car. Fast as a rocket. He pedals downhill, away from Sylvia's house, and the bike gets faster and faster. The wind's in his eyes, in his hair, ripping through his T-shirt like cold fingers on his skin and he keeps going, sailing right to the bottom of the road, feeling his legs pumping hard, hurting, a nice pain in his belly; all the bad things and halfway houses are behind him and can't catch up. He swoops in a tight curve at the end of the road and then bombs back, uphill, faster than all the cars stuck in the traffic, passing houses that blur into one another, plunging his feet down and rising up again, down and up, down and up, to the very top of the hill, straight past Sylvia's bungalow this time, straight past the Zebra on the sidewalk, all the way to the traffic lights and then he stops to get his breath.

Everything feels loose inside him, he's longer and stronger, and even though he's panting, he's full of air, dizzy and light. He smiles as he sees a black man on a racing bike, pumping hard just like Leon, slinking in between the cars and buses. His back is bent low, curved, no shirt on. He has a shiny bald head and wide yellow sunglasses. He looks like a wasp. His bike is red like Leon's but it's faster, with narrow wheels, slick as a bullet. The man angles his bike so his knees are almost skimming the road, then just as he's about to topple over, he turns the corner in one sweet and beautiful movement. Gone.

Leon pedals slowly back to Sylvia's. The Zebra is standing outside with her hands in her pockets. She's the best social worker in the world.

"There you go," she says. "You were made for that bike, Leon."

She opens the door to her car.

"I'll come back next week and, if she's a bit better, we'll see about a visit to Maureen. I'll take you myself."

17

After school, the next day, Leon asks Sylvia if he can go outside with his new bike. She's got the curtains drawn because it's sunny outside and she's watching her shows where people have to answer hard questions. She thinks she knows the answers when she doesn't. The man with the wig on the TV asks the questions and Sylvia says the answer right at the same time as the contestant, like she's clever. She didn't even know who won the soccer game. Eventually, Sylvia tells him to be careful of traffic and not to stay out too long.

Leon bikes up to the traffic lights. He parks at an angle to the corner, sits back on the seat, and folds his arms. People in their cars look at him; kids in the backseat can see his bike, his new BMX. He gets off, squats down, checks the tires, gets back on, twists the wheels, and watches people watching him. He looks big for his age, twelve or thirteen, and now, with his new bike, he could even be fourteen. As he sits he tries to remember the way Wasp Man went.

He crosses the road and turns the corner into a long busy street. He pedals on the pavement between stacks of vegetables outside the Pakistani shops. There are loads more black people than where Sylvia lives and lots of shops sell funny-looking vegetables in dark purple and pale green, things he's never seen in blood red and milky white, everything piled up on milk crates, spilling out onto the ground. He pedals over a squashed black banana and his front tire skids and slips. Clusters of old Indian men in turbans sit on little stools outside their shops, their long white beards dancing in the wind. Two black men sit on a square of grass with a chessboard between them, talking over loud music from a record shop. Black women in bright African headdresses walk slowly, holding the hands of their children, their big silver earrings swinging as they go. Some of the black men have locks standing up or hanging down their backs like furry black rope. Because the road is so narrow all the traffic goes slow and people in the cars shout at each other when they can't move forward. No one notices Leon.

He comes eventually to a crossroads. Down a narrow lane behind rusty iron railings, there is a huge, flat garden with lots of huts. He goes up to the sign, "Rookery Road Allotments." He pedals slowly past, down a little path that branches and curves, and everywhere he looks there are tidy rows of flowers and vegetables, garden sheds, greenhouses, crooked buildings made of corrugated iron and old windows, long plastic tunnels with plants inside, and, right by the gate, an old man is swinging a big curved knife, cutting down a bush. Leon watches him. That's the best knife he's ever seen and even though the man is old he's cutting through the bush like a soldier in the jungle. Right, left, right, left. The bush is hacked down to a naked, gnarled trunk.

Whoosh. Suddenly, a bike skims past Leon so close that he nearly falls. It's Wasp Man, with his bald head and yellow glasses.

"Easy, Star!" he shouts.

The man with the knife turns around and raises his arm in the air.

"Not in here!" he shouts. "Not in here!" He points the knife at a sign that says, "No dogs. No ball games. No cycling. No unaccompanied children."

But Wasp Man is still going fast along the little paths, so Leon gets off his bike and follows him to the edge of the allotment near a wooden shed. Leon wheels his bike right up to him.

"Yo, my friend," says Wasp Man. "You looking for somebody?"

Leon stares. The man is wearing tight black leggings and no top. His skin is brown like the wood on Sylvia's sideboard, brown like his dad's but shiny and muscly like the Hulk. He has three scars across his shoulder like he's been shot or attacked, another scar on his cheek. He's a warrior. He lifts his yellow wasp glasses. His eyes are black and when he smiles he looks like he's got too many teeth for his mouth.

"You lost?" he asks.

"No," says Leon. "I've got a bike like yours."

"Yeah? That's a good bike, Star. Let me see."

Leon gets off the bike and Wasp Man bends down. He handles the bike and runs it along the ground and back a few times, turns the pedals with his hand.

"Hold it," he says and takes a wrench out of his bag. "Good job I was just coming from work."

He unscrews something and pulls the seat up higher. He unscrews something else by the handlebars and pushes them down. He tightens everything up and pushes it toward Leon.

"Now you'll go faster. It's a bit small for you, you know. But this will fix it."

Leon sits back on and he's right. It is better. He rides round in a little circle.

"Yeah," says Wasp Man. "You got it." Then suddenly he says, "Get off. Quick. Now."

The man with the knife walks over to them and looks at Leon first.

"Who are you?"

Leon says nothing.

"Top of the morning to you, sir!" says Wasp Man. He smiles the big smile and salutes.

"Mr. Burrows," says the man, pointing the tip of the knife at Leon. "Children aren't allowed."

"Meaning?"

"Meaning that whoever he is, he's not allowed in here unaccompanied. Especially not riding a bicycle. Neither, for that matter, are you."

"I need to be accompanied, too?" says Wasp Man, still with his smile.

The man with the knife closes his eyes. Where the knife has been chopping at the hedge there are streaks of green on the sharp blade like alien's blood. The handle is made of black wood with a blue tassel on the end. It is so long that it nearly touches the ground. The man raises the knife and points the tip at Leon's neck.

"You know what I mean. Riding a bike. Cycling within the allotment boundary."

"Sorry?" says Mr. Burrows, turning his ear toward the man. "I didn't catch that. I'm not too good with Irish. Doing what?"

"It's Gaelic, not Irish, and on this occasion I was speaking English." The man takes a deep breath and repeats his words slowly. "Cycling. Within. The. Allotment. Boundary."

"Ah!" says Mr. Burrows. "You like your rules, don't you, Mr. Devlin?"

"They're not mine. I'm on the committee and, incidentally, so was your father."

"Yeah, well, he's not here and I am. I just come from work, and anyway, cycling is no crime. Don't worry yourself."

"I am not worried. Regulations, Mr. Burrows. They're not made by me, as you well know. They are committee regulations. And they're made to be adhered to."

"Aye, sir, I understand, I do," says Mr. Burrows and he tries to say it the same as Mr. Devlin with the funny accent.

Mr. Devlin stares and Mr. Burrows raises a finger.

"Oh, and by the way, Mr. Devlin, I think you finished your sentence with a preposition." He wags his finger in the air. "Against the rules."

The two men look at each other like they're about to start fighting but Mr. Devlin has a dangerous weapon and Mr. Burrows doesn't. Just when Leon thinks something is going to happen, Mr. Devlin walks away and Mr. Burrows makes a monkey face behind his back just the way Leon does when Sylvia tells him off.

"That man," he says, "has nothing else to do but lord it over people. Thinks he owns this place. So busy spying, he forgets to live his life."

Leon watches Mr. Devlin. He has a bit of a limp but, from the back, he could be young in his army boots and camouflage jacket. He's much older than Mr. Burrows and his white skin looks dirty or browned by the sun, but he looks strong. Maybe he's got scars as well under all his clothes.

"You want a drink, Star? Come."

Mr. Burrows unlocks the door of his hut. It's dusty inside, with folded-up chairs stacked at one end. A tall metal bin half-full of water has cans of soda floating on the top. On a little metal table, there is a set of dominoes in a wooden case. Leon's dad used to have a set of dominoes and his name was engraved on the lid: "Byron Francis." His dad used to let him play with them and line them up end to end, matching all the numbers. He picks up the case and rattles it.

"You're too young for them," says Mr. Burrows and lifts them out of his hand. "Big man's game."

On one side of the shed there are posters and pictures and on the other side there are three wide windows and, under the windows, there are rows and rows of little plants in black plastic trays. The shed smells of warm earth, sweet and fresh. Leon puts his face right up to one of the plants. The silver-green leaves are so thin and delicate that he can see threads of tiny veins like the veins on Jake's hands. And there are brown seeds in some of the trays that have burst open and white stems are bulging out, trying to escape. With the very tip of his finger, Leon presses down on the soil.

"Easy, easy," says Mr. Burrows and he leans down to look at what Leon has done.

"You see these?" he says. "Zucchini. I don't even like them but they grow good and strong. Yellow flowers."

He points to another tray.

"And these? Mangetout. Say it."

"Mange tout."

"Means 'eat all.' You can eat the whole pod, seeds and everything."

"What's in there?"

"Nothing yet. That tray is waiting for runner beans. Come."

Leon follows Mr. Burrows back outside.

"Cream soda," he says to Leon. "Kids love cream soda. Cool you down."

Leon pulls the ring off the can and glugs it back.

"You needed that, eh?"

Leon nods. "What's your name?" he asks.

"They call me Tufty because of my thick hair," says Mr. Burrows and he waits until Leon starts to smile.

"Yeah, lost my hair when I was your age. Never grew back. Linwood is what my mother named me but everyone calls me Tufty except that man over there. He thinks he's the boss. The general in a one-man army."

While Tufty drinks, he kicks at the stony soil.

"I got watering to do, weeding, seeds to plant, hoeing. Day like today," he says, "ain't really no digging day, Star, but you got to work with the seasons. Wait."

Tufty goes into his shed and comes back with two folding chairs that he sets in the shade.

"Come."

Leon sits next to Tufty and kicks the dry, stony soil like Tufty did. The pebbles roll under his feet and a bloom of gray dust settles on his sneakers.

Tufty's body covers the whole seat; he looks like he's sitting on nothing. He unlaces his special cycling sneakers and takes off his socks. He places his naked foot on top of the shoe and wiggles his toes.

"The sun," he says, closing his eyes and turning his face to the sky, "is a healer. When the sun comes out everybody smiles. World looks different. You can manage in the sun what you can't manage in the rain. That's what my father says. That's why he don't live here no more."

Leon looks up and closes his eyes as well. He remembers a day when his mom was pushing the stroller in the rain and Leon was holding on to the handle. She forgot the plastic cover and Jake was getting wet and she was rushing, bouncing the wheels in the puddles and splashing everywhere. By the time they got home they were all upset. His mom made a bottle for Jake and then when he was asleep she kissed Leon over and over and said she was sorry. She let him stay up late and watch TV with her under a blanket on the sofa. Then when he was in bed, she kissed him again.

"You're such a good boy, Leon. I'm sorry if I'm not the best mom. I love you, you know."

That's what the sunshine feels like.

Leon opens his eyes and looks around. There are no fences

between the gardens, just straight edges in the soil or grassy paths. There are other people gardening apart from Mr. Devlin. There's a woman in a pink sari in the next garden with her husband in a black turban. They're bending over, pulling weeds, talking to each other all the time in their own language. The woman keeps standing up and holding her back, so her husband points to a chair. She laughs and shakes her head, waves at a white woman wearing a vest who's digging her garden with a heavy iron fork that she stabs in and kicks, then turns over. She's the same age as Maureen and the vest is very tight on her chest. She's wearing a long, flowery skirt and a yellow bandana around her hair. She sees Leon looking and she waves.

"All help welcome!" she shouts.

The more Leon looks, the more people he sees and he realizes how huge the allotments are; they go on and on as far as he can see.

Tufty suddenly picks up a big iron fork and marches off to one end of his plot.

"Work to do," he says. "You take care, Star."

Leon watches him for a while and cycles away. He trundles between the little gardens, taking his time to see what people are doing. Some people have only flowers and a little lawn like Sylvia with deck chairs and parasols. Other people have long, straight rows of plants, bushy and neat. There are lots of plots like Tufty's, made into sections with a different plant in each section and some sections with nothing but dusty brown soil. There are no swings or slides but it's better than a park because everybody has their own bit of land to look after and they can do what they like with it. If Leon had his own patch he would make it into a soccer field or he would make a secret den with an underground tunnel.

Eventually Leon cycles back past Tufty toward the entrance and sees the man with the knife, Mr. Devlin. He is piling the branches and leaves into a wheelbarrow with the knife lying at his feet. Leon gets off his bike and goes a bit closer.

"Stay off that bike," says Mr. Devlin.

"What's that?" asks Leon, pointing at the knife.

The man turns his head slowly.

"Kanetsune," he says.

"Can I touch it?" asks Leon.

"No," says the man. "And if you remain here much longer you'll be trespassing."

"Are you from the army?" Leon says, making his bike balance on its two wheels.

The man picks up the wheelbarrow and marches away. Leon follows him down a little gravel path and sees him park the wheelbarrow and go inside a hut, except this hut is made of bricks with a proper roof and a chimney. It has two windows with iron bars across and a wooden door with three steel locks. All around the hut is a strip of grass with flowers and wooden barrels. There's stuff everywhere: a rusty wheel, a pile of pots stacked inside each other, the twisted branch of a dead tree, an old armchair with the seat missing, and a clothesline with a blue shirt hanging on it. Leon wonders if Mr. Devlin lives in a halfway house. He waits and waits but the man doesn't come back, so Leon pedals away, back to the corner, through the busy street with the vegetables on the pavements, over the traffic lights and down the hill to Sylvia's house.

18

Sometimes, on Saturday mornings, Leon can have the television all to himself to watch *Tiswas* and *Swap Shop*. If the cartoons are on, Sylvia will watch them with him but she talks all the time or paints her toenails, making a horrible smell. Everything Sylvia likes is purple because she wants it to match her hair. Afterward they have to go to the shop where Sylvia works part-time, to collect her money.

She always spends ages talking to the man who gives her the brown packet. He holds on to it until she tugs it away with a fake smile and when they get outside she calls him a bastard. On the way back she always gets her magazine and some cakes and Leon gets a comic. Sylvia sits at the kitchen table and licks her fingers and turns the pages and eats the cakes and licks her fingers again. She always buys Leon a doughnut but he can't have it until after lunch. Once Sylvia bought herself a bunch of flowers wrapped in a crinkly pink paper with a ribbon round it. She looked angry when she was putting them in the vase but when she saw Leon looking she smiled and said, "If I don't, who will?"

"My mom and dad have a massive garden," he tells Sylvia when she puts him to bed. "With lots of trees and grass and flowers and a shed. I used to grow everything with seeds that I planted myself. Zucchini and mangetout. I used to chop down trees if they got too big and dig the weeds out. My dad gave me a sharp knife and I used to help him. It's hard work but I don't mind. There's no one to look after it now if I'm not there."

Sylvia turns out the light.

"Well, why don't you go straight to sleep and have nice dreams about your garden? Night, night."

Leon hates it when the curtains move in the breeze but he's too scared to get out of bed and close the window. He turns over and tries to think of nice things like when Carol had a special bouquet for her birthday. It was wrapped in plastic with a bow made of white satin but because she didn't have a vase she had to prop the flowers up in the sink and then in the bath. Every time she looked at the bouquet she would say, "Must have cost a fortune." Later on that night, when his dad came, Leon heard her saying, "Byron, stop it!" but she was laughing, so he didn't have to worry.

All Sylvia's housework jobs last until lunchtime, when she makes him a sandwich and he can have his doughnut. But since he got his bike, Leon doesn't want to watch his shows.

"Can I go out on my bike, please?"

He stands near the back door with his hand on the knob. He always takes his backpack because he shows Tufty the soccer cards he's collecting or a picture of a bike because Tufty knows everything about them. He knows the way by heart now and he knows how to get off his bike at the gate if Mr. Devlin is around.

"Where?" she says, squinting because of the smoke from her cigarette.

"Just on the roads, on the sidewalks."

"All right then. But only around the block. You go up to the lights and right and then right again and you come to the bottom of the hill. Show me which is right and which is left."

He holds up the hand he writes with.

"Right," he says.

"Okay then. Now you watch that traffic. And if you get lost you ask a policeman. Second thoughts, if you get lost, ask a lady, any lady. You give them this address and you tell them to show you the way."

"Okay," says Leon and he opens the door.

"Hold on. What is this address, Leon?" She tilts her head to one side, looking like a teacher.

"Ten College Road."

Sylvia raises her eyebrows. "Off you go then. Back for your tea."

He puts his pack on and wheels his bike through the entry between the houses and out onto the road. He goes up to the traffic lights, crosses over, along the busy road, and all the way to the allotments. He gets off his bike at the railings in case Mr. Devlin is there and wheels it along the path by Mr. Devlin's brick shed and then, when he's absolutely sure Mr. Devlin isn't around, he gets back on so he can ride fast for thirty-seven seconds right up to Tufty's wooden hut.

It's a bright, bright day and because it's been raining all the green looks greener and all the blue looks bluer. The bloodred flowers in Mr. and Mrs. Atwal's garden have fallen over in the wind and beads of water drip from the cherry blossom onto Leon's back as he speeds past. Tufty waves when he sees Leon and calls him over. He hands him a packet of seeds.

"I can't read them little words, Star. Read this for me."

He hands Leon the packet and folds his arms.

Leon reads slowly but nice and loud.

"'Red-Flowered Runner Bean Scarlet Emperor is excellent for freezing and for showing. Runner beans are a good source of vitamin C and iron, and have a high fiber content. Height: ten feet. Spread: twelve inches.'"

"Hmm," says Tufty. "What does it say about when you plant it?"

"It says, 'Ideal for the kitchen garden. Flowering time July, August. Sowing months April, May indoors. Transplant outdoors when the risk of frost has passed, in full sun.'"

Tufty nods. "Okay, good."

"Has the risk of frost passed?"

"Well," says Tufty, "never can be sure. But it's the sixteenth of May. Sunny and warm. And in my little shed, they'll be safe. Yep, today's the day."

He goes back inside his hut and when he comes out the cycling pants are gone. Tufty's wearing baggy shorts, a sweater, and dusty beige boots with no laces. He puts a knitted hat over his bald head.

"Come in," he says to Leon. "You'll learn something."

Leon steps through the door and into Tufty's shed. The hut still has its special smell, like the gardens but stronger and sweet. Even with the folded chairs, there is lots of room inside. There is a little paraffin heater, a stool, a cooking pot, and some metal plates and mugs. If there was a bed this could be a halfway house as well. But there is dust and dirt on everything and piles of earth on the floor; tendrils of plants push in from the outside. Leon takes his backpack off and looks carefully at the pictures on the wall. They are all posters of black men: one in a suit and tie with a mustache, one who looks like a king, and another one with his fist in the air and a medal around his neck. Leon looks at them all one by one. They are all serious, not like Tufty with his wide smile and big teeth. The men look down at Leon and he imagines how they might talk and what they might say and if any of them would help him find his brother. He reaches out and touches the man with the medal. The poster crinkles and the man's chest contracts like he's breathing. Underneath the man in big writing it says "Black Power." Leon makes a fist and holds it up.

Tufty turns round and sees him.

"Yeah," he says, "he was a brave man. Now, watch."

Tufty rips the top off the packet of Scarlet Emperor seeds.

"Hold out your hands."

Tufty tips five seeds onto Leon's palms.

"Press one seed into each compartment. Like this. See?"

Leon presses the smooth, brown seeds down into the soil.

"Make sure it's covered over with the compost. You have to put them to bed so they can wake up. Keep them warm."

Leon carries on until all the compartments have one seed but there are still some left in the packet. Tufty folds the top over and puts them on a shelf. There are lots of other packets of seeds on the shelf and Leon takes one down. It has no writing on it.

"What are these?"

"These?" says Tufty, looking inside. He takes one seed out and holds it up to the light. He squints and shakes his head.

"Call them 'Take-A-Chance.'"

"Take-A-Chance," says Leon.

"Yeah, you plant them and water them but you don't know what you're getting. You just hope for the best."

Tufty puts the seed back in the packet and hands it to Leon.

"Keep them."

"Thank you," says Leon. He folds the top of the seed packet over like he saw Tufty do and puts it in his pocket.

"Look, now," says Tufty. "You got your seeds but you got to look after them. They got their blanket, they got food in their belly, but what else do they need?"

"Something to drink," says Leon.

"Right!" says Tufty, slapping him on the back. "Yeah, man. You got it. You do gardening at home?"

"No."

"Well, you're a natural then. Right, water is what we need. See that? Take it and fill it up from the soda bucket."

Leon fills a miniature watering can and dribbles water onto the seeds, drop by drop.

"Not too much," says Tufty. "Good, good."

"How big will they grow?" asks Leon.

"Taller than me and you," says Tufty as he walks outside. "Work to be done. Watch yourself, Star," he says. "Close the door after you."

Leon sees a ten-pence piece by the seed tray. It's got dirt on it and probably no one even knows it's a ten pence. He grabs the coin and takes his Take-A-Chance seeds out of his pocket. He puts them both in his pack and goes back outside.

He sees Tufty pick up the big garden fork and plunge it into the earth. Leon watches for a long time. Tufty sings to himself as he breaks the soil and turns it over, throwing stones over by the hedge. It's easy for Tufty because he's got big muscles. Leon feels the top of his arm and wonders when his muscles will grow. Then Leon gets on his bike and rides carefully along the little paths. The Indian lady waves at him and he waves back. He goes right to the end of the allotments where there's a tall wire fence and then he cycles on a different path toward the gate. He stops when he sees Mr. Devlin, gets off his bike, and wheels it over. Mr. Devlin is holding the Kanetsune again and wearing his army jacket.

Leon stares at it.

"Kanetsune," says Mr. Devlin. "Remember? Japanese."

Leon reaches for it but the man moves it out of the way.

"Too sharp. Dangerous for children."

On a deck chair outside the door of his hut, there is an old

wooden box with a lid. It is open and inside there are packets of
seeds squashed up.

"Are you planting Scarlet Emperor?" asks Leon. "Sowing
time is April or May."

The man looks at Leon and then at the seed box.

"I am. But not today."

"You have to transplant outdoors when the frosts have gone,"
says Leon. "That's in the summertime."

"Not quite that late, young man. Nearly."

Leon can see another small knife with a short blade on the
chair next to the seeds.

"Is that Japanese as well?" he says.

"That is a pruning knife. Needs oiling."

Leon shrugs. "I know how to oil a bike, my dad showed me."

Mr. Devlin walks to the chair, puts the seeds and the small
knife on the ground, and sits down. He puts the big knife on his
lap and picks up a bottle of linseed oil. Leon puts his bike on the
grass and walks over.

"Move that bicycle out of the way. It's a hazard."

Leon picks up the bike and rests it carefully against the brick
wall of the hut. He stands by Mr. Devlin and watches.

"Linseed oil," he says, "is for the handle here."

He shows Leon the handle. It's smooth, black wood with a
blue line running through it and a silky blue tassel on the end.

"Oil the handle. Never the blade."

"Is it sharp?"

"Pick that dandelion and pass it to me."

Leon picks the yellow-headed flower and gives it to the man.
Up close, Mr. Devlin has hair in his ears and nose. He has dirt
deep in the lines on his face and crusty, dry lips that make Leon
thirsty.

"The Kanetsune is the name for a group of knives. They have

steel blades. Sharp as a witch's tongue. Stroke the blade with the stem of the dandelion. Softly, now. Gently, like so."

He holds Leon's hand and draws the stem of the flower all along the edge of the blade but before it gets to the end, the stem splits open; half of it falls on the grass. Mr. Devlin takes a little breath in.

"Beautiful," he says quietly. "Imagine the damage it does."

Leon pulls his hand away. Loads of knives can cut dandelions. The little knife is on the grass and Leon picks it up and hands it to Mr. Devlin.

"You're a very determined boy, aren't you? What are you, twelve? Eleven? Sit down and take a piece of that cloth now."

Leon looks around.

"The T-shirt," says Mr. Devlin, "that there."

He points at a pile of cloth and Leon picks it up.

"No," he says with a sigh. "A piece of it, a piece."

He grabs it off Leon and with a swish of the big knife he separates a sleeve from the pile. Leon stares at the man.

"Wow!" he says.

"Yes, wow, as you say."

Leon uses the linseed to oil the handle of the pruning knife. It's very sharp and Mr. Devlin keeps reminding him, saying "careful" and "slowly."

"Do you have a name?" says Mr. Devlin after a while.

"Leon Rycroft. And I've got a brother. I know your name. You're called Mr. Devlin."

"Just Devlin. I used to be Señor Victor. Can you say Senhor Victor?"

"Senhor Victor."

Mr. Devlin stares at Leon and then whispers, "Or Papa."

"Papa."

"Ah," says Mr. Devlin.

Leon shows him the handle of the knife.

"Now wipe it over with a clean cloth."

Leon rubs it all over with the T-shirt while Mr. Devlin watches. "That's it," he says.

"Are you from America?" Leon asks.

"I've been called some bad things in my time. That's one of the worst. I am an Irishman, child. Dungannon is where I was born but I haven't seen it for many a year."

Mr. Devlin stops suddenly and turns his head like he hears something. Leon stops as well. Mr. Devlin mutters, "Twenty years precisely."

Leon wipes the knife along his leg.

"Don't do that," says Mr. Devlin. "You'll pierce your jeans and your mother will be after me."

Leon doesn't want to tell him about Sylvia or Maureen, so he finishes the knife and gives it back.

"You've used too much oil, look," says Mr. Devlin, wiping it off on his jacket. "On the other hand, you've been thorough and it hasn't leaked onto the blade itself. Use mineral oil for the blade. Or rapeseed oil."

He stands up suddenly and goes inside his hut. He is gone for so long that Leon gets on his bike. He goes round in a few circles and when Mr. Devlin still doesn't come out, Leon pedals back home with his new things in his backpack.

19

It's a long walk from the parking lot to the hospital. The Zebra walks fast and Leon has to trot to keep up with her. They go up in the elevator and Leon presses the button. Lots of people get in and squash him at the back, then they all get out at the same place and do lots more walking until they find Maureen. She is sitting up in bed with a white tube in her nose.

"At last," she says and she holds her arms open for Leon.

She smells different, she looks different, and she sounds different but when she snuggles him and rubs his back she is the same. Leon hugs her back and she laughs.

"Missed me, eh? Well, I've missed you as well. Can't wait to get home."

The Zebra starts walking away.

"I'm going down to the café. I'll be back in about twenty minutes, all right, Leon? All right, Maureen?"

Maureen waves her off and then looks at Leon.

"She all right? Does she get along with Sylvia?"

"I don't know," he says. "She got me a BMX."

"Did she now?"

"Yeah, a real one. It's red. It goes really fast."

"That's lovely, pigeon. And what about you? You getting along with Sylvia?"

Leon says nothing.

"She treating you all right?"

Her mouth is smiling but her eyes are sad.

Leon looks around the ward. There are lots of old ladies in nighties and dressing gowns. The room is too hot and smells of school dinners. All the visitors are looking at each other and chairs keep scraping across the floor. He can't see any nurses.

"The doctor said you're not dying," he says, "so why can't you come home and then I can live with you again?"

"I might not be dying but I feel like it sometimes."

Maureen lies back on her three pillows and closes her eyes but she keeps hold of Leon's hand.

"I'll be home soon. Don't you worry."

"I can go out on my bike whenever I want. I go everywhere. I found the allotments."

"Did you?"

Maureen's voice is far away.

"And there's lots of people up there that wave at me."

"Is that so?"

"Jake hasn't written to me yet."

"No, love."

"I don't know where he lives."

"No, love, nor me."

"When I'm in bed at night, I can't sleep properly."

"Really?"

"And I have to go to bed when it's still light."

"Yes, I know."

"The wind blows the curtains and it looks like someone's coming into my room."

"Well, they're not."

"My mom hasn't come back."

"I know, love."

The time goes slowly. Maureen's hand gets hot and sticky and he can hear the wind in her chest; it whistles like a recorder. A nurse walks up the middle of the ward and bends over him, whispering.

"Has your nana gone asleep, love?"

Leon looks at Maureen and realizes she is very, very old. She has lots of white in her hair now and soon she will look like the other old ladies and soon she will die.

"Is someone else here with you, love? Is your mom here?"

The nurse looks up and down the ward and takes his hand.

"Shall we go and find her? Or do you want to stay with your nana?"

The Zebra will come and take him back to Sylvia's. The Zebra will tell him not to worry. The Zebra will tell him he can't see Jake. That Carol isn't well. That's all anyone ever says to him.

20

There are lots of days when Leon goes out on his bike, even if it's only for ten minutes, and he always goes up to the allotments. Sometimes Tufty isn't there and sometimes Mr. Devlin isn't there but Mr. and Mrs. Atwal are nearly always there, digging and planting, and once Mr. Atwal gave Leon a curly stick of orange taffy, so sugary and sweet that it stuck Leon's teeth together and lasted for ages. Leon always waves just in case he has some more.

Today Tufty is there but he isn't alone. He's sitting on a fold-up chair with four of his friends, playing dominoes while an old man in a tweed coat watches.

The way Tufty slams the dominoes on the table it's like he's trying to break it in half. He nearly stands up off his chair and holds the domino high up in the air and when he mashes it down on the table, he says, "Yes!"

"What you got, Stump? Eh, what you got?" says Tufty.

"One," says a short fat man with a woolly hat. "One."

Then they all start talking and laughing and one of them pushes the dominoes into a heap. They talk loud, deep, all at the same time, in fast West Indian like his dad used to do except they are laughing all the time and making jokes.

As Tufty collects up the dominoes he notices Leon.

"Yo, Star!" shouts Tufty.

Leon gets off his bike and rests it against the hut. He goes up to Tufty, who puts his hand on Leon's shoulder.

"My friend this," he says to the other men. "He comes up regular to help me. You call him Star. Now, this is Castro, Marvo, Waxy, Stump, and Mr. Johnson."

The men nod in turn and get up, folding their chairs and handing them to Tufty. Mr. Johnson, who looks about a hundred years old, shakes Leon's hand.

"Pleased to meet you, young man."

Mr. Johnson has snowy-white hair in a little Afro and he hands Tufty a bunch of keys.

"Well, Linwood, I'm going," he says. "You're on your own tomorrow. Lock up good. This church meeting will last all day."

Leon sees the tall man with the ginger hair shake his head. His green eyes are narrow and red and his hair sticks up in dreadlocks all over his head. When he talks, his small brown beard bobs up and down. He makes a long hissing noise, drawing the air through his teeth.

"You still turning the other cheek, eh, Johnson?"

Mr. Johnson folds up the collar of his coat like he's cold. "Listen, Castro, you don't have the monopoly on anger, on a sense of injustice." He holds a finger in the air. "We have to organize. Black people won't get anywhere unless and until we form ourselves into a body which society recognizes, that can lobby the authorities and seek redress."

All the time, Castro carries on shaking his head. Even Castro's skin is ginger, brown and milky like a cup of tea, and he has freckles all over his face and down his neck. When he talks, his voice carries right across Tufty's plot. Mr. and Mrs. Atwal raise their heads.

"That's the old way, Johnson, when black people had to be grateful. Like when you and my father come to this country in your good suit and your pressed hair, doing as you're told, cleaning floors and driving buses."

Castro pauses and looks at each man in turn.

"Them days is gone. We don't have to be holding out our hat for the white man's leavings. If we come together to form something, it's an army. Not a—what you call it—lobby group. You think white people going to listen to monkeys? Monkeys is what they call we."

All the other men start talking at the same time while Tufty and Leon stand and listen. Tufty brings drinks and picks up the empty cans while his friends decide about their army. Leon can hear that the others don't like Castro's army idea but they don't like Mr. Johnson's lobby idea either. He helps Tufty tidy things up and, while they are still talking, Tufty takes a plastic soda bottle and fills it with water. He gives it to Leon and gets one for himself. Then he brings out the black plastic seed tray.

"Look," he says, "look what's happened."

The seeds have split and a strong curving tendril is shooting out like they are stretching out or waking up from a long sleep. Two little leaves, like closed wings, sit on the tip.

"These are babies," says Tufty. "Fragile. Babies need looking after. Come."

At the other end of Tufty's plot, there are tall wigwams made out of bamboo canes, two long rows. If you covered them over with leaves it would make a fantastic den or a hideout.

"You see here," Tufty says. "We have to put these seeds in carefully. Make a hole at the bottom of the stick like so, pour water in the hole. Drop in the baby plant. See?"

Leon kneels down and gently tickles the soil in around the hole so the seedling looks like it's always been there.

"You got it, Star. You really got it. Now pour on a bit more water. Don't drown it."

"Why have you put it by the bamboo sticks? Will they grow as well?"

"No, no," says Tufty, "these plants need support. They need to hold on to something strong while they're growing. They curl round the bamboo and then, couple of months' time, we get some beans." Tufty straightens up. "We got a lot to plant out. Look, I'll put them in the hole, you do the watering."

So, Leon follows Tufty from plant to plant, watering all around the bottom of the bamboo canes. He goes back to the water barrel and does the same thing again until it's all done. When they walk back to the shed, Tufty's friends are still talking. Castro is standing up, waving his arms and pointing to the street.

"You don't see what the police is doing to black people? Stop and search? You don't listen to the news, Johnson?"

Leon feels sorry for Mr. Johnson because he keeps trying to talk but Castro is too loud. Mr. Johnson speaks softly but Leon knows he's angry.

"Don't bite the hand that feeds you, Castro," he says. "Work with the hands God gave you." He looks at Leon and slowly closes his eyes. "Nobody listens anymore." Then Mr. Johnson puts his hands in his pockets and walks away.

Tufty holds his trowel in the air.

"Easy, easy. Keep it quiet, quiet. I'm already on a warning."

No one says anything for a few minutes and then Tufty claps his hands.

"You all going to Rialto Dance on Saturday? They give me a spot, so listen, let me try out my new poem."

They all shuffle round in their seats until they're facing him. He plucks a yellow flower from the ground and holds it up. He picks off one petal and then another and as he speaks he does all the actions, making everybody laugh.

"I call this 'Conspiracy.'"

She love me.
She love me not.
She love me.
She love me not.
So me take up me records and me good Dutch pot.
I step out quick before she changes her mind
And I walk with a swagger, never looking behind.
My mother say nothing when I go back home
But she work me hard, bend my fingers to the bone.
"Get up, Tufty, and wash the floor.
Open the window.
Close the door.
Carry my bag from the shop to the house.
Lay a fire for morning.
Lay a trap for the mouse.
Chop wood, wash dishes,
Peel yam, catch fishes."
And when I am sleeping she come in my room,
And wake me up to give me the broom.
Weeks I don't sit, months I don't rest,
I dream of my girl, my angel, my best,
So I crawl back begging to the girl I did leave,
"Save me from Mommy!"
I cry and I plead.
She loves me, yes, and I know for a fact
That she plan with my mother to get me back.

All his friends are laughing except Castro. Tufty waves his hand. "Wait, I got one more verse."

"Fucking girls! That's all you got on your mind, Tufty?"

Tufty smiles and holds his arms out. "Come on, Castro, man, chill out."

Leon watches Castro walk away, swinging his arms, kicking a stone all along the path.

21

Leon hates his new school. Because Leon missed a lot of school when he lived with Carol, the teachers keep saying he has to catch up but Leon is good at reading and writing and sums, and anyway, all the lessons are boring. The new school by Sylvia's house is even worse than the other ones and so is his teacher. He doesn't care about the Victorians and writing stories, he doesn't like it when they have to draw pictures about planets and stars, and he doesn't like school trips when they won't let you go to the toilet. And there are two boys in his class who have the same birthday and they both went to see the Jackson Five and they keep talking about it. At lunchtime, sometimes Leon plays soccer and sometimes he sits with Martin from the year below. Martin hasn't got any other friends and he lives with a foster carer too. Sometimes Martin gets into trouble for fighting. He always wins.

Sylvia had to come to his new school on Friday to see the headmistress and his new teacher. Leon couldn't listen at the door, because the school secretary was watching him. He had to sit still with nothing to do while the three voices in the next room talked about him. He knew what they were saying but he still wanted to hear. Eventually, the door opened and he went inside. Teachers are like social workers, with lots of different pretend voices and smiles. The head teacher coughed and picked up a piece of paper.

"First of all, Leon, we want you to know that Woodlands Junior School is an inclusive school. We want all our pupils to succeed."

She waited for him to say yes.

"This is great work, Leon."

She held up a picture he had drawn in art. It was a picture of Jake when he was grown up, looking like Bo Duke from *The Dukes of Hazzard.* He had yellow hair and he was standing by a red car and he had a gun.

"We can all see how hard you've worked on this picture. So we can see that when you want to, you can put a lot of effort into your schoolwork. This picture proves it. But, Leon, you have to work hard in all your lessons. Don't you?"

"Yes."

"We've spoken about this before but, this time, I want you to make a special effort, a really, really big effort, to pay attention in class. Yes?"

"Yes."

"And no swearing."

"Yes."

"Yes, Miss," said the head teacher. "Yes, Miss, or Yes, Mrs. Smith, or Yes, Mrs. Percival."

"Yes, Mrs. Percival."

"And no interrupting to go to the toilet all the time. You go once at the beginning of the morning and then again at break time. Yes?"

"But what if I want to go in the middle of the lesson?"

Sylvia shook her head. "Just hold it, Leon, like everyone else does. Put a knot in it till break time. That's what the teacher is saying. Or go before the lesson starts."

"Yes, Miss Sylvia," said Leon. He saw both the teachers look at each other when Sylvia started talking. They don't like her either.

Then his teacher started talking about effort and behavior with a voice she kept specially for when parents and other teachers were around. All the time he was watching her twisting her wedding ring around and around on her finger because they both knew that Leon wasn't going to get any stars on his chart.

On the way home, Sylvia looked in the window of a television shop. She said that one of the televisions had a remote control so you could turn the television off while you were still sitting down. Like magic. If Leon had a remote control he would lie in bed and turn Sylvia off, *click*, and the teachers off, *click*, and the social workers off, *click, click, click*. Then he would crush the remote control with a big hammer so they could never come on again.

22

At last. Leon has a whole week off school for half term. He goes to the allotment but Tufty isn't there, so he goes up and down the hill to see if he's getting faster. If he goes fast enough he gets a kind of fluttering, happy feeling in his stomach, like he's a superhero, like he doesn't have to stop at the top of the hill but could just ride straight over the cars and the roofs and the telegraph poles and fly away, across the city, looking down into all the gardens at all the children and all the babies and see where Jake is and Jake would wave and Leon would shout, "I can see you, Jake! I can see you!"

But always he rides home, parks his bike in the garden, and takes his backpack off.

Leon can hear the women's voices before he opens the back door. It sounds like a party. It must be Maureen. She's back. He runs into the living room. There are lots of women standing up with mugs of coffee and cigarettes and some sitting down with cakes and rolls, all talking at the same time just like Tufty's friends. But no Maureen. They keep saying she's coming out of the hospital soon but they aren't telling the truth.

Leon looks at each woman in turn but they don't even notice him. One of them is talking with her mouth full of cake; she has too many rings on her fingers and a crease in her neck. She throws her head back and laughs and he can see all the mashed-up cake in a creamy smudge on her tongue. Maureen wouldn't like her. If she was here, she would say "Shut your cakehole" or "Manners, please."

Sylvia sees him come in and ushers him back into the kitchen.

"Ham sandwich, milk, doughnut, and then off to your room."

Leon sits and begins to eat.

"This is what I think, Sylv," says the fat woman. "We can't trust the weather. Even in July. It could piss it down for all we know."

The other women are nodding, saying, "That's right."

"So I think we make two plans. The community center if it's raining, and if not, we block off the road and have a street party."

"Ooh, I can't wait."

"I think you need a license."

"What about the traffic?"

"A disaster if it rains."

"Exciting, isn't it?"

"The council have got an information pack."

"Tables and chairs."

They all start talking and it gets too noisy, so Sylvia holds up her hands.

"Pen and paper, pen and paper."

She opens the drawer in her sideboard and then sits down again with a pad and a pen.

"Barbara, you said you could run up some bunting?"

"Yes," says a woman from the sofa. "I'm going to put a pink *D* for 'Diana' on a red triangle and a pale blue *C* for 'Charles' on a navy triangle and in between white triangles with hearts on them."

They all say "Aaah" at the same time.

Sylvia writes it down.

"Maxine, Union Jack hats. Sheila, where's Sheila? There you are. Pasting tables, six of. Ann to call the council. Rose, you said you could lay your hands on some chairs. What else?" Sylvia points the pen. "Yes, Sue, you said savories."

Sue's eating, so she speaks out of one corner of her mouth. "Sausage rolls and quiche."

Sylvia writes it down and keeps giving people jobs until she has to turn the page over.

Leon finishes his lunch but stays where he is because there are too many people between him and the hallway. Someone passes round a magazine about the Royal Wedding and someone else says she is going to be a beautiful princess.

"A queen, you mean," says Sylvia and they all say, "Yes, a queen," and it goes quiet in the room until Sylvia stands up.

"We've got a lot to do. Next meeting at . . ."

"Mine," says Sue and they all get up with their handbags and magazines and bits of pastry and cake. Sylvia's list is still on the sofa. Leon can see it from where he sits in the kitchen. Her pen is falling between the cushions on the sofa and he hopes the ink will leak out and leave a stain. There is a jumbled-up mess at the front door as they all start to leave at the same time. Leon slips off his chair, skirts the sofa, picks up the paper, tucks it in his pocket, and tries to slip past. But they see him. Some pat his head or cheek and say "Bless him" or "Little love."

He goes to his room and sits on the bed. He reads Sylvia's list. Food, names, food, names, food, names. He folds the paper in half and in half until it's a heavy little square that will fit in his pencil case.

Because there's no school, Sylvia lets him stay up to watch the ten o'clock news. It's always boring and Leon doesn't really listen but at least he's not in bed. When Lady Diana comes on, Sylvia always turns up the volume.

"Look at that dress," she says. "Red. It's a brave blonde that wears red."

Suddenly, she jerks forward and covers her mouth.

"Oh my God! Carpenter Road!"

She runs to the window and pulls the curtains apart. She opens the door and looks up and down the road. Leon follows her. There are other people on the street with their arms folded, clustering together in little knots, walking up and down. An ambulance rushes past and then a fire engine, then a police car. Then another police car but this one stops and people walk over to it.

Leon stands on Sylvia's doorstep. There is the smell of a bonfire in the air and a hushed, exciting feeling. He knows where Sylvia's purse is. He backs away from the door and opens her bag. Her purse has a clasp at the top that he eases apart. There is a ten-pound note and some coins. He is quiet and silent and looks at the note and thinks what it would be like to have it. He would get on a train and find his mom. He would make a taxi take him there. And then they would both go and get Jake. He would buy some more cream soda for Tufty. He takes it out and feels it, soft and crinkly in his hands. He could fold it up with Sylvia's list and put it in his pencil case or inside his pillowcase. He stares at the ten-pound note then puts it back. He takes a twenty-pence piece and two tens. He leaves lots of other coins in the purse so she won't notice. He doesn't want them to jingle together in his pocket, so he clutches them in his hand, tight. He goes back to the door just as Sylvia is coming back in.

"Carpenter Road," she says. "They're running around breaking windows and robbing on Carpenter Road. Carpenter Road. Would you believe it? There's police down there by the dozen. There's two shops on fire. It's like Beirut, by all accounts."

She sits on the settee and lights a cigarette.

"Too bloody close for comfort."

Leon says nothing and she turns to look at him.

"It's all right, love. Don't worry. Come here."

She holds both of his fists in her hands. Leon feels the coins digging into his palm.

"You pay no attention. There's nothing happening on this street. We're safe here. Now you go along to bed."

Leon pulls his hands away quickly and goes to his room. He tucks the coins in his school shoes and puts them under the bed. He smells the tang of metal on his hands.

23

Leon's got a new Batman T-shirt and new white sneakers with black laces. If he wears them to the allotment they might get dirty but if he doesn't wear them no one will see them. Sylvia wants him to wear shorts because it's June but the only ones that he likes are the denim ones that Tufty has.

"Can I cut these up?" he says, showing her his jeans.

Sylvia squints her eyes.

"What?"

"I've seen other boys with cut-up shorts. Can I do it?"

Sylvia holds the jeans against him.

"Bit too tall for them anyway, aren't you? Hang on."

She takes the scissors from the kitchen drawer and cuts the legs off. She folds the ends over and makes them look neat but Leon will unroll them as soon as he gets outside.

"That suit you?" she says, holding them up.

He dashes to his room and puts them on. Now that he's got

his Batman T-shirt, his white sneakers, and his Tufty shorts, he looks really old, maybe even fifteen.

"Ooh, get you," says Sylvia and watches him open the back door and get on his bike.

"What's their names then, these friends of yours?"

"Who?" says Leon.

"These kids from the park. Why don't you get them to call for you?"

Leon shrugs and squeezes the brakes.

"I could bring you a picnic if you like."

Leon opens the gate to the entry.

"Bet you'd rather have your nails dipped in acid," she says as he pushes off. "Don't be late!"

He can hear that she's smiling.

Leon has forty pence in his pocket and stops at the paper shop. It's not like the paper shop where Maureen used to live, because that only sold papers and sweets and cigarettes. It's a paper shop with toilet rolls and tins of custard and soap powder and cabbages out on the pavement and if Sylvia runs out of anything she sends Leon to get it from the paper shop.

Sometimes it's an old Pakistani man who serves and sometimes it's a young one. The young one never looks up from the newspaper but the old man sometimes follows Leon around and asks him what he's looking for.

"Can I have a Curly Wurly, please?" he asks because all the chocolate and sweets are kept high up near the till.

The old man puts out his hand for the money.

"And some Toffos," says Leon.

"Twenty pence," says the man.

Leon doesn't like it when he has to pay first but he gives the man the money and the man gives him his sweets. Then he carries on looking at Leon like he hasn't paid.

"Did you see my window?" asks the man.

"No," says Leon. Then he notices that there is a big piece of cardboard in the bottom half of the glass door.

"You didn't see what happened? People running around smashing up shops and throwing stones. Why are you doing this?"

"I didn't," says Leon and he pushes his bike out of the shop. Leon only throws stones over by the fence at the allotment when he's helping Tufty dig his garden, so the Pakistani man is wrong.

It is just possible to eat the Curly Wurly and ride his bike at the same time. Curly Wurlys are very chewy and last ages but they also melt if you hold them too hard or if you put them in your pocket, so you have to eat them quickly.

He gets off his bike at the gate and wheels it past Mr. Devlin. Mr. Devlin's made a wigwam with bamboo canes just like Tufty's and he's standing next to it with a packet of seeds in his hand. He is swaying from side to side and when he sees Leon he calls him over.

"Come on, come on. Come here! Let me show you something, young man."

Leon smells sour whiskey on Mr. Devlin's breath.

Mr. Devlin takes a handful of seeds and lets them drop through his fingers around the base of each bamboo cane, four or five brown seeds in a little heap.

"Push them in, push them in. Don't just watch them."

Leon pokes them in with his fingers, each one in its own hole. He squats on the soil so he doesn't get his new shorts dirty and crabs his way round the wigwams, following Mr. Devlin, who's not walking straight and talking all the time.

"In São Paulo you have a longer season. That's the difference. No frosts. Cool nights. Wet. Ha! Soaked to the skin. Stupid boy. No, not stupid. Don't say that."

Mr. Devlin sounds like he's on the telephone, like someone is answering back. He looks at Leon suddenly and puts his hand on his shoulder.

"He had so much energy, just like me when I was a boy. Never still, never could sit still. Running full pelt. She never caught him."

Then Mr. Devlin goes to his halfway house and comes back with a battered khaki watering can and a plastic bottle. When he speaks, he sounds like a child.

"Would you help me with this, please? I'd be grateful if you would help me. Grateful."

They water the seeds together like Tufty showed him. Mr. Devlin has stopped talking. Leon looks at him as he waters his plants but his face is sad and his lips are thin.

"I have to go now," says Leon but Mr. Devlin doesn't even say goodbye. He slumps and trudges back to his shed, weaving from side to side, and Leon thinks he looks much older than usual.

There is music coming from somewhere, reggae music. Tufty must have a radio but when he gets to Tufty's plot he's nowhere to be seen and it's all gone quiet. Leon opens the shed door. Tufty's inside with a massive, massive, massive silver tape recorder. It's wider than Tufty's chest, with two round speakers on the front with dials and buttons and everything. Tufty's got a packet of batteries in his hand and he's taken the back off the machine.

"Wow!" says Leon. "What's that?"

"Boom box," says Tufty. "Panasonic 180 Ghetto Blaster."

"Is it yours?"

"Don't even ask what it cost. I can't afford it, you know."

"How much was it?"

"Take all your pocket money and multiply it by your age. I brought it up here to have some music while I'm working and the batteries just died. At least, I hope it's the batteries. The one time I bring this out of the house and look what happens. Anyhow, this thing breaks, it's going straight back to the shop."

Tufty clicks eight enormous batteries into place and fixes a plastic plate over them. He sits it up on the bench.

"Let's see. Cross your fingers."

Leon crosses all of his fingers and holds them up for Tufty to see. *Click. Doooouuufff. Doooouuufff.* The bass hits Leon like a train.

"Yeah, man!" shouts Tufty. "Feel that?"

Leon puts his hands over his chest and starts giggling.

"King Tubby, Star. You can't get better than King Tubby's dub."

Tufty turns the knob at the front and the bass, heavy as concrete, makes the whole shed shudder. *Douff, douff, douff. Douff, douff, douff.*

Tufty nods in time with the music and closes his eyes. He drops back, rolls forward, drops back, rolls forward, nods in time with the music, drops back. He's lost in it and Leon feels it, too. He feels a warm current of sound start in his belly and climb up into his neck. He starts to nod and sway and when he closes his eyes he feels it stronger, feels his arms rise up all on their own and his feet start shuffling on the wooden floor.

Douff, douff, douff. Douff, douff, douff.

There's no change in the music, just the cludding of the bass, on and on, over and over like the hammer of his heartbeat.

Douff, douff, douff.

When he opens his eyes, Tufty is standing with his arms folded, one hand hiding his wide smile.

"Yes, sir! You feel it! You really feel it! That's what righteous dub can do to you. Where did you go, eh? You went somewhere?"

Leon nods.

"Good?"

"Yes."

Tufty claps and laughs.

"Me and you, Star, in a good place. Yes! Come, I got more tunes for you."

Tufty plays Leon lots of different songs and tells him all the different singers: King Tubby, Bob Marley, Dennis Brown,

Burning Spear, Barrington Levy. All the names merge into one sound.

Douff, douff, douff. Black Pow-er. Douff, douff, douff. Black Pow-er.

When Leon gets back on his bike, he thinks about Jake and where he is and what he's doing and how he can find him. He thinks about Jake banging his baby drum in time to Tufty's music. Leon puts his feet on the pedals and his legs push down on the beat. *Douff, douff, douff,* all the way home.

24

Because the journey to the Family Center takes so long, Leon has to listen to the news twice. When the Zebra came he thought he was getting another present like the bike because she said she had a surprise for him. But it was much better than a bike. His mom has come back. He runs and gets his backpack and sits in the back of the car right away but then the Zebra stands at the door talking to Sylvia for ages. Leon rolls down the window so he can hear.

The Zebra talks about Maureen first.

"She's going to need to take it steady when she comes out."

"It's her weight as much as anything else."

"One of our best carers but I'm not sure she would be up to caring for another energetic boy like this one."

"My thoughts exactly."

"But she's so committed. Wish we had more like her."

"I'll be having words with her when she gets out, I can tell you."

"Leon misses her, doesn't he?"

"So do I."

"We're looking at a permanent plan for Leon. Long-term fostering is the best option obviously but those placements are not easy to find. Matching considerations come into play and various other factors . . ."

Sylvia starts talking about the Royal Wedding.

"Wonder what her dress will be like?"

"I'm not a royalist by any stretch of the imagination but I thought at least we'd get the day off."

"Disgraceful," says Sylvia and takes a little step back inside.

The Zebra leans in.

"Think about how much they've spent on it. All the pomp and excess. It's a showcase for the monarchy, a festivity, with all the heads of Europe being flown in. Who do you think is paying for that?"

"They've probably got their own planes."

"Then there's the hotels, the cars, the wedding breakfast."

"We're having a street party," says Sylvia with her hand on the door.

The Zebra gets her keys out of her pocket and jangles them up and down.

"Pretty girl, but I wouldn't want to be in her shoes."

"No?"

Sylvia waves at Leon, "Be good," then she twitches her face into a smile. "See you later."

On the Zebra's car radio, it's the same. The wedding and then the riots and the Irishman who starved himself to death, then the pope who got shot and then so much stuff that Leon just looks out of the window and imagines a plane flying in from Europe filled with all the heads of Europe. All the heads are bobbing around or falling off the seats like heavy balloons. Some of them are French and some of them are Spanish but no one can tell until they start talking in their own language. Leon starts to laugh and the Zebra sees.

"Looking forward to seeing your mom, Leon?"

"Yes."

"I'm pleased for you, love. It's an important day. You've waited a long time. It's quite a few months since you last saw her, isn't it?"

She pulls into the Family Center lot and turns off the engine. She shuffles round in her seat until she's facing him.

"Now, last time when your mom went to see you at Maureen's it wasn't a great success, so that's why we're here."

Leon nods.

"And things have got a bit out of hand recently, haven't they, Leon?"

Leon says nothing.

"Lying? Answering back at school? Taking things belonging to Sylvia?"

Leon looks at her.

"She notices, Leon."

He looks out of the window and the Zebra waits until he looks back.

"We need to take this one step at a time, all right? We want you to be happy, Leon. Honestly, we do, but it means you have to try to behave. Remember when I took you to see Maureen, you made me a promise? You remember your promise, don't you?"

"Yes."

"Which is what?"

"If I behave you'll take me to see Maureen again in your car."

"And?"

"And I have to stop stealing."

"And?"

"And Jake is with his new mom and dad."

"Yes, but that wasn't part of the promise, Leon, that was—"

"And I can't see my mom every time I ask."

The Zebra closes her eyes and scratches her forehead.

"I know it's hard, Leon."

Then she turns to the window and says, "Fucking hard."

She coughs.

"So, your mom's inside, in the Family Center, over there. She's still not well but she says she can manage a visit. She's had a long journey as well, so she might be tired."

"Did she come with the man?"

"No, we had to go and fetch her. Two hours to get there and two hours back. Lovely journey it was for me on the highway at eight o'clock in the morning. Come on and bring your bag."

The Family Center smells of strong coffee and cleaning solution, like a hospital without the doctors. Social workers sit at their desks and there are people everywhere sitting on chairs, waiting for something. A woman with a broken arm is shouting and a social worker is writing everything down in a file because social workers need to know the date people shout and the date people visit and the date they take children away. Leon knows what's written on the paper: June 8. She's shouting. She has a broken arm. Her two children are screaming and running along the corridors.

Leon can't see his mom anywhere but he follows the Zebra, who seems to know every single person in the whole place.

"All right, Pat. All right, Leslie. Glynis! Glynis! Hello! Haven't seen you for ages. I'll be back in a minute, just got to get this access visit started. All right, Bob. You supervising this access? No? Who is then?"

The Zebra is talking to a man in a checked shirt. He's on the phone but talking to her at the same time.

"Bob? I said who's doing this access visit?"

"Bernie's just finishing. She can take over."

The Zebra stares at him.

"I don't think so, Bob."

She tells Leon to sit down while she goes into the office but he can still hear.

"How is she? Where is she, Bob?"

The Zebra sounds annoyed and Leon realizes that she's in charge of Bob and Bob doesn't like her.

"Family Room. She hasn't bolted. She's had a sandwich and a coffee. She's smoking like a chimney."

"Well, she hasn't disappeared, so we're making progress."

"She went for a walk down the corridor a few minutes back, muttering to herself. I think she was looking for the toilet or the way out or something but then she just went back to the room. She's been asking for you anyway."

"Me?"

"Well, like when are you coming and what's the delay."

"No good deed . . ." says the Zebra.

She sees Leon at the door.

"Come on, love."

They walk further along the corridor to a small room with two sofas and a coffee table with toys on it. The toys are for babies but Carol is playing with them. She's holding a little doll and turning it around and around, up close to her face like she's trying to read something. She doesn't even notice when Leon comes in and the Zebra has to tell her.

"Carol? Carol? We're here. Leon's here."

She turns slowly and smiles but she's not really looking at him. She has her hair parted on the wrong side and she's skinny, even skinnier than before, and her jeans are too baggy. But most of all, she looks like she's been crying for days and days, like her eyes are made of liquid, like she's been asleep and had a nightmare, like she's never been happy in her whole life.

She puts her arms out to him, just like she used to, and hugs him tight. Leon feels a fresh worry for his mom because no one is looking after her. She holds him by both shoulders.

"Can't believe how grown up you are. Can't believe it's you."

Leon sits down and takes off his pack.

"How are you, Leon?" she says, lighting a cigarette.

There's so much smoke in the room that the Zebra opens the windows and begins wafting the clean air inside.

"Carol, could I ask you to stand by the window if you want to smoke? It's not good for children. Other people will need to come into this room after you. Women with babies. Families. Thanks."

Carol doesn't move. Leon opens his bag and looks inside at all the things he's collected. Sylvia said he also had to bring some papers.

"This is my school report," he says.

Carol puts it on her lap.

"Are you smart?"

Leon looks at the Zebra standing by the window with her arms folded.

"Yep," she says. "He is."

"You being good?"

Leon nods. "And I got a B in Math."

Carol begins reading the report on her lap. Turning the pages slowly and looking up from time to time and smiling at him. Then she looks at the Zebra.

"Is this a supervised visit?"

The Zebra walks to the door.

"Would you like a drink and snack, Leon? All right for a drink, Carol, or would you like another coffee?"

Carol doesn't answer. She's taking ages reading the report and Leon is getting angry. Even he reads quicker than Carol and he's only nearly ten.

"I'll bring you a coffee, shall I?" shouts the Zebra as she lets the door slam. Carol looks up.

"She's not nice, is she?"

Leon shakes his head.

"And she looks like a fucking badger."

Leon grins and Carol sniggers and they begin to laugh and

once they start, they can't stop. Leon feels the laughter come rushing out like a river, hurting his belly and his throat, pouring out of his mouth. And Carol's the same. She's rocking to and fro on her seat and holding her chest. Tears are in her eyes but they're good tears. Leon doesn't have to worry. She's pointing to her hair and trying to talk but it's no good, she's laughing too much. Then she starts making little animal movements with her hands and Leon has to hold his neck because it's aching and his jaw hurts and the pain makes a clean white space in his mind. He wants to laugh forever.

Then Carol gets down on her hands and knees and starts snuffling around Leon's legs like a dog and it's still funny. Then she starts yapping like a dog and pawing at Leon's trousers. She isn't laughing anymore and neither is Leon. She's trying to tickle him, scrabbling her fingers on his chest, but she's doing it too soft. He can hardly feel it through his T-shirt and he can smell her tobacco breath, strong and sour. She has her head to one side and her eyes wide open.

"Remember, Leon? Remember?"

"Yes."

"Remember?"

"Yes, Mom."

He holds her hand still and she rests her head on his knees.

When the Zebra comes back with the coffee, Carol gets up and sits back on her chair.

"Everything all right in here?" asks the Zebra. She raises an eyebrow at Leon like they have a secret. Carol lights a cigarette and walks to the window. She blows the smoke out at the trees. There is fresh daylight outside but Family Centers always have bluish lights that make everything look worse, the toys, the files, the people. When the Zebra leaves, Leon goes and stands next to Carol.

She holds his hand and squeezes it.

"Are you coming back? Are you coming back for my birthday?"

Carol closes her eyes and takes a very long, shaky breath. Leon thinks she's going to cry.

"Do you see Jake, Leon?"

"No, they won't let me."

"Nor me," she says. "Nor me. Do you remember him, Leon? Remember when he used to get his temper up?"

Leon says nothing.

"He had so much life in him, that kid. Like his dad."

"He used to sneeze five times," says Leon, "or six. He used to get bubbles in his nose at bath time."

"Did he? He had that cough that time and I had to take him to the doctor's in that pouring rain. Remember?"

Leon opens his backpack and takes out Big Red Bear.

"Look," he says.

"That's lovely," she says.

"It's Jake's. Maureen gave it to me."

"Did she buy it?"

"I don't know. Have you still got the photograph of Jake?"

Carol looks out of the window, left and right, like she's looking for the man in the sports car.

"Hate these places," she says. When she sighs, her whole body shakes and the squeezes of Leon's hand get quick and sharp. She leans against the windowsill and starts knocking her head on the glass.

Leon doesn't know if he can remember how to do Jake but he has to try and find Jake's voice in his throat. He makes the wrong noise a couple of times but then it comes.

"Yeeeyyii, yeeeyyii, tatta, tatta."

Carol looks at him.

"Yeeeyyii, yeeeyyii, tatta, tatta."

Leon moves his hands like Jake moves his hands when he's banging a toy in his high chair.

"Leon! Leon! Ta-ta, ta-ta."

"Is that him?"

"That's how he said it, Mom. Just like that."

They hold each other and he can feel her chest heaving and her jolting sobs. Leon has to tell her.

"I could be him, Mom," he says. "You could come back for me and, sometimes, I could be him."

25

In Leon's dream he's standing in a cooking pot with white flames licking up the sides. He is slippery with oil and can't get out. He's an ogre's dinner. Then he's running in bare feet on scorched sand, acres and acres of it in every direction, but there are no hiding places and if he doesn't keep running, a giant's foot will come out of the sky to squish him flat. If only there was some water. He's calling out but his throat is cracked and sore and every time he opens his mouth someone says no. So he says no back and they say no louder, so he says no and no and no and then Sylvia wakes him up.

It's dark outside and all the lights are on.

"Come on, come on," Sylvia says, making him sit up. "Drink this. That's it. All down."

She puts her hand on his forehead and his cheek.

"Burning up," she says. "No wonder you're making such a racket."

He gulps the water down and throws the quilt off.

"I don't feel well."

"No, love," she says. "Don't look it neither. I'm going to get you some more water. You stay there."

Leon's back is sticking to the sheets. He tries to open the window but Sylvia catches him and tells him to get back into bed.

"I'll do that," she says and when she opens the window a beautiful, cold breeze comes into the room and makes him feel better.

"Now, drink this and take these two pills. Says you've got to be twelve on the packet but you're about the size of a twelve-year-old. Can't hurt."

But the pills are lumps of chalk and it takes him forever to swallow them. His throat is raw and his head is hot.

"All right, love. Don't cry," Sylvia says and takes his hand. "I think you've got the flu, that's all. Won't kill you. I expect you've got a touch of the miserables as well. No wonder. Come on. Snuggle in now and I'll help you cool off."

She slides Leon's comics off the bedside table and begins to fan him, little puffs of cold air all over his face and back. Sylvia isn't as nice as Maureen but she is smarter.

"Can you tell me a story?" he asks.

She says nothing for a little while then she sighs.

"I could really do with a cigarette but that won't help you sleep. All right then. Now let me think."

She takes so long thinking that Leon thinks that maybe she can't be a fan and tell stories at the same time and he would rather have the fan, so he says nothing.

Sylvia stops suddenly.

"Here's one I remember," she says and starts the fan again.

"Once upon a time there was a man who was peacefully driving down a windy road. Suddenly, a little bunny skipped across the road and the man couldn't stop. He wasn't going very fast but he hit the bunny head-on. Smack. The man stopped the car right away and he quickly jumped out of his car to check the scene. There, lying lifeless in the middle of the road, was the Easter bunny. The man cried out, 'Oh no! I have committed a terrible crime! I have run over the Easter bunny!' The man started sobbing quite hard. What was he going to do? How could he put it right? And then he heard another car coming. It was a woman in a red convertible."

"What's a convertible?" asks Leon.

The fan stops and Sylvia says, "A car with no roof. Do you want me to carry on?"

"Yes," says Leon, "with the fan as well."

"Anyway, the woman stopped and asked the man what the problem was. The man explained, 'I have done something horrible. I have run over the Easter bunny. Now there will be no one to deliver eggs on Easter Sunday. All the children will be sad and it's all my fault.' 'Don't you worry,' said the woman and she ran back to her car. A moment later, she came back carrying a spray bottle. She ran over to the bunny lying dead in the road and she sprayed it. The bunny immediately sprang up, ran into the woods, stopped, and waved back at the man and woman. Then it ran another ten feet, stopped, and waved. It then ran another ten feet, stopped, and waved again. It did this over and over and over again until the man and the woman could no longer see the bunny and it disappeared into the woods. When it had gone, the man shook his head, 'Wow! What is the stuff in that bottle?' The woman replied, 'It's hair restorer. It brings your hair back to life and adds a permanent wave.'"

It isn't a story, it's a trick.

"Get it?" asks Sylvia. "Hair meaning hare. Hair on your head and hare meaning rabbit. Do you get it?"

She has stopped being a fan now and Leon feels sleepy.

"Is that the end?" he asks.

"Well, no. The rabbit has gone off to have his adventures.

Like you'll have adventures in your life. We all have adventures, some are good and some are not so good. You're in the not-so-good phase."

"What else happens to him?"

"That's enough for one night."

Sylvia gets up and opens the window a bit wider. She turns the light off and closes the door.

"I'll come back and check on you in a bit. Sleep time now."

When Leon wakes up, the sun is shining outside. He's still too hot but his head has stopped hurting. He gets up and goes to the living room.

Sylvia is watching the TV with a cup of coffee and a cigarette.

"Here he is," she says, smiling. "How's the soldier?"

Leon goes into the kitchen, gets a drink of water, and sits next to Sylvia.

"I'm hot," he says. "Do I have to go to school?"

"School? It's one o'clock, boy. You've missed school for today. Here, take another couple of these."

He swallows another two tablets, nestles down onto the sofa, and closes his eyes. He remembers what Maureen told him about not having bad dreams by thinking of nice things. He tries hard to think about Christmas and his birthday and the presents he might get. He thinks about the Incredible Hulk and he looks down at his chest. One day, if he gets really angry, his chest will grow enormous and he will burst out of his clothes and nobody will be able to stop him doing anything. He thinks about being strong and having powers like Superman or Batman and then he feels Sylvia covering him up with a blanket.

Once, when he was little, he was in the park with his mom and she covered him over with a blanket. He was lying on the grass. He remembers the smell of the earth and the feel of scratchy leaves on his legs. The sky was far away and everything was still and quiet. His mom was singing to him but it was more like a whisper and his dad was there as well. His dad was reading the newspaper and he was leaning against a tree. Leon had a blue and red ball and an Action Man and they left the Action Man at the park and his dad promised to get him a new one. And he did. But that was later. While they were at the park, under the tree, under the blanket, under the white sky, he fell asleep with his mom's hand on his back, with her song in the air, and when he woke up, he was in his bed and it was nighttime. He wonders if there is another boy in that bed now. He thinks about that boy playing with his toys and using his things and he can feel the anger inside bubbling around and making his chest heave.

He throws the blanket off and sits up.

"Too hot?" asks Sylvia.

"Can I go back to bed, please?"

As soon as he is in his room, he gets his red backpack from his cupboard and puts it on his lap. He looks inside and counts his things. He opens the pockets with the zippers and looks inside at all the things he's collected and then he puts it next to the bed. The full feeling in his chest has gone. He gets back into bed and closes his eyes and sees his mother's back, sees her jeans and her cardigan and her sneakers disappearing down the corridor at the Family Center. And he doesn't see her turn around and wave, because she didn't.

In the morning, he's better and he's starving. Sylvia puts her hand on his forehead as he eats four Weetabix with sugar sprinkled on top.

"Better stay off school for one more day. All right?"

Leon runs to his room and gets dressed. He takes his backpack and goes back to the kitchen.

"Can I go out on my bike, please?"

Sylvia looks at him with one eyebrow higher than the other.

"How do you feel? It's hot out there, you know? Go on, but half an hour tops. All right? How long did I say, Leon?"

"Can I have two hours, please?"

"No, you get back here for lunchtime. It's ten thirty now. That's an hour and a half. Go on."

26

There is hardly anyone at the allotments. No Mr. Devlin. No Tufty. Only a few old men in distant plots and Mr. and Mrs. Atwal sitting on chairs by their shed. Leon waves as he cycles past. He rides through the allotments, past Mr. Devlin's plot, past Tufty's plot and past five other plots, to the edge of the allotment where there are scruffy bits of land that no one wants, where tall, forgotten plants sprout seeds and prickly leaves, coarse and sharp, where there are gnarled trees and overgrown paths. And an old shed.

Leon parks his bike at the back of the shed and tries to open the door. It's made of heavy planks of wood nailed together. He has to pull it hard with both hands and when he steps inside it bangs behind him, clashing against the corrugated iron roof that shudders and moans. A heavy lump of light comes in through a broken pane of glass but the other window is covered in a veil of dust. No one can see him but people might have heard the door. He peeks out. Nothing. Ropes of curling plants stick to the walls; spiders' webs, thick as cotton wool, nest in the corners and hang between the wooden struts that hold up the roof. There are dead moths and butterflies caught in white sticky traps. The whole place smells of hot soil and dry wood, not like Tufty's shed. There are plastic plant trays upturned on the floor, a metal chair on its side, and a crooked wooden table leaning against the wall, its legs splintered and uneven. Nobody looks after this shed. Nobody wants it. Leon leans against the heavy door and props it open with his backpack to let in some fresh air. He looks out of the gap in the glass. There are no neat rows of plants nearby, there are no wigwams, no water barrels, just wild sprouting plants as high as Leon's knees, clumps of coarse grass, dense, uneven bushes. Leon sits down on the step of the shed. It's perfect.

By the time Leon cycles back toward the gates, lots of people are around and some of them wave at him. He stops at Tufty's shed and goes to inspect the Scarlet Emperors. The shoots seem to grow taller every single day, working their way up toward the sun, coiled tight around the bamboo canes, plaited together, bright green heart-shaped leaves along the stem like a picture from "Jack and the Beanstalk." Leon always gives them a bottle of water when he passes, even if Tufty's not around. He fills the plastic bottle from the water barrel and drips water over the base of each until the dirt is black and sodden.

"There you are, little plant," he says, but as he's speaking he has a funny feeling. Something reminds him of Jake and he straightens up quickly as though he can hear him cry. Leon feels Jake so close that his heart begins to bang in his chest. *Jake! Jake! Where are you?* He turns around but everywhere he looks there are just old people bending over with their spades and forks, no babies, no children.

Maybe he heard something. Maybe Jake is living nearby. The

social workers could be lying when they said they didn't know. Again, he turns around and around, his eyes darting from the sheds to the hedges, everywhere and beyond, to the trees and to the tops of the houses and beyond and beyond, to the flats and maisonettes that he cannot see and beyond to the house where Jake lives without him.

He turns again, his eyes scanning the ripped white clouds, the hazy blue. How old is Jake now? If he can walk he might have escaped from his new forever family and he might be trying to find Leon like Leon is trying to find him. Leon feels the sun on his head and the full feeling in his chest and the pounding of all the questions that nobody answers and then all Tufty's plants float up past his eyes like wisps of dancing, fluttery green feathers.

When he wakes up, he is in Mr. Devlin's shed, sitting in an old leather armchair, and Mr. Devlin himself is leaning against the door.

"You're sick," he says. "There's a drink of water next to you. Look. Drink it."

Leon sips at the water from a metal army cup.

"When you've had that, get straight home. You shouldn't be out. You have a temperature."

Leon sits up straight but his legs are empty and weak.

Mr. Devlin puts his hand out.

"No, not yet."

His voice is different now. Soft like Maureen's.

"Just sit. Sit still. You'll feel better in a short while. It's the sun."

"My bike," says Leon.

"Yes, yes. Of course. Don't move. I'll go and get it."

Leon gets up slowly and looks around. He likes Mr. Devlin's shed. Everything is all piled up and there are lists of things pinned to the walls. There is a walking stick tied to the ceiling with bunches of onions hanging off it and upside-down plants tied up with string. There is a wooden bow and arrow up there as well, turning in the breeze from the door. It's too high for Leon to touch and it's all dusty like it's been there for years. There is an old brown and green rug on the floor with a hole in the middle and painted wooden boxes on their sides with pots in, old seed packets with faded pictures, an old toy train, a gas mask and a metal can with a lid, the white skull of an animal and a bird's wing. On the shelf above him are lots of old books, more books than there are at school, and a fancy teapot. There is a wooden spear with a carved head propped up in a corner. There are tools everywhere and cans of oil. Everything is old but nothing is dirty.

And tucked behind all the interesting things are photographs of boys, lots of them, dozens; there are five or six different brown boys in the pictures and then lots and lots of one boy in particular. In some of the pictures he's a baby and in others he's three and then five and then seven or eight. He's so pretty he could be a girl. But best of all, on an old wooden bench are lots of knives and some of them haven't got any covers. Leon looks everywhere but he can't see the Kanetsune. Up high, just out of reach, is something that looks like a pistol. It's a real pistol. He can see it just on the edge of the shelf next to a dirty glass jar full of brown liquid. If he had something long he could reach it and knock it down. But he would have to catch it carefully otherwise it would blow everything up. Or he could stand on the arm of the chair and . . .

"Here it is," says Mr. Devlin, wheeling Leon's bike to the door of the shed.

Leon is standing near the knives.

"You mustn't touch those," he says and his gruff voice is back. "Best get off home now, if you're better."

"What are all those things?" Leon asks.

"They are things that belong to me," Mr. Devlin says and holds the door open wide.

"Is that a real gun?"

But Mr. Devlin doesn't answer. Leon wheels his bike all the way home because he still doesn't feel well, but there are things in Mr. Devlin's shed that he wants to see again.

27

Leon has swollen glands, so he has to miss a whole week of school. Sylvia says he has to tidy his room properly and help her take the weeds out of the front garden. He has to clean his school shoes. He has to help her rearrange the airing cupboard. He has to sweep the path and finally he has to go to the supermarket to help her carry some of the stuff for her street party. She buys lots of tins of salmon and bottles of juice and the bags are so heavy they cut into Leon's fingers.

Sylvia pulls a cart that is full to the top with tea bags and jars of coffee, bags of sugar and trifle mix.

"We're starting early. A little bit here and there and, on the day, we won't have so much to get. It's only six weeks now."

But Leon just wants to go to the allotments, go to his shed, and make it nice. Get it ready. He has taken a tea towel from Sylvia's kitchen and a little hand broom from under the sink. He has got some tape for the hole in the window and lots of other things. And he needs to get a padlock, because Mr. Devlin has a padlock and Tufty has a padlock and they do things properly. So after he has done all his jobs, he puts his backpack on and goes to the front door.

"Oi," says Sylvia. "Where you going?"

"On my bike."

"Where on your bike?"

"The big gardens."

"You mean the park?"

"Yes," he says quickly, "the park with the railings."

She looks at him for a while, then she lights a cigarette.

"What's in the bag?"

"Nothing."

"Like what? Give me an example of 'nothing,' Leon."

"Like a ball in case I see any of my friends."

"Two hours," she says and he races out the door.

It rained in the morning and it rained the day before so the road is slippery and black. He gets off his bike at the allotment gates in case Mr. Devlin is there and wheels it in. Mr. Devlin is kneeling down with a trowel. He raises it as Leon goes by. Tufty is standing with Castro with the ginger hair but as he waves at Leon his face changes. Leon looks behind. A group of men are walking into the allotment behind Leon. They haven't come to look at the plants and they're not wearing the right clothes for gardening. They have their hands in their pockets and one of them is kicking stones. They walk straight toward him and they look angry. Leon knows that they have come to take him away for stealing.

The Zebra warned him. Sylvia must have complained to her. He thinks about all the things he has stolen and what he will say. He tries to think of clever answers but all the time he wants to go to the toilet and he can't move. Sylvia has sent them to lock him up. The men are close now. Leon drops his bike. People are staring at the men, Mr. and Mrs. Atwal and Mr. Devlin and

everybody working at the allotments, because they aren't keeping
to the path and some of them are walking on people's plants.

Leon takes his pack off and holds it in front of him. He'll
say sorry and give everything back. He feels the pain in his chest
again and wishes he was the Incredible Hulk and he could fight
them all and run away. But the men walk straight past him and
surround Castro and Tufty.

One of them is the leader. He has a leather jacket and a thin
mustache with a leather belt under his belly. He's smiling at Tufty.

"Linwood Michael Burrows? Long time no see. Never took
you for a Percy Thrower."

Three of the other men have gone into the shed and Leon
can hear things being thrown around. The whole shed seems to
be moving. Another man is walking around, treading on things
and kicking stones.

"And Earl Parchment, aka Castro. Either of you two fancy
helping us with our inquiries, to coin a phrase?"

Tufty says nothing but Leon watches him move his feet apart.
He sees Tufty make his lips small like he's trying not to let the
words out and Leon knows exactly how he feels. Castro opens his
arms wide.

"You blood-clat, Babylon! You beast boys can't come in here
for we. You don't have nothing on we."

"Sorry?" says the man. "Didn't catch that." He takes a step
back and looks around. All the people in the allotment are looking over.

"DC Ronald Green, Springfield Road police station, folks,"
he shouts. "Nothing to worry about. A driving matter."

The other policemen start to laugh and DC Green puts his
finger to his lips and says, "Sssshhhh.

"Now," he continues, "it so happens, I'm not looking for either of you this time. Where's Rainbow? That's what I want to
know. He's your mate, isn't he? Your 'brethren,' your 'spar,' your

'idrin.' That's the lingo, isn't it? And as for you, Castro, my little carrot head"—he pushes Castro in the chest—"don't come with any of your blood-clat bullshit here. I don't like it."

Tufty holds Castro's arm. "Leave it, Castro, man. Leave it."

"Yeah," says the policeman. "Listen to your reasonable friend. He likes the quiet life, just like his old dad. Does as he's told. Don't you, Tufty? Always just a bystander, aren't you? Perhaps your balls haven't dropped yet, is that it?" DC Green pretends to shudder. "That's an image I don't care to dwell on. Anyway, as I was saying, we're looking for Rainbow. Or, as we know him, that shit-stirring windbag with the tea cozy on his head, Darius White. Where is he?"

There are five policemen in all. Leon counts them but none of them are wearing police uniforms like the lady who gave him the doughnut when Maureen was taken to the hospital.

"He's done nothing," says Tufty.

"Oh? That's not what I hear. There was a disturbance on Carpenter Road a few nights back, incited, I do believe, by the ever-eloquent Rainbow. We heard he was leading a pack of you all right down the middle of the road, chanting and spear-chucking and war-dancing. He was shouting something. What was it now?"

DC Green looks around at the other policemen.

"Down Babylon," one of them says and they all laugh again but it's not real laughing.

"That's it! Down Babylon. Yes, he had posters and placards and everything. Learned to write at Her Majesty's pleasure, so I understand."

Castro spits on the ground.

"Yeah, Rainbow speaks for all of we."

"Then you were there, eh, Castro?"

They surround Tufty and Castro until Leon can't see them anymore but he can hear Castro shouting in fast West Indian. Mr. Devlin is standing close. He beckons Leon toward him, so he runs over and Mr. Devlin rests his hand on his shoulder. Then the fighting breaks out. Leon's glad that he's standing by Mr. Devlin because of the Kanetsune. He's seen Mr. Devlin using it and, although he doesn't look strong, Leon knows that he really is and he could chop down people just like he chops down bushes and trees. Three of the policemen grab Castro; he starts to buck and struggle but he can't get free. DC Green stands back and shoos everybody away.

"Resisting arrest. Nothing to see. Off you go. Off you go."

It takes four police officers to drag Castro out of the allotments. He's shouting and fighting and twisting his body. One of the policemen has his arm locked round Castro's neck and Castro's trying to pull it off. Spit comes out of Castro's mouth like he's a wild dog. One of his shoes comes off. His jeans are pulled down to his ankles and DC Green is smiling all the time and tightening the belt on his trousers.

Tufty is shouting, "Leave him! Leave him! He can't breathe!" But DC Green points one long finger and holds it against Tufty's chest, prodding and poking with every sentence.

"Excitable, isn't he, your mate? Whereas you've always been sensible, up to a point. Now, if you'd like to save him a couple of nights in the cells and yet another offense on his rather dense list of priors, you could tell us where to find Rainbow."

Tufty takes a step away from the policeman. Everyone is watching Castro being dragged away but not Mr. Devlin and Leon. They are watching Tufty. He goes into his shed and he comes out with a shovel. He holds it like a sword right up in DC Green's face then slams it into the ground. It slices through the wet earth just in front of the policeman's toes. It judders back and forth and then stands dead straight.

"This is my land," says Tufty. "My piece of the earth. My fucking land."

DC Green puts his hands in his pockets and laughs. He

throws his head back and laughs so loud that all the fat on his belly wobbles.

"Oh, dear me, Linwood. Something rattled your cage, has it? You all make me laugh. You're all the same with your big mouths and your big lips and your 'pussy' this and 'ras-clat' that. But when it comes to it . . ."

He kicks the shovel and it falls to the ground.

"Spades don't scare me, Linwood. Not one bit."

The policeman walks slowly away, kicking a stone in front of him and whistling. Nothing happens for a few minutes then Tufty looks straight at Mr. Devlin. He opens his arms wide, splays his fingers.

"What? You got something to say? I didn't invite them in here. Don't say nothing, all right? Don't open your fucking mouth."

He picks the shovel up, goes inside the shed, and throws it down. Everybody goes back to their gardening except Mr. Devlin. He looks at the mess that the police have made of the path. He looks at the plants their black boots have trampled.

"They're the same all over the world," he says. "Small minds, big feet."

He walks away.

Leon has been told over and over always to ask a policeman for help but these policeman didn't even have uniforms on and they didn't give Castro a chance. Leon walks over to Tufty's shed and looks inside. Tufty is sitting on a stool, picking up pieces of paper. All his posters have been ripped off the wall. The man with the fist and the Black Power has had his head ripped off. Tufty's seeds and little baby plants are in a terrible mess on the floor.

"Don't come in here," he says and his voice is sharp like he is still talking to the police. "Can't you see it's all a mess? Don't walk in here with your shoes on. I have to see what I can save."

But most of the plants are broken or stamped on. All the pictures are torn. Tufty picks one up and shows the pieces to Leon.

"You see this man? He says we mustn't fight. Says we can all live in peace. Says don't cause no trouble."

Leon can only see half a black man's head.

"Yeah? You see him? Well, they killed him. Yeah, shot him dead."

Tufty stands up suddenly and looks around, kicking the plants and the torn posters and slamming his stool against the wall and flinging the plastic pots all over the place and making even more of a mess than before. When he stops, he's panting.

"Let me tell you, Star. Stand up for yourself. All right? You see me?" He stabs himself in the chest with his finger. "I try, you know. I try hard. Keep my head down, don't cause no trouble. It's how I was brought up but sometimes—" Tufty kicks the side of the shed so hard that one of the planks comes loose.

"Go home," he says.

Leon backs away, picks up his bike, and pedals home to Sylvia.

But at bedtime, Leon can't sleep. He doesn't want to be in his room on his own and he creeps along the hallway and pushes the door open a little bit. Sylvia is in the sitting room watching one of her programs. He can hear her shouting the answers louder than usual. She's drinking her favorite dark brown beer with the white foam and laughing when she gets the answers wrong.

"Blankety Blank!" she shouts or "Tiebreak!"

Leon opens the door wide and Sylvia turns around.

"Five minutes, you!" she shouts. "Bed at the end of this."

They watch until the end of the program, then Sylvia herds him back to his room. She stands in the doorway while he gets into bed.

"What's up?" she says.

"I saw some policemen today and they were fighting with two black men."

"Well, as long as you keep out of trouble you've got nothing to worry about."

"Can you tell me about the rabbit's adventures?"

"What?"

Sylvia sits down heavily on Leon's bed and flicks her cigarette ash into the palm of her hand. "Rabbit?"

"The one with the permanent wave."

Sylvia laughs so hard that she can hardly breathe. She takes ages to stop and then she goes to the bathroom and flushes her cigarette away. She comes back and takes a deep breath.

"Right. Rabbit. Let me see."

She's smiling now and Leon can smell the beer on her breath; he sees how she's trying to sit up straight.

"All right. Well, the rabbit ran off into the woods. He's still waving but obviously the man and the woman have gone now, so he's just waving at the other animals. He waves at a squirrel and the squirrel waves back. He waves at a beaver and a weasel and, what else, a badger, yeah, a badger, and they all wave back and they say to themselves, 'Wow, what a really friendly rabbit.' So word gets around in the woods that there's this nice little rabbit going about and everyone starts looking out for him. Anyway, he gets into the middle of the woods and, he sees a bear. And he waves at the bear and the bear calls him over. 'How you doing?' says the bear. 'Yeah, I'm fine, thanks,' says the rabbit. 'Do you like it in the woods?' asks the bear. 'Yeah, it's great,' says the rabbit. 'No problems?' asks the bear. 'None, no,' says the rabbit. 'I'm A-one okay.'"

Sylvia is a little bit drunk.

"The bear says, 'That's great. I wonder if I could ask you a question.' 'Fire away,' says the rabbit. 'Well,' says the bear, 'you know when you go to the toilet, for a number two, how do you get the shit off your fur?'"

Leon starts to laugh.

"'The shit?' asks the rabbit. 'Yeah,' says the bear. 'Do you find it difficult to get the shit off your fur?' 'No,' says the rabbit. 'It comes right off.' 'Great,' says the bear and he picks up the rabbit and wipes it over his arse."

Leon and Sylvia lie on the bed together, rolling from side to side.

28

Sylvia wakes him up early the next day. The skin on her face looks even more creased than usual and her eyes are hardly open.

"Rough, rough, rough," she says as she sits at the kitchen table.

"Are you pretending to be a dog?" Leon asks, smiling.

She looks at him and points at the kettle. Leon fills it and flicks the switch. Then she points at her handbag and he passes it to her. She digs around inside and then shoves it across the table and puts her head on her arms.

"Your fault, this is," she says. "You and your bloody social workers booking themselves in at half past bloody eight."

Leon finds her cigarettes, takes one out, and puts it in her hand.

"Thanks, love," she says. She drags her head up and it lolls around on her shoulders. She lights the cigarette and blows the smoke up into the air.

"I've got about half an hour to look gorgeous."

Leon says nothing.

"It's a new one. A big cheese. The boss of the boss, something like that. A bloke at any rate. Sounds all right on the phone. You never know, you never know."

Leon says nothing.

"Could be my lucky day."

She takes a mirror out of her bag and squints into it.

"Not too shabby, Sylv. Not too bad at all."

In half an hour they are both ready. Leon only took a few minutes to get a wash and then Sylvia told him to tidy up the kitchen. Sylvia spent all the time in her bedroom, muttering and swearing. When she comes back she looks the same as she did before but she has some lipstick on and it's too bright. And it's on her teeth but Leon is scared to tell her.

She punches all the cushions on the sofa and fills the kettle.

"I used to be married, you know. Yes, didn't know that, did you? And Maureen. We were sisters that married brothers. She got the good one and I got the bast—the loser."

Sylvia goes to the front window, moves the net curtains aside, and looks up and down the road.

"Then there was someone else. And he left me as well. Up here."

She taps her temple.

"Not just me. Took leave of his senses, as they say. Cuckoo."

Sylvia carries on tapping her temple even when she's not talking.

"I couldn't see it but Mo knew it from the get-go. Said he needed to sort himself out. Don't we all."

She lets the curtains drop.

"Look, here he is. Let him in, let him in. Wait. Quick. Now."

Leon opens the front door and a man holds his hand out.

"You must be Leon. I'm Mike."

He has a perfect social-worker smile and a hot, damp hand. He has a checked shirt and shiny purple boots with yellow laces.

He has short hair that sticks up like a brush and an earring in the shape of a cross that judders when he moves. Leon moves aside to let him in.

"Is Sylvia about?" he asks.

Sylvia comes out of the kitchen, showing her pink teeth and creased face. Mike holds his hand out.

"Mike Dent, Independent Reviewing Officer for Leon. We spoke on—"

"Come in," says Sylvia and she points to an armchair. "Coffee?"

"Black no sugar, please."

While Sylvia is gone, Earring gets some papers out of his briefcase. Leon can see he also has a Mars bar in there and Leon wonders if he has brought him a present.

"How are you, Leon?"

"All right."

"We've not met before, have we?"

"No."

"Well, I'm an Independent Reviewing Officer. I'm the person in charge of making sure we're taking care of you properly and we're listening to what you say. Part of my job is to talk to you face-to-face so I can be certain you're happy and well. You're old enough now to have your wishes and feelings taken into account and for you to tell us what those wishes and feelings are. I also have to think about what your needs are from our point of view and then make sure that all your needs are being met. All right? Do you understand what I've just said, Leon?"

"Yes."

"I've come today to give you some more information on what's happening with your placement and also what the plans are for you in the long term. And also to ask you how you are. And also to ask you if there is anything you're not happy with. We do this from time to time to make sure that we are taking good care of you. Okay? Do you understand this, Leon? Is there anything you want to ask me?"

Earring begins writing something on a notepad. "No questions so far?"

"No."

"And Sylvia? You getting on with Sylvia?"

"Yes."

"You're a sizable lad for nine. Let's see, your birthday is on . . . ooh, it's in a few weeks' time. Looking forward to it?"

"Yes."

"And what would you like for your birthday? Bet you've been talking to Sylvia about it all the time. I know I did when I was your age. Couldn't wait for my birthday to come around. Pestered the life out of my parents."

"Yes."

"Right, and you had an access visit with your mom on the, let's see, eighth. How was that? Was it good to see your mom again?"

"Yes," says Leon and he remembers Carol's brown-stained teeth and her brown-stained fingers when she picked up her bag. "Leon," she said, "I can't manage myself, let alone you." She squeezed his hand and walked out of the room. He ran to the door and watched her get smaller and smaller as she walked down the corridor. She had to press a buzzer to get out and while she was waiting for it to open, Leon thought she might turn around and wave. But she didn't.

"Leon? I said how about school? Do you like your school?"

"No."

"Okay, then. Thanks for this coffee, Sylvia. For the first part of the meeting, I'd like to speak to Leon on his own. Is that okay?"

Sylvia walks back into the kitchen.

"Right. Okay, let's make a start."

Earring speaks too quickly, like he's running out of time.

He asks all the questions the Zebra asks but faster, writing and talking or putting ticks in boxes. It goes on for ages, then he sits back and takes a breath.

"Are you happy here, Leon?"

"Yes."

"What's it like living with Sylvia?"

Leon looks at the door to the kitchen. He sees Sylvia behind it with her cigarette.

"Where's Maureen? When am I going back home?"

"By 'home' you mean back to Maureen's?"

"Who's got all my other toys?"

"Which toys?"

"Me and Jake had lots of toys and we had to leave them all behind. I had lots of Action Men that my mom and dad bought me. I had seven. No, eight. And now I've only got one."

Earring is looking through his papers and doesn't speak for a moment.

"One-sixty-four B Benton Avenue South? You mean when you lived with your mom?"

"Yes, and I took some of them to Tina's, to Auntie Tina's house. Jake took some of his as well but he left to go with the other people. Where is Jake? Where does he live?"

"Let's take this one question at a time, okay? Right, when you went into care, Leon, and when your mom left, I'm afraid she also left all her property in the maisonette. She no longer has a tenancy there. That means someone else lives there now and I don't know what has happened to all her possessions. I'm sorry about that."

Leon says nothing.

"Now, if there was stuff at Auntie Tina's, that's Tina, Tina—" he looks at his papers—"Tina Moore, then I could certainly try and follow that up for you and see if there's anything she forgot to pass on to us. Let me just write this down so I don't forget."

He writes slowly and then taps the paper with his pen.

"What else? Yes, right, you asked about Jake. Do you understand about adoption, Leon?"

"Yes."

"What is adoption?"

"Am I getting adopted?"

"Is that what you would like, Leon?"

"No. I want Jake to come back."

"Adoption is where you get a new family, a new mom and/or a new dad. And you go and live with them. Adoption is forever, Leon. It means you don't go back to your first family. You live with a new family all the time you're growing up."

"Where is he?"

"Jake is living with his new family."

"Where does he live?"

"He lives far away, Leon. Well, not that far, but he has a whole new life."

"Why can't I live with him?"

Earring picks up his coffee cup and looks inside like he's trying to decide whether to drink it or not. He puts it back on the table.

"This must be very hard for you, Leon. Jake was adopted because he was a little baby that needed looking after. You both needed looking after, actually, but sometimes adoption is best for some children and fostering is best for other children."

"You said he would write to me."

"Me?"

"The other one."

"The other social worker? Yes, well, he might. Is that something you would like, a letter from Jake?"

"I've been waiting ages," Leon says and he decides to go to the toilet in case he starts to cry but, as soon as he stands up, some tears spill out and Earring sees them.

"Leon," he says, "this is a very difficult thing to understand. You must miss him."

"He misses me!" Leon shouts. "He's crying for me! I heard him!"

"Is that what you're worried about, Leon? You think Jake is unhappy?"

"He needs me," says Leon. "Only I can look after him."

Earring makes a little shaking movement with his head. His Adam's apple bobs up and down in his throat.

"It was a really, really hard decision to make to split you up from Jake, Leon. Really difficult, Leon. We tried to think of a way that we could keep you together and a lot of people sat around a table and after a long, long time, we couldn't find a way that was fair to both of you. We want you and your brother to be happy and have the best chance in life and sometimes that means finding that happiness in different ways. Has anyone explained this to you before?"

Leon says nothing.

"Do you think you'd like to talk to someone about how you're feeling, Leon?"

Earring isn't writing anymore but he's making little dots on the paper with the end of his fountain pen. The end of the pen is like a little metal knife. It could be dangerous and it could kill someone. It could kill Earring if Leon picked it up and stabbed him through the soft bit of his eye. He would push the pen in and write on Earring's brain: "I fucking hate you. Black Power. From Leon."

Earring's mouth is moving and he's blinking and, all the time, he's trying to be Leon's friend.

". . . arrange for you to see someone, special advisors trained to help children who have been through a difficult time. Would you like that?"

"Jake will forget about me."

"Well . . ."

"I won't forget him but he might forget me."

"I think—"

"You're making him forget. You took him away so he could forget about me. You only care about him. You think you know what he wants but you don't. Only I do."

"Leon—"

"Only me. No one else. They don't know how to look after him."

"I think you—"

"He misses me."

"I'm sure he—"

"He might be upset and you don't care."

Earring puts his pen down and Leon knows every word that he's going to say. He knows he will turn his head a bit to the right then the left, he will talk slowly using baby words because he thinks Leon is stupid, but whatever words social workers use they all mean the same thing.

"It's very difficult—" he starts.

Leon runs down the hallway and slams the bathroom door. He picks up the toilet seat and bangs it down. The noise makes him jump. He unravels all the toilet paper and shoves it down into the toilet bowl and then puts the towel in it and then Sylvia's dressing gown from the back of the door. He tries to close the lid but the toilet is too full, so he just pulls and pulls the seat until his arms hurt and his fingers tingle and his face is all crooked and then finally it breaks and rips out of its socket. Leon catches himself in the mirror. He thought he would see the Incredible Hulk with green skin and a chest as wide as a double bed and a ripped shirt. But he looks just the same. He is nearly ten and he is black and Jake is one and he is white. That's why Jake is adopted. That's what Maureen said and she's the only one who has never lied.

Sylvia knocks on the door.

"You all right, love?" she says.

Leon sits on the edge of the bath. He's wet himself.

"Leon?"

Sylvia opens the door. She doesn't say anything. Leon can feel the pee itching his legs and he wants to take his jeans off but he can't move. The pee is in his sneakers as well and in his socks. Sylvia closes the door and he hears her go down the hallway. He can hear her voice and Earring's voice and it sounds like an argument.

Leon takes everything off, even his underpants, and goes into his bedroom. He puts his tracksuit trousers on with his school shoes and he sits on the bed. Sylvia will tell him to leave. She always said she wouldn't stand for any nonsense.

He finds his backpack and he makes sure that everything is inside. He has all his important things and all the zippers are done up. He hears the front door close and he hears Sylvia coming back, so he goes to stand at the window so he doesn't have to look at her.

"Made a right mess of that bathroom, haven't you?" she says. He can hear the cigarette in the corner of her mouth.

"What were you thinking?"

Outside in Sylvia's garden there is a black and brown cat walking very slowly on the grass with his head down. He is going carefully like a soldier in the jungle. He's trying to catch something but Leon can't see what it is. It might be a mouse or a rat or a bird. Once, Leon's mom bought him a kitten but it made him sneeze, so his mom gave it away and bought him a dog with a battery in it. Leon wanted a real dog but his mom said no. Then Leon remembers Samson and the way Leon's dad said he would hold his paws and break his heart open. Leon starts to cry.

Sylvia is still standing in the doorway. He can hear her breathing and smoking. He can hear her getting angry with him and telling him to leave. He drags his sleeve across his face, turns around and picks up his pack, and waits for her to say it.

"Where you going?" she asks.

Leon says nothing.

"If you think this fool is putting them pissy clothes in the washer and tidying up, you're mistaken. Put your bag down. Come on."

She puts her hand in his neck-back, just like Maureen does, and nudges him into the bathroom.

"Jeans, sneakers, socks, pants, all of them in the bath. Come on. I'm standing right here and watching."

Leon does it.

"Fish my best dressing gown out of the toilet and put that in the bath as well and try not to get any of that wet toilet paper on it. And don't make such a bloody mess on the floor neither. Watch it. Careful."

Leon does it.

"Now, run and get two shopping bags from under the sink. Quick. I'm counting to ten."

Leon runs and comes back in eight.

"Now put your hands in there and get every single piece of toilet paper out and into one of the shopping bags. And when I say every single piece, what do I mean?"

"All of it."

"You bet your sweet life."

She stands and watches him. It takes ages and she says nothing. When it's all done, she takes the shopping bag and twists it around by the handles and knots it in the top, then she puts it in the other bag and does the same. The linoleum on the floor of the bathroom is all wet.

"Right, pick up the clothes out of the bath and bring them into the kitchen and be quick. Don't let them drip. Come on."

They run down the hall together, through the living room and into the kitchen. She drops the shopping bag into the trash bin and then opens the door to the washing machine.

"All in," she says, "the sneakers as well. All in."

Leon feeds everything into the washing machine and watches while Sylvia puts in the soap powder and turns it on.

"Wash your hands."

Leon does it. She points at a chair. Leon sits down.

"Ever hear the phrase 'Don't shit where you sit,' Leon?"

"No."

"What do you think it means?"

Leon says nothing.

"No? Well, I'll tell you. It means don't fuck up a good thing. It means that if you get bad news or someone gets on your nerves, you don't make trouble or ruin things at home. Home is where you live, where you sleep, where you eat, where people look after you. Don't shit on your own seat. You shit on someone else's seat or find another way to sort things out."

Leon nods.

"Now," she says, lighting another cigarette, "I don't know if you've any idea what I'm going on about, so I'll say it nice and simple. We get along. I like you and you like me. Yes?"

"Yes."

"And more important than anything is the fact that my sister, Maureen, who ain't well, loves us both."

Sylvia smokes her cigarette for a bit.

"So I'm going to look after you until she's well again. That means I need a dressing gown. That also means I need a working toilet and I don't need attitude."

Leon nods.

"Now, if that mincing prick comes back here with any of his nonsense, I'll sort him out. I don't know what he said to upset you because I couldn't hear properly from where I was standing but you leave him to me. He's already had the rough edge of my tongue. That's the first thing. The second thing is, I don't like any of that nonsense in the bathroom. How much money have you got in your bag?"

Leon says nothing.

"I'm taking two pounds off you for a new toilet seat. I'll take fifty pence a week out of your pocket money till it's paid off."

She puts the kettle on and makes a cup of coffee. She gives Leon a drink of juice and a packet of chips.

"In a minute, you're coming to the bathroom with me, we're mopping the floor with bleach and then you're getting in the bath. Bet your legs are itching."

Leon nods. She smiles.

"Serves you right," she says. Then she stops still and looks off into the distance. "I wet the bed till I was nine, and I shared with our Maureen. She stood up for me, she did. Said it was her so I didn't get into trouble."

Sylvia stirs the spoon in her mug.

"Hope she gets better."

29

Something is wrong. For days and days Sylvia is on the phone
and when Leon comes in the room she says goodbye or tells him
to go outside or she starts to whisper. She hasn't forgotten about
the toilet paper and her best dressing gown. She hasn't forgiven
him for shitting where he sits.

Leon measures himself using the window ledge in his bedroom. When he was nine the window ledge was the same height
as his elbow but tomorrow, when he's ten, people will notice how
he's grown. Leon breathes in deeply and sees his chest grow. He
feels his arms and shoulders for muscles. He needs to get strong
if he's going to carry a heavy weight.

He cycles up to the allotment straight after school. It's a
sunny day and there are lots of people doing something to their
little gardens. Mr. Devlin calls him over.

"Off the bike, boy."

Leon gets off and rests the bike on the ground.

"Have you seen your handiwork?"

"No."

"Come and look."

They walk to the wigwam of canes and each little plant has begun to twist around the cane. Some of them are loose and tall and some of them are stubby and strong.

"Will they get to the top?"

"And beyond. Eight feet or more. So you see, there's no harm done if you delay planting. And planting in situ has many advantages. The seedlings aren't disturbed. You put the seed where the seed grows, where it belongs, and then you don't move it. Best results? Do what I do."

He pours a gentle trickle of water on each seedling.

"Of course, if you have a proper greenhouse, like Mr. and Mrs. Atwal over there, you can get a jump on this method. Start them off in a seed tray or a three-inch pot. Replant them after a few weeks. They'll come up all right, I suppose. Yes, yes, and the ever-present Mr. Burrows likes to tell us all about his achievements, but I'll tell you this, there is a rightness about planting seeds the way people have planted seeds for generations."

Leon looks at Mr. Devlin's neat rows of runner beans.

"Not quite broadcasting but fairly close. There was a field outside the schoolhouse, just under an acre. Very quiet, on the outskirts."

"Why do they call them Scarlet Emperor?"

"*Phaseolus coccineus.* South American in origin. There are many varieties, in fact. When they get more mature, you will see the most beautiful red flowers, scarlet flowers. And another thing." Mr. Devlin squats down and touches the delicate new leaves of the plant with his dirty fingers. He looks happy. "The Scarlet Emperor is a whole plant. That means you can eat the flowers, you can eat the beans, and you can even eat the root. This sort of plant can keep you alive for many weeks if necessary, if that's all you had. There is a type of protein in the bean, even the bean pod itself is nutritious, the flowers are both attractive and flavorful, and there are tribes in Mexico who boil and eat the root. And then, of course, if you're away from home, you can dry the beans and cook them. Never eat them raw. Never. Magnificent."

Mr. Devlin's eyes are twinkling and bright. He stares at the wigwam and then looks at Leon.

"How old are you?" he says.

"I'm ten tomorrow. It's my birthday."

"Ten years old. Summer baby," says Mr. Devlin. "A ten-year-old boy. You're well grown for ten. Well developed."

"I'm going to have big muscles. I'm going to carry bricks in my backpack until my muscles are strong. I saw it on a TV show."

"Bricks?" says Mr. Devlin. He puts his hand around Leon's upper arm and squeezes. "I have something better than bricks. Come with me."

He takes Leon into his shed.

"Let me see," he says and begins moving things on the shelves and behind the chair. He keeps dropping things onto the armchair: a pair of brown leather shoes that are all moldy and creased, some china plates with chips on them, a tiny kettle, and a rolled-up checkered blanket. These are all things that Leon would like to touch but then he drops the gun on the blanket and Leon gasps. It doesn't go off but Mr. Devlin wasn't very careful with it. Then he throws more things on it, some magazines and a clock and some plastic rope.

"Yes, good. That's the thing. Look here."

Mr. Devlin is holding some weights like bodybuilders use; they're made of black iron. He holds one out for Leon but when Leon takes it, it drops out of his hand. It doesn't look heavy but it is.

"Steady now," says Mr. Devlin.

He crouches down, picks up the weight, and closes Leon's hand around it. He shows him how to bring it up and down, watching him closely, breathing in and out, smelling of oil and dinners and old people.

"Do you feel it?" he says.

Leon nods.

"Where do you feel it?"

"In my arms," says Leon.

Mr. Devlin presses Leon's chest.

"And here?"

"Yes," says Leon.

Mr. Devlin presses Leon's back.

"And here?"

"Yes."

"Hmm. Now, a boy's muscles are sinewy and undeveloped. You can't build muscles on a boy, neither should you. A little light work doesn't hurt but no vigorous bodybuilding. Not yet."

Leon brings the weight up and down again just to show he can do it. After a while, Mr. Devlin smiles.

"Very good," he says and stands up. "Here, take this."

Leon takes the other weight and puts them both in his pack. It's heavy now and difficult to hold. Leon takes his time doing up the zipper and making them fit straight at the bottom and all the time Mr. Devlin is standing at the door watching him.

"Hey, you!"

It's Tufty's voice outside.

Mr. Devlin turns round.

"Yes?"

He steps out of the shed and Leon hears Tufty shouting.

"What the fuck is this?"

Leon quickly goes to the old chair; he moves the magazine, the clock, the rope, and all the other things. He feels around until his hand closes on the butt of the gun. He grabs it and puts it in his pack. He mustn't touch the trigger. He puts the pack on. It cuts into his shoulders as he steps outside.

Mr. Devlin has his hands on his hips.

"Listen, Burrows, it's not my idea. It's the rules. Your father has sublet the plot to you. Subletting is prohibited, as you know. There was some discussion and—"

"I said what the fuck is this?"

Tufty is shaking a piece of paper in Mr. Devlin's face.

"It's in the rules. However, if you're unhappy, there is an appeal procedure."

"Liar."

"I don't care what you think, Mr. Burrows. There was a committee meeting last night and—"

"Bullshit! What committee meeting? This is about them police the other day. You see me do anything? You see me start any argument? I did nothing. This isn't about no fucking subletting. This is about racism, pure and simple."

"Holy Mother, you're ridiculous. I have nothing to gain by getting rid of you. This is between you and the committee. I have no dog in this fight."

"This ain't no fucking fight. And I ain't no fucking dog. You're just a foot soldier, man. You ain't no general here. You don't like it when you're not in charge, do you? You go around cutting down bushes with your fucking knife. Who told you to cut down the bushes? You think this is the jungle or something? Tend your own fucking business, man."

"General? I never claimed to be a general, you damn idiot."

Tufty notices Leon then.

"Yeah? What you doing with that boy in there?"

"What did you say?"

Mr. Devlin stands up tall but he is still shorter than Tufty.

"You heard me. I seen them pictures you got in there. Little boys on your shelf."

Tufty pulls Leon toward him.

"You don't go in there, you hear me. Stay away from that man. He don't like black people unless they're under sixteen. Yeah?"

"How dare—"

But Tufty is towering over Mr. Devlin. He holds the paper up in the air and then flings it in Mr. Devlin's face.

"My father's been on this site for twenty years. How long you been here? Eh? How long? My father's gone home for six months. Six months. I told you that. You know that. I've been coming here with my father since I was five years old. You think you can come here and tell me anything? He's coming back when he's good and ready and when he does, he will find everything just how he left it. You get me? You ain't throwing me off this site. Don't send no fucking Ku Klux Klan orders to my father's house. Next time, I don't play so nice. You get me?"

All the time Tufty is walking forward and Mr. Devlin is walking backward, right into his shed.

As soon as Mr. Devlin is gone, Leon goes and gets his bike. It will be hard to pedal with the weights on his back and with the gun in between them. He goes all along the path to his halfway house and tugs the door open. He lets it close gently, silently, but as soon as he puts the weights on the crooked table, both legs break off and the weights crash on the floor. Leon peers through the glass but there is no one nearby to hear. He takes the pistol from his backpack and holds it up to the light. It's all black, shiny and smooth. It feels heavy in his hand and fits perfectly. He points it at the door. *Poof.*

30

It's the fifth of July. Finally. Saturday. At last. Leon's birthday. He wakes up early. Sylvia hasn't even mentioned his presents or anything and every time he tries to say something about it, she's talking on the phone or planning her street party for the Royal Wedding. He thinks about the Action Man that he got for his last birthday and his other Action Men that he had to leave behind. He had lots of outfits and different guns and they are all still at his old house where he used to live with Carol.

He gets out of bed and walks slowly along the hallway in his pajamas. Sylvia is standing at the back door with a cigarette. She turns around when she sees him.

"Here he is! Ten years old and nearly looking me in the eye. Bloody hell! You've grown overnight, haven't you? Come here."

She bundles him into her skinny arms and kisses him on the cheek. He can smell her body and her cigarettes.

"There's a birthday kiss for you. I don't give them away very often. Not these days."

She opens a kitchen cupboard and takes out a little box wrapped in glittery paper.

"That's from me, love," she says. "And here's your card."

Then she opens the door to the cupboard where she keeps the vacuum and pulls a massive box out.

"And this is from Mo!"

Leon looks at his two presents.

"Can I open them now?"

"Go on then."

The paper is hard to get off the little present because there is so much tape but inside is Darth Vader in a cardboard box. Luke Skywalker and Han Solo are good but Darth Vader is evil and Leon wonders if he will have a bad dream if Darth Vader is in his bedroom.

"Thank you, Sylvia."

Sylvia pushes the other box over to him.

"Wait till you see what's in this."

There's so much paper it takes ages, but he keeps going.

"It's an AT-AT Walker!"

Sylvia helps him take the cardboard box off and all the little bits of wire that hold it in place and then Leon puts it on the carpet. Then he makes it walk up and down and moves its head and fires all the guns.

"Is it good, then?" asks Sylvia.

Leon is still playing with the AT-AT when Sylvia sits down next to him on the carpet.

"Ooh, that's a long way down. Now," she says, "here you are. You've been waiting on this and, between me and Maureen, we made sure you were going to have it on your birthday. So, here."

She gives him a strong, brown envelope with his name typed on the front. It feels like there's a card inside.

"Do you want me to open it for you?" Sylvia says. "Open it carefully."

So he does. There's a photograph inside. It's Jake. He's sitting up and he has a lot of blond hair just like Carol's. He's wearing a pale blue top with a velvet collar and a mini pair of jeans. He has no shoes on but his feet are much bigger than they used to be. He's smiling and he has a lot more teeth. One arm is reaching out for Leon.

Jake is smiling but Leon can see he's tired and he doesn't like having his picture taken. Anyone can see that. Leon doesn't want to turn the photograph over because he knows the address will be on the other side, so he just pretends he can't stop looking at Jake, which is true anyway.

"There should be a letter in there as well."

Leon puts the photograph down carefully by his AT-AT and takes the letter out. It isn't written by a baby, it's typed.

"What does it say?" says Sylvia.

"'Dear Leon, I know it is your birthday so I have sent you a photograph of me. I am very happy living with my new mom and dad. I have got lots of toys and I like playing with cars and trucks. I have my own bedroom with pictures of bears on the wall and I go to nursery to play with my friends. I hope you are as happy as I am and hope you have lots of presents on your birthday. Lots of love from Jake. Three kisses.'"

"There you go!" says Sylvia and she strokes his back. "See? He's very happy."

She goes into the kitchen then and says he can have whatever he wants for his birthday breakfast. He can have chocolate cereal which she bought specially or he can have beans on toast with grated cheese or he can have biscuits with icing on or anything that's in the cupboards because it's his birthday and he can choose.

Leon has Choco Pops with Pepsi Cola and he opens all his birthday cards. One from Maureen, one from the Zebra, whose name is Judy, one from Beth, the other social worker who sometimes collects him from school, one from Sylvia, one from someone called Ian from-the-center-in-brackets and one from Sylvia's friend, Sue. Sue's card has a one-pound note in it. As soon as he opens the cards, Sylvia puts them on the sideboard.

"Happy?" she says.

"Yes."

After breakfast, Leon takes all his new things to his room with his photograph. He puts his new toys on the bed and then turns the photograph over. There is an address printed in big gold letters.

"HALLADAYS"

287 DOVEDALE ROAD

DOVEDALE HEATH

Leon puts the photograph in his backpack and then he takes it out again. He reads what the letter says. He reads it twice. He's angry with the person who wrote the letter and put three kisses on it and makes Jake sleep in a bedroom all on his own. He puts the photograph next to his bed and gets dressed.

Mr. Devlin is watering his plants when Leon wheels his bike into the allotments. Leon stops and they both look over toward Tufty's shed but he isn't there. Mr. Devlin waves him over.

"It's your birthday, isn't it? Today, you said."

"Yes. I got an AT-AT and Darth Vader and some money."

"Good. And I've got something for you as well. I don't think our friend Mr. Burrows will object to this."

He goes into his shed and comes back with a brown paper bag.

"I've been watching you. Come with me."

Leon follows him to one of the plots between Tufty and Mr. Devlin. It's overgrown and untidy; no one looks after it.

Mr. Devlin points to a spot on the earth.

"Stand there."

He walks with long steps to a bush with green berries on it.

"That's about twelve feet. It's about one-quarter of a standard plot. It now belongs to you. It's your small patch of the planet. It's arranged with the committee and I'm your sponsor."

He opens the paper bag and gives Leon a small fork with a wooden handle and a trowel that matches it.

"Now you have to look after it, young man. You have to weed it and plant some seeds and water them. You're in charge of them. Do you understand? It's hard work. It might look easy but it isn't. Responsibility never is. What does responsibility mean?"

"When you're in charge of something."

"That's only part of it."

"And it means you have to look after something and it's always there in your mind even when you can't see it, because you're thinking about it all the time and you have to make sure it's safe and everything you do is about looking after that thing and making sure it's all right even when you don't want to do it. Because that's your job."

Mr. Devlin nods and waits a little while before he speaks again.

"Very eloquent. Yes. And now this one-quarter plot belongs to you. Look."

He puts his hand in his pocket and takes out a packet of seeds.

"Scarlet Emperor. You remember we planted those seeds over there? Remember? Start with those. It's not too late in the season."

"I haven't got the wigwam," Leon says.

"We will do it together. Later."

Leon's backpack is so heavy. He has some tins of food from Sylvia's cupboard inside and a bag of sugar and a blanket from the airing cupboard. He puts the pack down and looks at his plot. Then he looks at Tufty's plants in neat and tidy rows and Mr.

Devlin's and Mr. and Mrs. Atwal's and all the others. Like Mr. Devlin said, it might look easy but it isn't.

"It seems to me you might need a little help to get you started. Get the seeds in the ground and—ah, here is just the man."

Mr. Devlin moves away from Leon. He goes to the edge of Leon's little plot. Tufty's bike skids to a halt and he gets off. The two men look at each other for ages but no one speaks, so Leon tells Tufty about his present.

"He gave you these?" says Tufty, weighing the tools in his hand. "He give you any other presents? He give you anything else?"

"Some seeds," says Leon.

"They ain't enough. You need more than these to start with. Come."

Leon turns to wave at Mr. Devlin but he is already walking away.

Leon's plot has some raised beds. That's what Tufty calls them, raised beds. They are mini gardens surrounded by wood. He has four of them and some raspberry bushes. The raspberries are sour. The best plot in the whole allotment is Mr. and Mrs. Atwal's and the second is the woman who wears long skirts, but third is Tufty's.

"Right," he says, "we got to clear the beds first, then we work on the path."

"It's my birthday today," says Leon.

"Yeah, yeah. I remember. You told me."

"I'm ten."

"Yeah?"

Tufty makes Leon sit down on one of his fold-up chairs and then he gives him a can of pop.

"You can't do hard work on your birthday, Star. You got to take it easy. Did you get your presents yet?"

"I got an AT-AT and Darth Vader."

"Yeah? That's good."

"And I got some money."

"Nice."

"And Mr. Devlin gave me these tools."

"They're good old tools, Star. Nice handles." Tufty slaps him on his shoulder. "Ten! I remember being ten. You got no worries yet, Star! You got to enjoy it. Yeah, wish I was ten again, sometimes."

Leon looks at his backpack with the tins inside and thinks how far he has to go on his bike.

"How did you get your muscles, Tufty?" he asks.

"Me? Just born this way. I used to do a bit of martial arts when I was young."

Tufty springs up onto his feet and kicks the air; he sweeps one hand around in a circle and then stabs the air with the other.

"You want me to teach you some moves? Come. Stand up. Stand like this."

Leon stands with his feet apart.

"First thing you got to know is kung fu means 'work hard,' so this ain't easy. Not if you want to get it right. Okay, first you need to get your stance right. A firm stance is going to keep you on your feet. You know, if someone comes for you and you're standing right like this"—Tufty spreads his legs wide—"this is horse stance. If you're in horse stance it's difficult to knock you down. Then there's this, this, this."

Tufty is moving and punching the air and waving his arms and he looks like nobody could beat him.

"Come on, copy me."

Leon does everything that Tufty does, stances, stretches, punches, blocks, and it takes a long time.

"Yeah, yeah, you got it. You do those moves every day and you get muscles. You get muscles and no one can fuck with you."

Leon copies Tufty carefully.

Tufty moves like a cross between a soldier and a ballet dancer, graceful and dangerous.

"When people fuck with you, you got a choice. You fuck back or you swallow down."

He raises one leg a few inches off the floor and draws a circle in the air. He stares straight ahead but his chest is going up and down. Leon knows he's angry and he's thinking about the policemen who trampled on his posters and took Castro away.

"Swallow down enough times and you start to choke."

He stops suddenly and puts his foot on the ground. He blows all the air from his belly and closes his eyes.

"Or you learn to accept. Let go. Breathe easy."

Tufty brings both hands together like he's praying. Then he turns his head quickly to look at Leon. "But you know what's best?" he says. "You need some classes. They got classes up on Carpenter Road."

Leon sits down and drinks his can of soda.

"You could get your mom to take you. I'll show you where. Or your dad can take you. It's not far. Where do you live?"

"Ten College Road."

"So, it's not far. Tell your mom you want to do it. Okay? You got some good moves there."

Leon stands up. "I've got to go now."

Leon picks up his tools and puts them in the paper bag with his Scarlet Emperor seeds. He puts the bag in his pack and it's even heavier than it was before.

He waits until Tufty isn't looking, then wheels his bike quickly to the halfway house. He tucks it out of sight, crouches down, heaves the door open, and places the tins and the blanket and the sugar on the floor. He will have to make it tidy another day.

Sylvia has everything ready when he gets back. There are sandwiches on the table and little sausage rolls and mini cakes.

"It's not too late to change your mind. We can ask that boy from up the road if you like. He's about your age."

"No," says Leon. "I don't know him."

"I'm sure the boys from your class would have come if you'd asked. What about your friends from the park?"

Leon says nothing.

"It's just going to be me and you and a couple of my friends, Leon. It's not much of a party, kid. You sure?"

"Can I go out on my bike later?"

"Again? After tea you can have another hour. What's at the park anyway?"

"Swings and slides. Some kids have got skateboards. I can go down the ramp on my bike."

"You can bring one of your friends back here sometime if you like, you know. You should have friends, Leon."

"Can I put the TV on?"

"They'll be here soon. Go and wash your hands. Put your bag away."

Leon gets more presents when Sylvia's friends come. Felt pens, a car, three pound notes, and a soccer ball. And more cards as well. The sideboard is full up. He has chocolate cake and sweets and Pepsi Cola and an enormous bag of Revels all to himself.

Sylvia's friends talk about riots in another city and the Irishmen who are dying on a hunger strike.

"I wouldn't mind a bit of that," says Sue with a piece of cake on her plate. "Don't remember the last time I was hungry."

The others laugh and say she's terrible. Rose stands by the door and shakes her head.

"He's got to be strong to go through with it. He's a believer. Imagine believing in something so much that you kill yourself."

"They don't just kill themselves though, do they?" says Sue through half a sandwich and then they all start arguing about the IRA and the bombs and why people fight each other and where it's all going to end. While the argument is going on, he hears Sylvia talking in a whisper.

"Not one single word from his mother. No, not a card, nothing. I had a hard time getting bloody Social Services to play ball. They promised him a photo from his brother, you know, the one that got adopted. Getting on for six months now. Would they get it done? No. Jerks, the lot of them. Anyway, me and Mo decided on a pincer movement. Her from her hospital bed, screaming blue murder, me from here, and eventually that Judy with the hair got it sorted. Yeah, got it this morning, thank God. Just in time. Cheered him up it has, little soldier."

Leon can feel their eyes on his back. He knows what their faces look like and how they feel sorry for him and how much they hate his mom. Why can't they be quiet so he can watch the TV or play with his toys? Why can't they all go to their own houses and feel sorry for him from there? He wishes that when he turned around he would be in his own house with his own toys. His mom would be sitting on the sofa with her furry frog slippers. Jake's on her lap and she's singing to him. Jake is wriggling because he always wants to be with Leon but his mom is saying, "Sssh, little monkey. Sssh." And every time Leon moves his mom says something like, "Don't, Leon. You know he won't sleep if he can see you." So Leon has to turn the TV down with no sound and lie on the carpet so Jake thinks he's not there, keep as quiet as a mouse, playing with his toys until Jake is asleep, but always his mom falls asleep as well. Everything goes quiet and Leon sits down next to Jake and looks at his perfect lips and his perfect face.

Leon gets into bed and keeps the light on until Sylvia comes to find him.

"You still up?" she says, pushing the door open.

"Where's Dovedale Road?"

"Dovedale? Across town. Main road, lots of shops and houses. Why?"

"I heard it on the TV."

"Had a nice day? Look at him, eh?"

She picks up the photograph of Jake and then holds it away from her face.

"You can see the resemblance. You really can."

Leon says nothing. He reaches out for the photo and puts it back beside his bed.

"Can I buy a map?"

"A map of where?"

"Just a map of the streets."

"You can buy what you like, love, it's your money. I'm turning this light out now."

"Can I buy a compass?"

"Whatever you like. Sleep time now."

"I can't sleep."

"Too excited, I bet. And too full of sugar."

"Can I have a story?"

Sylvia switches off the light and sits on the edge of his bed.

"Where were we?" she asks.

"The rabbit was with the bear."

Sylvia laughs.

"Yeah, I remember. All right, well now. The rabbit is covered in poo, isn't he? The bear takes off because bears are like that. They don't stay around when they're needed. No. Bears think they're the only ones who've ever had their hearts broken or had the stuffing knocked out of them. The rabbit might have needed a friend, but no, bears just think of themselves. You can't reason with a bear. Not on your life. Bears are selfish and when they've had their fun, they barge their way back into the woods and disappear."

She stops like she's trying to remember the rest of the story. She takes a very deep breath and starts again.

"Anyway, the rabbit hops all over the wood, smelling bloody

awful. He can smell himself, the other animals can smell him, the birds can smell him, and he's desperate for a wash. Every time he goes up to an animal to ask where the river is, they hold their noses and run off. Eventually, after a long, long time, he stumbles across the river, flowing all lovely and blue through the woods. He runs up to it but there is a pig standing on the bank. The rabbit thinks the pig is going to run away but when he looks carefully, he sees the pig has a wooden leg. 'Hello, pig,' says the rabbit. 'Oh, hello, rabbit,' says the pig with the wooden leg. The pig sniffs the rabbit and says, 'Oh dear, you better get in the river and get clean,' so the rabbit does, but all the time he's thinking to himself, why has that pig got a wooden leg? In the end, his curiosity gets the better of him and he asks the pig, 'What happened to your leg, pig?' 'Well, I'll tell you,' said the pig. 'My master lives on a farm and one night I noticed that the stables were on fire. So I shouted as loud as I could and woke the farmer, who rescued all the horses.' The rabbit was amazed. 'So did you get burned in the fire and lose your leg?' 'No,' said the pig, 'the fire spread to the chicken coop and I had to run into the stables and get the master.' 'So did something fall on your leg?' said the rabbit. 'Oh no, because then the fire spread to the farmhouse and I had to run in and wake the mistress and get all the children out. I ran to all the bedrooms and pulled them out one by one. I let the youngest one ride on my back until we were out in the garden and we were safe.' 'Wow,' said the rabbit. 'You must have got injured bringing them downstairs,' said the rabbit. 'No,' replied the pig, 'but the farmer said I was a very special pig and when you have a pig like that, you don't eat it all at once.'"

Leon decides he won't ask Sylvia for any more stories and he turns over.

"Night, love," she says and closes the door.

31

The next day, Leon doesn't get to his plot until after teatime. First of all, Sylvia takes him and another boy to the pictures to see *Raiders of the Lost Ark*. The boy is called Timmy and he is special. Timmy's mom works at the supermarket with Sylvia and whenever they meet they keep saying how good Timmy is and saying "Bless him" and "Good as gold." But Leon has to sit next to him in the cinema and he talks all through the film, turning around and jumping in his seat. And he spits. Everyone looks at Leon all the time and tells Timmy to be quiet. Then Sylvia gets angry and says that they should shut up and mind their own business. All the kids laugh and swear and Leon wants to go and sit on his own because people might think that Timmy is his brother.

He has to say thank you to Timmy and let him play with his AT-AT, so by the time he gets to the allotment it isn't exactly getting dark but it's the time of the afternoon when everything looks exciting. He has his tools still in his bag and he pedals as fast as he can to the allotment and then wheels his bike to his plot.

Someone has taken all the weeds out of his raised bed. Some-one has made all the paths nice and tidy and someone has put some wigwam canes up at the far end.

Leon puts his hand deep into the crumbly soil. It's cool and black underneath and he can squeeze it into a ball. The whole raised bed is just waiting for him to plant something. He can see specks of insects burrowing away from the light and a tiny black spider marching across a stone. Underneath him is a whole world of insect lives that nobody ever thinks about. Leon lies down on the earth and feels them marching and burrowing and finding their dinner and making their nests and bumping into each other. Hello, spider. Hello, beetle. He looks up at the pale blue suede sky and closes his eyes. He feels the roots of all the trees and the flowers mingling in with one another, making a giant web that sucks all the goodness and the rain up into their leaves so they can make apples and roses and all the strange vegetables that grow in the Asian shops. Leon's going to have the best plot on the whole allotment. He's going to grow the plant with the yellow flow-ers and baby peas and mangetout and Scarlet Emperor. And he's going to need more seeds.

Leon sits up and brushes the dirt out of his hair. Tufty isn't around and his shed is always locked so Leon can't go and have a look at his seeds, but Mr. Devlin's halfway house has the door wide open so Leon walks over.

Mr. Devlin is slumped in his armchair. He has a small blue glass in his hand and his eyes are closed. Leon tiptoes inside. The room smells of beer and old clothes. Every time Mr. Devlin breathes out, a small bubble of spit forms at the corner of his mouth. It goes big and small, big and small, as Mr. Devlin snores and blows, snores and blows. Sometimes, Mr. Devlin has the same old-lady smell as Sylvia, and Leon notices that he wears the same clothes every day, whether it's sunny or it's raining. His hair is gray and long, just like his face, and sometimes Leon thinks that Mr. Devlin might actually be a tramp.

Leon walks quietly around the shed looking at more and more of Mr. Devlin's special things. He sees there are bottles of drink in the corner by the door, whiskey and stuff that his dad used to like. Leon carefully picks one of the bottles up and unscrews the cap. The smell reminds him of his dad at Christmas and his black granny that he only met once, just before she died.

His granny's house was full of furniture and ornaments. All along the mantelpiece there were little china dogs and birds and a pink lady with an umbrella. There were pictures on every wall and a big map of Antigua in a silver frame. Every room smelled of spicy meat and it was so hot inside that Leon felt sick. The old lady sat in an armchair with a blanket over her knees. Leon's dad told him that she had had her feet cut off because she had diabetes and wouldn't stop eating cakes and Leon kept thinking of the stumps under the blanket and what they looked like.

"This him, Byron?" said the old lady, looking at Leon.

"Yes, Mommy," said Leon's dad and pushed Leon forward.

The old lady held Leon's wrist and brought him up close to her face. She had a dark, sunken face, sunken eyes with a dot of pure black at the center that darted from side to side. Tight plaits of cane row stuck out of her scalp like sharp white bones and Leon kept thinking where his feet were going in case he trod on her stumps.

"He look like your father," she said, turning Leon from side to side.

She smiled at him.

"Leon? That's your name?"

"Yes."

"You look like your grandfather, Leon. He had your pretty face, same nose. You look like your father too. He just tell me now about you. Just last week. He knows I'm dying. I know I'm dying. So your father just tell me now he has a son. All these years I never knew about you. We could have been friends."

She spoke slowly, pushing her face up close; her moist breath smelled of medicine. She asked him lots of questions about school and his favorite programs and what he wanted to be when he grew up, so Leon said a fireman because he couldn't think of anything else. But she wasn't really listening and she kept closing her eyes.

Then she started coughing and Leon's dad had to get her some water. As soon as he left the room, Leon's granny pulled him even closer.

"You be a good boy for your mother. I never met your mother, so I don't know her, but I know what a good son is. I know how a good son can make your life wonderful and a bad son can bring you heartache. So you be good for your mother. You look after her. Take care of her. I wish I didn't have to leave you, Leon. I hope you remember me."

She let his wrist go and put a five-pound note in his hand. Leon walked backward away from her. His granny looked at his dad and shook her head.

"Oh, Byron."

"Sorry, Mommy," he said. Leon had never heard that voice before. He'd never heard his dad sound like a little boy.

Leon had to have some rice and meat and then his dad took him home. Leon never saw his granny again. One day afterward, his dad told him that she'd died. He was wearing a black suit with a white shirt and a black tie. He was drunk. He kept saying the same thing over and over.

"I got no one now. I got no one now. I got no one now."

He pulled Leon toward him and started crying until Carol told him to stop.

"You're scaring him, Byron," she said. "Go and sleep it off."

Leon knows that Mr. Devlin is sleeping it off as well. He can smell it in the air.

Leon listens carefully but there's no one nearby. Mr. and Mrs. Atwal aren't talking in their own language and the lady with the long skirt is nowhere around. Just Mr. Devlin breathing. Leon tiptoes up to where Mr. Devlin keeps all his knives. He can't take the big knife, because Mr. Devlin uses it every day and he would notice if it was missing, but he could hold it and touch the very edge of the blade and see how it felt to swish it in the air. He has almost got his fingers on the handle when he feels Mr. Devlin's hand on his neck.

"Leave it."

Leon's hand hovers in midair. He doesn't move.

Mr. Devlin drags him back away from the bench and pushes him down on to the floor.

"Sit."

Leon sits cross-legged like he does at school assembly. Mr. Devlin sits up straight in his chair. He pours some drink into his blue glass and drinks it down in one gulp. His eyes are small and red.

"Thought we were friends," he says.

"I just wanted to feel it."

"Sit still."

Mr. Devlin puts his glass down and feels across the bench for a small knife. His hand moves like a spider and all the time he carries on looking at Leon. His hand finds the small knife and a block of wood. He picks them both up and starts peeling the block of wood with the little knife, looking from the wood to Leon and from Leon back to the wood.

"I used to be good at this," he says. "You have yourself a wide forehead. I've been looking at you. I started this from memory, some weeks ago."

Little pieces of wood are flying onto Mr. Devlin's lap and on to the brown rug. Leon picks one up.

"Pine, I'm afraid. Just pine." Mr. Devlin is squinting. "It's too soft but then I'm old now. My whittling hands aren't what they were. Can't do what they once did."

He holds the piece of wood away from him and looks at Leon again.

"I used to use walnut or mahogany or ziricote. I had some skill, used to have some skill. Look."

He gestures to the wall behind him and for the first time Leon notices lots of carved things, a lion and an elephant, a truck and the life-size head of a woman with plaits. And then, at the very front, little heads of children. All boys.

"Miguel, Lorenzo, Gustavo, José, Enzo. And Gabriel," he continues, but he has a different accent like he's talking in another language.

Mr. Devlin looks behind him and points at the different heads.

"Pedro Gabriel Devlin. I wanted Gabriel. She wanted Pedro. Every other child in Brazil is Pedro."

He laughs and Leon sees that he didn't brush his teeth properly. Mr. Devlin carries on chipping away at the wood and Leon watches him. Mr. Devlin has to hurry up because it's getting uncomfortable on the floor and Leon's thirsty. Tufty always has a drink for him but Mr. Devlin doesn't.

"Are they your children?"

Mr. Devlin begins to giggle. It starts in his belly and then goes up to his shoulders and then it's in his throat and his nose and finally he starts to laugh so that he can't carve anymore and his hands are shaking.

"What? All of them? Forty-seven children?"

"Why did you carve them?"

"After school. I would take one or two of the boys. I had a workshop. Like this. I was loved. They loved me."

Mr. Devlin starts peeling the wood away. It comes clean away from the sharp blade.

"Shuffle forward. Here, to me," says Mr. Devlin and Leon does as he's told.

"Think you can do this?"

"Yes."

"Here."

Mr. Devlin gives him the knife and the block of wood. Leon is just about to start when Mr. Devlin covers Leon's small hand with his own. He guides it along the curve of the forehead.

"Like this. Slowly. But firmly. Along the grain. Slowly."

A rind of wood curls away and falls on the ground.

Leon looks up and Mr. Devlin grips his hand tighter.

"I wouldn't change a thing," he says. "Better to have loved."

The wooden handle digs into Leon's palm and the blade is pressing down on the wooden head, making a mark. Mr. Devlin grinds his teeth together and shouts.

"Keep the fucking rules! Isn't that what I said? Isn't that what I told him? Isn't it? Slow down, I said. Over and over, I said it."

He leans forward and covers Leon in a damp blanket of sourness.

"Don't run!"

He stands up suddenly and Leon drops the knife and the wood on the floor. Mr. Devlin stumbles against the shelf and picks up one of the heads and holds it to his chest.

"Look at him! Look!"

Leon stands up and takes the head. It's a baby's head and the baby is asleep. Leon hands it back. Mr. Devlin puts it back on the shelf next to another head that is the same baby but a bit older. He picks it up and points to his nose.

"Does he look like me, do you think?"

There are four heads altogether of the same baby getting older and older.

"It's my fault, she said. My fault for shouting. He wasn't looking. My fault. Always my fault. Always will be my fault. Forever and ever. Amen."

Mr. Devlin picks up the biggest baby's head. It's different from the others; it has more hair and its eyes are open. He sits back down in his leather chair. He puts the baby on the table next to him, picks up his blue glass, fills it with his whiskey, and gulps it down.

"This is my favorite. I like to sit here with him. I tell him stories."

He fills the glass again and, just before he drinks it, he points at the door.

"Go home," he says. "Go on. Get out."

Leon backs away. He stops at the door and watches Mr. Devlin throw his drink to the back of his throat. He drops the blue glass on the carpet, closes his eyes, and slumps back in his chair.

Leon walks slowly to his plot. He understands why Tufty doesn't like Mr. Devlin. It must have been Tufty who did all the work on Leon's plot.

The allotments are quiet. This would be a good time to go and put his things in the secret shed. He looks around. There are one or two people in faraway plots but they won't notice. But then maybe Mr. Devlin might come out and catch him. He picks up his backpack and walks slowly. If anyone asks him where he's going he'll just say he's looking for ideas of what to plant. As soon as Leon gets near his shed, he crouches in the long grass and opens the door. He rushes inside and closes it behind him. It's dark inside. He can hear birds flapping nearby, a scratching noise on the roof. Leon picks up the tins he left and stacks them in the corner by the heavy weights from Mr. Devlin. He forgot the broom. Maureen would say his shed was a pigsty. She would make him tidy up and make it spick-and-span. He uses one of the plastic trays to scrape the leaves and dirt into a pile by the door. He picks up the chair and sits down. There are still a lot of things to bring. A bed, something to eat with, spoons, a bowl and a plate, more food. He uses his fingers to keep count and then takes the two trifle mixes out of his bag and puts them on the chair. He stacks the tins underneath and folds the blanket over them. He will fix the window another day. He closes the door behind him.

Leon uses his little spade and his little fork to dig the soil in his raised beds. He plants his Scarlet Emperor seeds at the base of each cane the way Mr. Devlin did. He places them in the little hole and covers them over with soil, presses it down softly. He waters them from Tufty's water barrel, taking care to let the water trickle and not flow. It takes a lot of going to and from and when he's finished he sees there's still lots of space for other seeds. If he grew carrots, he could take them home to show Sylvia and she would be surprised, because all of her carrots come out of tins. And he could show Maureen when she gets better and she'd smile and say how clever he was. And if he saw Carol again he could cook them and make her eat them so she could get better. But all his Scarlet Emperor seeds have gone and he doesn't want to spend any of his money on carrot seeds because he's going to need every penny. He looks at the padlock on Tufty's shed and wonders if he could get inside. Tufty wouldn't mind.

The door isn't locked. The padlock is just hooked on the outside for show so Leon pulls the door open. Someone grabs him, pulls him inside. It's Castro.

"Shut the door," he whispers and he shoves Leon against the wall so hard that the door slams and makes a noise.

"And keep quiet. Quiet, you hear me?"

The whole shed smells sour and bad. And he doesn't look like he looked when Leon first saw him. His red hair sticks out from under a dusty woolen hat and his clothes are dirty but his face has changed the most. He has blood on his lips and one of his eyes is swollen and closed. There are Tufty's cans of soda all over the floor and Castro has made a bed out of Tufty's clothes.

Castro rubs the dirty window and looks outside.

"You see Tufty?"

"No," says Leon.

"Where you live?"

"On College Road."

"Where is Tufty, man? I thought he come up here every day? He don't come every day?"

Castro turns and looks at Leon and points to his bag.

"You got food in there?"

"No." Leon stands with his back to the door with his backpack squeezing against it. He thinks of his precious things and what he will do if Castro tries to take them.

Castro rubs his hands over his face.

"I need a drink."

Castro is close. Leon can smell pee on his trousers.

"I know where there is a bottle of whiskey," he says.

"Where?"

Leon points. "In the shed over there."

"Somebody in there?"

"He's asleep."

"Run get it. Quick."

Leon turns around and puts his hand on the door and then Castro grabs him and pulls him back. His voice is slow.

"Anyhow you don't come back, anyhow you tell someone you see me, anyhow the police come here for me, anyhow you open your mouth."

Leon says nothing.

"You get me?"

Leon steps outside and closes the door behind him. He walks

to Mr. Devlin's shed, thinking all the time if he can just run back home and what Castro would do to him. Who is the worst, Castro or Mr. Devlin?

The door to Mr. Devlin's shed is open and Leon stands just out of sight. He can hear snoring inside. Slowly, slowly, he peeks in. Mr. Devlin's mouth is open; Sylvia would say he was catching flies. The blue glass is still on the carpet where he dropped it and Leon's wooden head is on his lap. Just inside the door is the tray of whiskey bottles. If Leon's arms were longer and rubbery, he could stay where he was and his arm could go inside all on its own without Leon having to tiptoe on to the wooden floor and hope it doesn't creak and choose the fullest bottle which is in the middle of the pile and lift it up straight so it doesn't knock into all the others and it's so heavy he thinks it might slip out and smash to pieces and wake Mr. Devlin who has already told him off once and who might kill him with his Kanetsune.

Leon can feel his heart pounding under his T-shirt and he can feel the anger for Castro bubbling in his throat. It makes him want to smash the bottle against the wall. It makes him want to wake Mr. Devlin and say, "Watch this!" It makes him want to take the big curved blade and march to Tufty's shed, kick the door off its hinges, and stab Castro and tell him to fuck off. All the anger makes him want to fight Castro for making a mess in Tufty's shed and drinking all the soda.

Mr. Devlin doesn't move. His snore is like a whistle and a grumble and he just carries on sleeping as Leon steals the bottle, and then Leon sees the pruning knife right next to the baby's head, the one Mr. Devlin talks to, the one he loves. The one he speaks to and tells stories to. He moves quickly, silently, one step at a time until he has them, and then quickly, silently, he steps outside. He pushes the head and the knife in his bag, twisting and wrestling with the zipper, then he runs with the bottle back to Castro.

"Yeah, man!" says Castro and pulls the cap off. He scrunches up his eyes when he drinks and then coughs.

"Yeah, fucking hell, man. Yeah. Feels good."

He's talking all the while and looking out of the window between gulps from the bottle.

"If Tufty don't come soon, you have to go fetch him."

Leon shuffles backward. He puts his hand on the door to push it.

"Don't fucking move, you hear me?"

But Leon is through the door before Castro can catch him. It's starting to get dark outside. He runs and runs, not even stopping to get his bike, because he knows Castro is behind him with his bad breath and his one eye, so Leon runs and runs and the pack is smashing into his back with every step but he runs and runs and runs and then something hits him full in the face and he falls over. He tumbles and rolls onto the dirt, catches his elbows on sharp stones.

"Easy, Star!"

Tufty gets off his bike and lets it fall. He pulls Leon up onto his feet but Leon can't stand up and his legs won't work properly.

Tufty squats down and holds Leon steady.

"What happened? What's wrong?"

Leon likes the sound of Tufty's voice and the feel of Tufty's hands on his shoulder. He likes the way Tufty looks worried and the way the lines have appeared on his forehead and his eyebrows are close together.

"Somebody trouble you, Star?"

Tufty looks over at Mr. Devlin's shed.

"He touch you? You running from him?"

"I'm thirsty," Leon says.

But Tufty stays looking at Mr. Devlin's shed. He stares at it like he can see Mr. Devlin lying on his chair inside, like he can hear his whistling, grumbling whiskey breath.

"Come," Tufty says eventually. "I'll get you a soda."

Leon doesn't move.

"What?"

Leon says nothing.

"Come then."

Tufty picks up Leon's backpack and puts it over the handlebars of his bike. Then he takes Leon's hand like he's a little boy going to school. The nearer they get to Tufty's shed, the more Leon tries to go slow. He shuffles his feet and tries to hang back but Tufty pulls him along.

"You want to get on the bike? It's too high for you but you can try."

"I want to go home now," Leon says. "My back's hurting."

"Yes, get a drink first. You don't look good. Take five minutes, get yourself right."

As they get near his shed, Tufty slows down. Leon watches him because he doesn't know what Tufty will say about Castro making a mess. He sees Tufty looking at Leon's bike on the ground, then at the padlock that has fallen off the bolt by the door. Tufty's voice is quiet when he speaks.

"Somebody inside there, Star?"

"Yes," says Leon.

"You been inside?"

"Yes."

"Police?"

"No."

"White man?"

"No."

"Black man?"

"Castro."

Tufty stops.

"Castro," he says and he looks around the allotment. "You see anybody else? You see any police?"

"No and Mr. Devlin is drunk. He's asleep."

"Good."

They walk quickly to the shed and Tufty pulls the door open. Castro is standing just inside, holding the garden fork up in the air.

"Fucking hell, Tufty, man. I nearly stab you!"

Tufty pulls Leon inside and shuts the door behind them.

"Shut up, Castro. Keep quiet."

"I couldn't see nothing, it's too dark. I was keeping watch for you."

"Keeping watch for me? It's not me on the run, Castro."

Tufty looks around the shed.

"What you doing here, Castro? You can't stay here."

Castro shrugs his shoulder and grabs the whiskey bottle off the shelf.

"You think I like sleeping in a shack, Tufty? You see this?"

Castro points to his eye.

"You think I like being blind? You think I have choices, Tufty? You think I can check into the Hilton, lie down, and sleep? You think I can run up to the hospital and tell them, 'Police beat me?' You think I can go to my mother's house and get a dinner? Tell me, Tufty."

Tufty kisses his teeth.

"You're drunk, Castro. Keep quiet."

Castro drops down onto his bed, sucking from the bottle. He looks like Jake when he's hungry. Tufty takes the bottle off him and stands it on the side.

"What happened, man?"

"They charge me with resisting arrest but I get a solicitor up at the Cross. The solicitor start talking about technicality and they have to let me go. The magistrate throw it out. Next day, them same police catch me up by the Law Center. I was standing in the entry waiting to go inside. One solicitor there told me I could sue the police from last time. Remember the time they

mash up my place and their dog bite me? Yeah, well, the solicitor told me I could get compensation so I was just going in to
see them. Three police pull up in a beast wagon. Right there on
the street they attack me. Didn't say nothing like 'Get in the car,'
never even try to arrest me. They don't usually beat you till they
get to the station, Tufty, but these people out of control. They just
grab me and throw me down the entry. Start search me and box
me down. Three of them. I mash one of them full on his fucking
mouth. Bam! Anyway, the solicitor come out of the Law Center
and they did stop. Said it was a routine search and I just run off."

"Fucking hell, man."

"Yeah," says Castro, "hell is what it is."

Tufty looks at Leon.

"You better go home, Star. And listen . . ."

"I won't tell anyone, Tufty."

Tufty puts his hand on Leon's shoulder and squeezes. "It's
getting dark outside. Ride carefully."

32

The whole house smells of toast. It's the big-shop day but it's been raining since Leon woke up. The wind is swirling around outside and making the windows rattle. It looks like it's going to rain forever. So there's only bread to eat. Sylvia has toast for breakfast and Leon has the rest of the Weetabix, then they both make toast for lunch; Leon has one slice with raspberry jam and the other slice with a cheese triangle.

Leon moves the net curtains aside and looks at the silver raindrops weeping on the window. Some drops stay where they are for ages but others hit the window and immediately start racing, joining up with little drops until they become a fat river that runs all the way to the windowsill and drips off the edge. Leon tries to guess which raindrop will start moving first. He chooses two drops next to each other, one for him and one for Jake. Jake's starts to move immediately. It's got a weaving, sliding movement, veers off to the right somehow, picks up miniature droplets on the way, hovers near a running stream and tries to join in but it's going too fast. When Leon's raindrop moves, it's just straight down, all on its own, glistening, shuddering in the wind, straight down, fast and true, all the way to the bottom. He wins easily and the game is over.

The TV is boring. One channel has horse racing and another has cricket and Sylvia has a rule that they both have to agree on the program. She turns on a black-and-white film with dancing. A little girl with ringlets keeps walking around and singing, so Leon doesn't agree on the program, but Sylvia says because there is a child in it, he should be interested. Leon sits on the floor with his AT-AT.

"If you pull that stunt again, Leon, I'm taking that bike to the secondhand shop."

She has been talking about him being late over and over since last weekend. She was standing at the front door looking up the road when he cycled up. She pulled him off the bike, told him to get in, and started asking questions but she didn't leave him any space to answer, which was great.

"I've been worried sick. Where have you been? I nearly came out looking for you. Have you seen the time? It's going dark. One hour, you said. I'm going to get you a bloody watch. Hour, my ass. Where have you been anyway at this time of night? Anything could have happened. Didn't you think? I've been sitting here watching the news. Have you seen what's happening? Thought you might have been attacked. I had no idea where you were. Where were you till this time? There's some sort of fight up on Nineveh Road. You haven't been up there, have you? Did you see anything? You can't be at the park at this time of the night. Where were you?"

She shut up and looked at him.

"What's the matter?"

"I fell off my bike," he said. "I hurt my back."

She turned him round and pulled his T-shirt up. She looked

at the scratches on his elbows and the marks where his backpack had pounded into him.

"Bloody hell," she said and from then on she was nice and didn't tell him off anymore. But then the next day, and every day since, she goes back to where she left off.

"No more coming in late, all right? Or that bike goes."

Leon says nothing.

"Sunday tomorrow," Sylvia says. "Another week bites the dust."

He can feel her eyes on him. She's not watching the singing girl, she's watching him. She does this sometimes but usually it's when he's eating his dinner or when he's falling asleep. She looks at him like he's a photograph or someone she's met for the first time. Sometimes, she looks soft and reminds him of his mom.

"It's my birthday soon, you know. August," she says.

He turns around and looks at her. She has her head to one side like she's trying to measure him.

"I was thirteen when I grew up. I was fourteen when I went to work and seventeen when I got married. I was only a bloody child. You don't get married at seventeen."

Leon turns back to the television.

"How old is your mom, Leon?"

Leon shrugs his shoulders.

"They say age is just a number," she says, lighting a cigarette. "They're right. One bloody number for every year you've been alive."

Leon remembers when his mom got birthday cards she kept saying she was old, but she was very pretty, so no one noticed. Sylvia isn't pretty anymore and that's why she's sad.

"Can I go to Carpenter Road to the place that does kung fu?"

"Kung fu?"

"It's where you learn to fight."

"Kung fu? There's nowhere like that on Carpenter Road."

"There is, someone told me."

"Who?"

"A boy's dad at school. He goes."

Sylvia raises her eyebrows and blows the smoke up toward the ceiling.

"Suppose it might keep you out of trouble. That's the stuff where you chop bricks in half, isn't it?"

"It's for making you strong and so no one can knock you over."

"Is it? Might come with you then. I'll talk to your social worker about it. But you know what? We're going to starve if we stay in any longer. Come on. Coat."

Leon keeps his hood up. They take the bus because of the rain and just as they go to cross the road by the traffic lights, Sylvia takes his hand.

"Quick!" she says and she tugs him close to her and she doesn't let go even when they are safe inside the new supermarket. He doesn't want everyone to think Sylvia is his mom, so he runs to find a cart. The new supermarket has a man dressed as a brown bear outside, handing vouchers to people as they walk past. Sylvia and Leon both think of the rabbit story and smile at each other. Sylvia even checks his bum as they walk past.

The supermarket has a massive toy section and Leon asks if he can stay and look at the toys while Sylvia does the shopping.

"I'll be back in ten minutes. You stay right here till I come back."

There are so many things that Leon wants and so many things he has never seen before. He even looks at the girls' toys, because they have a doll that's the same size as a baby and if you press its belly the mouth opens and it tries to say something. He looks at the Legos and the games and the balls and the videos and the dolls and the paints and pens and paper and the soldiers and the guns and the plastic knives but nothing is as good as the stuff in Mr. Devlin's shed. He wanders around the aisles look-ing for Sylvia. There's loads of stuff in the supermarket that he could take. Loads of stuff he needs for his halfway house. He goes up and down every aisle and then he hears Sylvia's voice. She's talking to someone.

"Got used to the little bugger if I'm honest, Jan. You know, someone to make the dinner for."

The other lady asks Sylvia about Maureen.

"She'll never be the same, they told me. She had a sort of stroke, then an infection when she was in the hospital. Plus pneumonia. Looks bloody awful but she has lost a bit of weight while she's been in. I want her to come to me when she comes out so I can look after her and keep her hands off the cakes. She's not having a parade of foster kids tramping through her life neither. Not if I have anything to do with it. I'm going to see to that first of all. She's giving it up. She can get back on her feet and put herself first. Twenty-two years she's been doing it and Social Services have taken her for granted. Taken the piss, they have. They're always giving her the worst kids with the most problems. Maybe when she was young it was all right but not now. It's done her in."

Leon walks down another aisle and looks at the breakfast cereals with cartoons on the boxes and then at the porridge and the muesli and he wonders how long it will be before Jake can eat Choco Pops and Rice Krispies and Sugar Puffs. He walks to the baby-food aisle and looks at how much things cost. The most expensive things are little mini jars of baby dinners. One's called "Chicken and Vegetables" and another is "Beef Casserole" but they look exactly the same. The baby wipes are also expensive and so are the diapers. There's ointment to think about as well, because Leon made sure that Jake never had diaper rash when he was looking after him. Leon remembers how Jake used to wriggle when he was wiping his bum and always kicking his legs so the diaper wasn't on properly. Leon remembers the weight of Jake in his arms and the feel of his brother's arms around his neck, his fingers pulling his hair, the smell of him.

The little jars of baby food feel heavy in his pockets.

Sylvia nudges him in his back. "There you are! I thought I said stay in the toys."

Leon walks to the bus stop with Sylvia and makes a list of all the other things he will steal.

33

When he gets to the allotment, Leon rests his bike against Tufty's shed. Tufty is wearing a vest that looks like a net. It's tight on his chest and it makes his muscles stand out. He's wearing his denim shorts and flip-flops. Only girls wear flip-flops but Leon won't say anything. Leon walks over to his plot to check and see if his Scarlet Emperors have come up. He teases the soil away from the base of one of the bamboo canes and sees a little split in the seed and a sturdy, cream-white coil bent over, pushing its back out toward the sun. He covers it again quickly. Then he sees two green leaves on a white stalk sticking an inch out of the soil. He peers close. The two leaves are folded together, hugging each other like they're scared to come out. They are so fine and delicate, Leon wonders if they will survive. They shudder in his breath.

"You see anything?" shouts Tufty.

Leon nods.

"They're growing, Tufty! I can see them coming out!"

Tufty smiles his wide smile.

As Leon looks he sees lots of shoots and leaves coming up; every seed is going to grow tall and strong. He looks up to the top of the wigwam and imagines them snaking all the way up to the sky.

What else can he plant? Leon remembers all the seeds on Tufty's shelf.

"I wish I had some more seeds," he says, "like the ones in your shed."

Tufty laughs. "You want some?" he says. "It's a bit late for planting anything now but come, let's look."

They bring Tufty's seed box out and sit on two fold-up chairs with a can of soda each. Tufty has ginger beer and Leon has Tango; the sharpness zings on his tongue and makes his teeth ache.

Tufty starts rifling through the seed box and picking out packets that he drops onto the ground.

"Carrots for seeing at night."

Drop.

"Courgettes are soft to the bite."

Drop.

"Peas so sweet on your tongue."

Drop.

"And broccoli to keep you young."

Drop.

"Come, Star. Look. Here's tomato. What can you say about tomato?"

"Tomato to make your sauce."

"Good!" says Tufty and drops it on the ground and picks another packet.

"Now the hard bit. We got peppers next. What rhymes with sauce?"

Leon screws his eyes up.

"Peppers as big as a horse."

Tufty throws his head back and shows all his teeth. When he laughs, his shoulders shake and he claps his hands.

"Yes, man! You got the gift."

"Do you write poems about children, Tufty?"

"Sometimes, if the mood takes me."

"Do you work in a school?"

"Me? Nah, man. Bike shop. I mend bikes for Mr. Johnson. Remember Mr. Johnson? He's got a little bike shop up at the Cross. I used to go up there after school and he gave me a job. Taught me everything. It's just me there now because Mr. Johnson is old, old, old. Older than my father."

"Have you got children, Tufty?"

"Yes, yes."

Tufty gathers up the seeds and puts them on Leon's lap.

"Plant them. It's not too late. Put a seed in a hole and just hope."

Leon doesn't move.

"Where are they?"

"You got a lot of questions today, eh, Star? Well, they live with their mother. We don't see eye to eye so I don't get to see them too often. They don't live here. They live far away."

"Are they babies? Are they boys?"

"Girls, seven and five. Two girls."

"I've got a brother."

But Tufty isn't listening. He's staring at the trees, at the sway and lean of the branches in the wind. Leon knows where he's gone. He's gone off to play with his little girls, to push their swings in the park or catch them at the bottom of the slide. He's smelling their hair and holding them. He's feeling their arms around his neck as he lifts them up. He lets Tufty think about his children for a while and then Leon picks up his seeds.

"I've got a brother, Tufty," he says.

Tufty doesn't move. His eyes are open but he's still in the park or tucking his girls up in bed.

Leon takes his new seeds over to his plot and pushes them in, one hole each, two inches deep, long straight rows. Then the watering, back and forth with his plastic bottle. If he had a watering can, he would look like a proper gardener. Tufty is still on his chair when Leon finishes. He's reading something and when he sees Leon he folds the paper in half.

"Right. Sit down," he says. "I made a new poem. 'Ode to Castro.' Wrote it last night but not sure how it will come out. Sit down, tell me what you think. You listening?"

Tufty stands up and as he talks he takes a step to the left and then a step to the right, bouncing on the balls of his feet.

I don't want to be a warrior
I didn't come for war
I didn't come for argument
For policeman at my door.

I didn't come for least and last
For the isms and the hate
That you pile upon me day by day
Till you crush me with the weight.

It was you that took me off my land
Took my name, my ways, my tongue
Sold me cheap, from hand to hand to hand
Made slaves from all my young.

We are not a warrior
We are Africans by birth
We have truth and rights and God besides
We have dignity and worth.

We have lost the way we used to live
And the way that we behaved
We are the consequence of history
We are the warriors you made.

When he gets home, Leon tries to remember the words of the "Ode to Castro" and tries to sound like Tufty, move like him, open his arms wide, bounce on his feet. He walks around his bedroom talking quietly so Sylvia can't hear.

"We have dignity and worth," he says.

Sometimes, when Tufty is talking, Leon thinks about his dad. Tufty and Leon's dad don't look the same and they don't talk the same but Tufty tips his head to the side when he talks, he makes shapes in the air with his hands and that's like Leon's dad and that's what makes Leon remember the last time he saw him, before Jake was born.

It was Christmas Eve. Leon's dad came to the front door and Carol was wearing the zipper of her jeans down because of the new baby. Leon's dad looked her up and down and kissed his teeth, which meant he was annoyed and trying not to shout. He was carrying a black trash bag and Leon wondered if his present was inside it. Carol said he couldn't come in.

"You got your fancy man in there, eh, Carol?"

"Please, Byron," she said, "I don't want to—"

"I hear he left you. That right? He's gone back to his woman."

"I don't know. It's none of your business."

"I hear you're running around the place trying to find him. Making a fool of yourself. You don't have no pride, Carol?"

"I'm not running around. Who told you that?"

They both noticed Leon at the same time, listening by the door. Carol told him to go back into the living room, so he did, but if she made his dad angry he might forget to leave the black bag.

Leon's dad was trying to talk quietly but he wasn't good at it.

"He's left you. You know it's true. You was just his fancy piece. That's what I hear. The man has a woman and child. He don't want you, Carol. But you know what? It's good because I don't want no white man coming in here and abusing my son."

"What?" said Carol. "What are you trying to say? What are you talking about? He's never even seen Leon. And you can't talk. All the time you come around drunk. It's you that abuses him if it comes down to it."

His dad did a fake laugh.

"Yeah, yeah, Carol, all right. I don't want no argument with you. I didn't come to upset you. I just come to say I got my date today. Crown Court next week. So if I don't come back, let me give you this for Leon. Just a few things. Let me see him before I go."

"Leon!"

Carol moved aside so Leon could get past. His father grabbed him and crushed him to his chest. He smelled of bitter cigarettes and the dumpling shop and Special Brew. Leon and his dad have the same type of hair but Leon's dad has short locks that stick out all over the place, like a hedgchog. Leon's dad is dark chocolate brown but Leon is light brown, like toast, and looks like Carol. But right then his dad just looked tired and sad.

His dad let him go and handed him the bag. He knelt down and held both of Leon's hands.

"You can't open it till Christmas, right? Look, I put a knot in the top. You can't undo it. Christmas, Leon, and that's tomorrow morning, right?"

He looked at Leon for a very long time and kept trying to say something but nothing came out. Then he hugged Leon again and kissed him twice, his rough face scratching Leon's cheek.

"Now go," he said at last. "Put it under the tree."

Leon took the bag. It was heavy. There were at least two

presents inside, clunking together. Leon wanted to be happy but when he saw his dad walk away he wanted to run after him.

His dad had been to Crown Court before and he didn't come home for a long, long time. That time his mom kept crying for him and saying she missed him but this time she didn't care.

34

Sylvia is on the phone. She's talking and painting her toenails at the same time. It makes her voice sound different. Blue veins track all the way up her legs and disappear under her dressing gown. She should pull the dressing gown down but she doesn't notice things like that. She has a pair of glasses resting on the end of her nose, the phone squashed under her chin, a pot of nail varnish in one hand and the nail brush in another. So she hasn't got a free hand to pull her dressing gown down and cover her pale blue underwear.

Leon looks away but he carries on listening because she's talking to Maureen and it's all about how she's getting better.

Sylvia talks in a squeaky voice.

"So what did he say in the end?"

Leon can't hear Maureen so he has to imagine what she says.

"That I can come home, Sylvia."

"Really?"

"Yes, Sylvia."

"When?"

"Tomorrow, Sylvia."

Sylvia stops dead still.

"Tomorrow?"

"Yes, Sylvia."

"Tomorrow as in tomorrow?"

"Yes, Sylvia, tomorrow as in Monday."

"Monday?"

"Morning, Sylvia."

"Monday morning?"

"I'll get a taxi to your house, shall I, Sylvia?"

"Yes, that's it. Get a taxi here and I'll be waiting."

Sylvia looks up at Leon and puts her thumb up.

"We'll both be waiting. He sends his love."

"Send him my love back, Sylvia."

"She sends you her love, Leon."

"I haven't got a time yet. They don't tell you anything around here, Sylvia."

"Don't worry about a time, I'll wait in all day if necessary. Like you say, they'll keep you in the dark till it suits them."

"Got to go now, Sylvia."

"Yes, yes. You get off. We'll be waiting."

With only eight of her ten toenails painted, Sylvia stands up and does a silly hopping dance on the carpet, keeping her toes curled up. She looks like a mad person and Leon doesn't laugh even though Sylvia is happy. Leon's happy inside.

Then for the whole day it's jobs, jobs, jobs. There's nothing wrong with his room but he has to clean it. He has to wipe the windowsill with a clean cloth and put his toys in a neat row. He has to make his pillow puff up and put his shoes in pairs. Then he has to clean the bathroom mirror because Sylvia says he does it the best but that was a lie. He has to put bleach in the toilet and then some green stuff that's supposed to smell like pine trees but it just smells like school.

All the time, Sylvia is running backward and forward with eight pink toenails and two plain ones. She puts fat rollers in her hair and doesn't get dressed for hours.

"Spring cleaning," she says, forcing her hands into some yellow rubber gloves. But she is wrong again. It's summertime.

They open every single window and door, sweep the two paths, the one that leads up the garden and the one at the front. Then Sylvia puts on her working jeans and fills a plastic bowl with hot soapy water. She gets a scrubbing brush from under the sink and carries it all out to the front garden.

She looks up and down the road.

"Beautiful day, isn't it?"

Leon nods.

"Now," she says, dipping the brush in the bowl and squatting down by the front door. "This is a lost art. The ancient ritual of the scrubbing of the front doorstep."

The brush makes a scratching noise on the concrete and the suds turn black. Sylvia is talking all the time and nodding her head like there's an invisible person agreeing with her.

"Yes," she says, "every Friday morning before the weekend. Or was it a Saturday? Yes, Saturday. Crack of dawn you'd hear our old lady with that tin pail. Clunk, clunk, clunk from the back to the front. All weathers. Oh, if that wasn't a hint to get your ass up out of bed, I don't know what was. Yep, seven o'clock on a Saturday morning. Vowed I wouldn't turn out like her and here I am on my hands and bloody knees for our Mo who doesn't give a shit in the first place. You're nuts, that's what you are, Sylvia Thorne née Richards. Potty. The neighbors think you're mad. Mo thinks you're mad. You know it yourself. But that's who you are and there's no changing now. No, nor wouldn't want to. There's filth on this step and it's coming off."

She's scrubbing so hard that she's swaying from side to side.

"Mo won't even notice, will she? No, she won't. But you'll

know, Sylvia. You'll know you scrubbed your front step like it was Leighton Buzzard 1952. There!"

She stops and wipes the back of her hand across her forehead and tests the rollers to make sure they haven't moved.

"Make us a cup of coffee, Leon, love. Don't just stand there and look at me like I'm a Martian. This is normal behavior where I come from."

Leon makes her coffee in her favorite mug and puts two biscuits on a plate. He puts everything on a tray and then adds a teaspoon in case her biscuit collapses when she dips it in. He brings it out to the front and when Sylvia sees it she gives him a kind smile and stands up, arching her back forward and then backward.

"What would I do without you, eh?" she says. "You're lovely, you are."

Even though her face is very old, Sylvia has young eyes and sometimes he can see that she used to be pretty. When the TV was black and white, she says, that's when she was pretty, when everything cost a shilling and she used to go dancing at the Locarno. Sylvia is prettier than Maureen but Maureen is nicer and Maureen is coming back. That means that Leon will go back to his second bedroom. His first bedroom was when he used to live with Carol and Jake. His second bedroom was at Maureen's house where he and Jake used to sleep. He remembers the wallpaper and the lampshade and the way the light came through a gap in the curtains. His mom came to that room and saw the photo of Jake and fell down. His third bedroom is next to Sylvia's. It won't take him long to pack his things.

Sylvia gets in the shower and when she comes out she has her hair in a different style.

"What do you think?" she says.

"It's higher."

"Higher and?"

"Bigger," says Leon.

"Bigger and higher," she says.

Leon nods.

"And is that good in your world, Leon?"

She sounds angry so Leon says nothing.

"You've got a babysitter tonight. I'm going out."

Crazy Rose comes to look after him.

"Hello, Pete," she says.

"Leon, Rose. His name is Leon. Leon. He's ready for bed, so just send him off when you're ready. He's as good as gold. Won't make a fuss."

"Like your hair, Sylv!" says Crazy Rose and she walks all the way around Sylvia so she can see it from every angle.

"Did you do it yourself?"

"Me and the rollers and a can of Silvikrin Extra Hold."

"It's worked anyhow, hasn't it?"

"Do you think?" says Sylvia, pushing it up at the back. "It's not too high?"

"Goes with that dress and them shoes."

"Ten ninety-nine from British Home Stores," says Sylvia, putting one foot forward like a ballet dancer. "The dress was on sale and I took it in. Always had a tiny waist."

"Well, have a good time, Sylvie, love. We'll be all right together, won't we, Pete?"

"Leon," says Sylvia.

Crazy Rose puts the TV on and they watch a film about a shark and then she falls asleep, so Leon changes the channel. He is still awake when Sylvia comes back.

"Rose? Rose?"

Sylvia has to shake her loads of times to get her to wake up.

"Oooh," she says, "was I asleep? How long have I been asleep? Where's Pete?"

Sylvia cocks her thumb and tells Leon to go to bed.

"Come on, Rose. I've saved my taxi for you. It's outside."

Leon stays on the sofa. He's taken seventy pence out of Crazy Rose's purse and he's already put it in his backpack. He also took her nail file with its purple plastic cover. He saw a film once where someone used a nail file to escape from prison. They put it in the lock and then the door opened.

When Crazy Rose has gone, Sylvia starts taking grips and pins out of her high hairstyle and it all comes down, wild and fluffy. She has black makeup under her eyes.

"Bastard didn't turn up, if you want to know, Pete," she says.

Leon gets up.

"We're going to move to the seaside, that's what we're going to do. Me and Mo. Hastings. Or Rye. I'm going to make her do it. Give this all up and retire to the sea. A little cottage next to a pub."

She's swaying a bit from side to side as she lights her cigarette.

"Fuck this shit," she says, waving her arms around. She flops down on to the sofa and a single belch pops out.

"Begging your pardon. Make us another one of your marvellous coffees, Pete."

She begins to giggle.

"Pete! Pete! Crazy fucking Rose."

Leon makes her a cup of coffee and puts extra sugar in it because Sylvia looks sad. He takes it in on a tray with the biscuits and a spoon.

He puts it carefully on the floor and sits next to Sylvia on the sofa. She doesn't say thank you and so he doesn't say anything, either. The room is so quiet he can hear the traffic on the road outside, just a few cars and a siren far away.

Then Sylvia begins to cry. She puts one hand over her eyes and the other hand, with the cigarette, starts shaking. Leon takes the cigarette and puts it in the ashtray, then he sits back down.

Sylvia's crying gets worse and her hair starts bobbing up and down. He holds her hand because that's what she did when he started crying when he was sick.

"Sorry," she whispers. "I'm sorry."

Then Leon puts his arm round her shoulder.

"Don't cry," he says. "Maureen is coming home tomorrow."

35

Leon knows Sylvia won't wake up early, because she never does when she's been drinking so, as soon as he gets up, he looks through every single thing he's collected and all the things he has in his backpack.

He has nine pounds and forty-seven pence plus his granny's five-pound note, which he's saved for ages, a nail file, a writing pad and a pen, four Curly Wurlys but one is broken in the packet, a can opener, two small cans of baked beans that he can heat up, his Take-A-Chance seeds, his garden tools from Mr. Devlin, a comic, Sylvia's favorite brooch in case he has to sell it for money, a can of soda with a dent in it, the gun, a key ring in the shape of a gun, a green plastic gun, the head, an axe with a wobbly handle, a map of Bristol, a map of London, a bar of soap with a crack in it, baby dinners, the photograph of Jake with his address on the back, a mini packet of cornflakes and a mini packet of Rice Krispies, some coins that aren't English, a knife, the letter from Jake, his best Action Man wearing a beret, Big Red Bear, two diapers and a pacifier, a tea towel from Sylvia's cupboard, and a baby's blanket.

When he puts everything inside his pack it's so full he can hardly zip up the top. He will never be able to carry it all at the same time. Maureen will ask him what's inside and he will have to pretend it's all toys. Then when he takes the pack back to her house he can hide some of the things under his bed. He's going to have to leave the things that he's stored in his shed but when Maureen brings him back to visit Sylvia again, he can see if his plants are growing and collect anything he leaves behind. Leon might have to wait to do his plan now that Maureen's back. He might not have to do it at all.

When he has made his breakfast, Sylvia shuffles into the kitchen. She puts the kettle on and pulls the belt on her dressing gown. She sits down at the kitchen table and puts her hands together. She has lots of folds on her face and the black makeup is now on her cheeks as well as her eyes. But her hair isn't high anymore.

"Listen, Leon, I'm sorry. I'm bloody sorry. What was I saying last night? Was I talking rubbish? Anyway, the point is, whatever's going on in my life, it's not fair to put it on you. It's not like you're having such a marvelous time, either."

She gets her cigarettes out of her pocket and lights one. Leon starts to make her a cup of coffee.

"Mo will be here sometime today. I'm hoping she'll move in for a few days. Or even for good."

Leon splashes himself with hot water and nearly drops the kettle.

"Careful, love!"

Sylvia is up quick as a flash and takes the kettle off him.

"You all right? Let me see."

But Leon moves out of her way and sits back down.

"You're not hurt, are you?"

Leon shakes his head. Sylvia is ugly in the mornings and her old lady smell is very bad. She can make her own coffee. She's wrong about lots of things, so she is wrong about Maureen moving in. Like she said, she talks rubbish sometimes.

They have to wait for ages and ages before Maureen comes. He hears it first. He hears a car pull up outside and he runs to the door. Maureen is getting out of a black taxi. She has a suitcase with little wheels on it and Leon runs to get it.

Maureen opens her arms wide.

"Here he is!"

She grabs Leon and squeezes him hard and he squeezes her back.

"Stop it!" she whispers. "Stop growing so tall! You're going to be a giant and we won't get you through the door."

She doesn't let him go.

"Oh, I've needed a good hug, I have. That's better than all the pills in the world."

Then Sylvia comes and Leon has to move out of the way.

"Get the bag, Pete," she says. "Come on, Mo, come on. Inside and sit yourself down. You shouldn't be pulling that suitcase."

Sylvia bosses Leon around and makes a pot of tea. She's bought a round cake with sprinkles on top and jam in the middle. She puts it on a plate and cuts it into slices.

"Get you!" says Maureen and she winks at Leon. "Have you gone all fancy while I've been away?"

"This," says Sylvia, "is your last piece of cake, Mo. You've got to promise me about your eating and drinking."

"Me? Drinking?"

"Eating then, sugar, cakes. You know what I mean."

"All right, all right, don't go on, Sylvia."

Leon likes it when Maureen uses her no-nonsense voice with Sylvia. They are all quiet while they eat the cake. Then Maureen gets up and cuts herself another slice and looks at Sylvia while she does it.

"Do you want a bit more, Pete?" Sylvia says.

"Who's Pete?" asks Maureen. "Why you calling him Pete all the time?"

"Oh, it's a joke. Crazy Rose started it."

Maureen looks at Leon and raises an eyebrow.

"She's a bright spark, is Rose. Did she fall asleep midsentence like she usually does with her tongue hanging on her bosom?"

Maureen makes such a funny face that Leon begins to laugh and then Maureen and Sylvia join in. When nearly all the cake is gone, Leon asks if he can go out on his bike.

"I've heard a lot about this bike," says Maureen. "Where do you go?"

"The park," says Leon.

"What park?"

"The one with the railings."

"All parks have railings, Leon. How do you get there?"

"Up the road."

"Hmm," says Maureen, "you can show me this park tomorrow. Bathroom first, wash your hands and face. You've got crumbs everywhere."

Leon goes down the hall and opens the door to the bathroom but he doesn't go in. He stands quietly near the living room. Sylvia is talking.

". . . good kid, all in all. No trouble at all. Got used to having him here."

"Where's this park he keeps talking about?"

"Oh, it's up there on the main road. You pass it on the bus. He's all right, Mo. Look at the size of him. He can take care of himself. You should be worrying about yourself."

"He's gone a bit quiet," says Maureen.

"Kids are like that at his age."

"He's going to be six foot and then some, that one," Maureen says, "and good-looking."

Leon smiles and feels the muscles at the top of his arms. Then Sylvia starts again.

"Listen, you and me have got to have a talk about the future, Mo."

"Not again, Sylvia, for God's sake. I've just got here."

"And you're staying here. You're moving in with me. It makes sense. I can keep my eye on you. Neither of us is getting any younger. You haven't got a guy, neither have I now. Two of us could halve our bills. I've got two bedrooms going spare. No stairs to climb. I've thought about it a lot and it's for your own good. You don't want to have another stroke, Mo. It's nearly finished me off. You're moving in with me."

"Am I? You've decided, have you? That's nice. I've got no say, I suppose."

"Then, well, we don't have to stop here. What's keeping us from moving? Nothing. Mo, what do you think about Hastings?"

"What are you talking about?"

"Sell it all. Pool what we get. How much do you think we'd get? We'd have enough for a two-bedroom cottage, that's for certain. The sea, Mo. You love the sea."

"Hastings?"

"By the sea."

"If only."

"Why not? You love the sea, Mo."

"It's been a good long while since we had a proper break, I know that much."

"What's stopping us?"

"I can think of a few things."

"Just give the idea a chance for a few minutes, Mo. Stop thinking of why not all the time."

Sylvia's getting loud and Maureen doesn't say anything for ages and then when she does her voice is different, it's all soft like when she used to tell Jake a bedtime story.

"I do love the sea. I've always wanted a place by the sea. Walking on the beach. Them lights that they put around the pier. A little springer spaniel or something. I'd lose this weight, wouldn't I, with all that walking? I love that curve in the bay, great sweeping curve, like a giant smile. It's mild down there even in winter and you'd have the sea to look at. To listen to. What is it about the sea? What is it when you look out at the sea and feel calm? Hastings, though, it must have changed since we were there."

"Just me and you, Mo," says Sylvia.

"Or a Lakeland terrier. Or a . . . what was the dog the Turners had?"

"Bedlington."

"Pedigrees are expensive though, Sylv. And Bedlingtons can be a bit bouncy as well. We could get a rescue dog. I'd rather have a little mutt. A little crossbreed, quiet, well behaved. If it was up to me, I'd have beams in the ceiling and a stable door at the back. I don't like cobbled streets, though, not with my ankles. I'd like it to be at the bottom of a little lane with hollyhocks on both sides. They're the tall ones, aren't they? Don't want much of a garden when you've got the sea and I've never been much good with plants. Local pub. Local fish-and-chips shop. Sound of the waves at bedtime."

"Just you and me, Mo."

Leon walks into the bathroom and flushes the toilet. He watches the water swirling around, turning blue and then settling in the bottom. He flushes it again and spits into the water, watching his saliva dissolve and disappear. He wipes his hands down his trousers and goes into his room.

Jake looks at him from his photo with his hand stretched

out, trying to pull his hair or take his truck or sit on his lap. Leon lies on his bed, closes his eyes, and puts his hands on his stomach in case he's going to be sick. He feels all his blood turning to clay, feels Sylvia's plans settle like an anchor on his chest, squeezing his throat into a narrow iron tube, filling his lungs with her sour perfume, her intimate odor. On his palms, he feels the squeeze of his mother's fingers, her secret messages, her physical decay, her distractions, her stained fingers, brown as rotten fruit. And, deep in his brain, he can hear something screaming and wailing, the new realization that Maureen is just like everyone else.

He picks up his backpack to feel how heavy it is. Yes, he will be able to carry it on his bike all the way to the allotment. Yes, he can put the heaviest things in the empty shed. Yes, he's good on his bike and strong. Yes. Castro won't have found his hiding place. Yes, he can do it. He can. So long as no one else finds his halfway house and steals his things while he's away. Yes.

When he goes back to the living room, they are still talking about the seaside and when Maureen sees him she takes his hand.

"Think I'll come with you for a little stroll up to the park," she says.

"I'm not going now," he replies and sits down in the armchair.

"Changed your mind?"

"Yes," Leon says. "I've changed my mind. I want to stay at home with you."

He smiles. Just like Maureen has a soft voice and Sylvia has three or four different voices, Leon can have a pretend voice as well.

Then the whispering begins. They go into the kitchen but he can hear because only his face is watching the TV; every other inch of him is standing between them in the kitchen, watching their lips. Maureen will have her arms folded.

"You didn't tell him then?"

"No," says Sylvia.

"Good. Leave that up to me. I want to tell him before the social workers get to him. But I'll wait until the time's right."

"How soon will it be official?"

"Any day now but you know how bloody slow they can be. Social Services do everything in their own sweet time as you know."

"And it's for good?"

"Permanent, as far as I'm concerned. I'm stopping work apart from him."

Then he can't hear because the kettle's boiling. They'll drink more cups of tea and coffee and eat cake and sandwiches and talk about people he doesn't know and the seaside all the time while they make their plans about him, while they make their plans without him. Then Sylvia starts talking about houses again and how many bedrooms they can afford. And Maureen is nodding. They keep saying it will be permanent and secure and Leon sees how fat Maureen is and how ugly Sylvia is and how they both want to get a dog instead of him.

Then all of a sudden they both scuttle into the living room and stand in front of the TV.

"Where's that?" says Maureen.

Leon wasn't paying attention so he doesn't speak.

"Hold on," says Sylvia. "If it's a news flash it will be on ITV as well."

Maureen changes the channel and the news flash is on the other one too.

". . . area of high deprivation. Most recent reports tell of fires burning in streets and clashes between police and gangs of youths following the death in custody of a local man from the Union Road area. What began as a peaceful demonstration outside Springfield Road police station has escalated into running battles between police and rioters with several police officers and civilians being taken to the hospital. Witnesses have reported looting and damage to several shops in the area and additional police officers are being sent in from forces throughout the region. We will keep you updated throughout the night."

36

It smells like bonfire night. There's a feeling in the air like when something exciting is going to happen. Something exciting has already happened. Leon has done a brave thing. He's a burglar. He's James Bond. He's climbed out of his window so quietly that he couldn't believe it himself. It was difficult dragging the back-pack out but he did it in the end.

He scuttles around the side of the bungalow and unchains his bike from the drainpipe by the back gate. He pushes it through the path that leads between the houses, crouching down beside it like it's moving all on its own. The pack is really heavy and it drags him down but as soon as he gets out on the street he can straighten up. He pushes hard up the hill away from Sylvia and Maureen. They won't notice for ages because they're watching the news on the TV. Even when they do notice, they won't care anyway.

He is sweating but he keeps going. His face feels funny and his lips feel swollen from crying. He thinks of Maureen going into his room in the morning and how she will cry like when they lost Jake. She'll run and tell Sylvia and they'll start crying together because it will be too late. His throat hurts now and he has to drag his sleeve across his eyes to see where he's going. If anyone sees him they will think it's the smoke that's making him cry.

There are lots of people standing on street corners and someone shouts at him to stop but he pays no attention. He's never heard so many police sirens. It sounds like a film or a TV show and even though Leon wants to see where the fire is, he's got to be careful because he has a long, long way to go to get to Dovedale Road and then all the way back to his halfway house and then all the way to Bristol. Two hours the social worker said but that was in her car. He's got a map in his bag and, including the money he just took out of Maureen's purse, he's got more than twenty-three pounds.

Usually when he thinks about seeing Jake he feels happy. But for some reason he's crying and he wonders if Jake will remember him. Babies change a lot when they start to grow up. How will he know what Jake looks like and how will he get into the house where they are keeping him? At least he's got the nail file from Crazy Rose.

He looks behind him at how far he has come from Sylvia and Maureen. He will put the heaviest stuff in his shed at the allotment and then only take the most important things to Dovedale Road: some candy for himself, baby food for Jake, his money, his map, and the photograph.

When he's got Jake, if anyone stops him and says, "Where are you taking that baby?" Leon will show them the photograph to prove that it's his brother. When your brother is white it can be difficult to believe that you're related. He hopes Jake can walk on his own because, if not, Leon will have to carry him. He wonders if Jake will fit in the backpack. He's seen some of the African women carrying their babies on their backs, so it can be done. It makes him feel better to think he has a backup plan if he can't steal a baby buggy or if Jake can't walk or if he's too heavy to carry in his arms or on his bike.

Finding Carol might be more difficult but he'll deal with that problem when it comes. If there's one thing he's certain of, it's that his mom wants to see Jake again. He imagines her face when he knocks on her door and holds Jake in front of him. She'll burst into tears and pick him up, hold him close to her chest, and say, "My baby, my baby," and she'll probably crumple down like she did before but this time it will be out of happiness and Leon is strong enough to help her up all on his own. Every social worker he's ever had has told him that his mom loves her children but she just can't manage. Well, all that is going to change. Leon has learned a thing or two since he was nine. He's been shopping at a big supermarket with Sylvia, picked out the cheapest and best food, and put it in the cart. He's learned how much things cost and how to take them cleverly when you haven't got enough money.

Looking after Jake won't be a problem; it never was. Looking after Carol can be tricky and if he'd done a better job in the past, he wouldn't be in this position now, pedaling hard with a heavy bag all the way to the allotments when it's getting dark and when he's a bit scared. He was stupid to go and see Tina and ask her for some money. It was her fault that his mom went into the hospital and that was what started everything going wrong. That's a mistake he won't make again. Twenty-three pounds is a lot of money. It can last two people and a baby for weeks if they all stay together.

He gets off the bike at the entrance to the allotment. He expected the gate to be locked, that he'd have to wheel around and climb over the brick wall. He even brought his bike lock just in case but the gates are wide open and one of them is hanging off its hinges.

He goes slowly. He can hear voices, shouting and swearing.

He stops. Maureen might have noticed that he's left home and she might call the police. If she does, they will be looking for him and it might be better to just go back. The sound of the men swearing at each other makes him want to get back on the bike and climb back through Sylvia's window but if he isn't brave and if he turns back at the first sign of trouble he'll never get to Bristol. And anyway, as he gets closer he can hear it's Tufty and Mr. Devlin and they have always hated each other. It's just them arguing as usual. It doesn't mean anything bad's going to happen.

He has to make sure they don't see him. He can just make out their shapes, standing in front of Mr. Devlin's brick shed. Mr. Devlin's flashlight is pointing at the ground but Tufty's light dances everywhere, the beam making wild shapes in the air. Leon wheels his bike slowly along the far path behind Mr. and Mrs. Atwal's plot. As usual, Tufty is doing all the talking but Mr. Devlin seems to say just as much with fewer words.

"Is that so?" he says. "Show the government? Is that so?"

Tufty is shouting and Leon knows he will be pointing his finger, right up close to Mr. Devlin's face.

"That's what you do, isn't it? You and your IRA. It's a protest. Get it? A protest. Except we don't bomb people in their beds like you Irish people."

"Oh, every Irishman is a terrorist, is that what you're saying?"

"You sit in your shed half-drunk, talking to yourself. You don't know what's going on in the world."

"Is that so?"

"You think it's funny? Why you smiling? You think it's funny that the police kill black people?"

"Don't be so fucking—"

"What? Don't be so fucking what? You don't believe me? There's hundreds of people on the street tonight. You know why? The police killed a black man last night, someone I knew. Yeah, my friend. Castro, man. They took him to the police station for some bullshit reason and kicked him to death. Castro, they killed him."

"Listen—"

"Yeah, so don't laugh when you're talking to me. Don't laugh."

"I am not fucking laughing."

Leon can hear the drink in Mr. Devlin's voice. "I'm sorry about your friend," he continues, "but that doesn't mean they should be running through here like this. Look at this place."

Leon stands still. He can see now that the flower beds have been trampled. The water barrels have been pushed over and the lines between the plots aren't straight anymore.

"You ever been angry?" says Tufty. "I don't mean you run out of whiskey and the shops are shut. I mean down in your belly. You ever been angry in your balls?"

There is a long silence. Tufty and Mr. Devlin must be staring at each other, waiting for each other to blink. Leon stands still too because it is so quiet and he is so close that they might hear him. He hopes that whoever made the mess in the allotments hasn't been near his shed.

"Of course I've been angry."

"Yeah? Anybody make you into a slave? Put you in chains?"

"Oh, for pity's sake," says Mr. Devlin, "a history lesson now. Fix the gate with me, can't you? The gate. You're acting like a child."

"Who you think you're talking to?"

"Well, don't make excuses for them then. They're savages."

"Savages? You calling black people savages? You fucking—"

Leon hears the scuffle but can't see it. Both men are grunting and gasping, the flashlight beams skimming across Leon's chest like a laser. Leon wheels his bike slowly until he is level with Mr. Devlin's shed. He's about to move when he hears Mr. Devlin cry out as he lands on the ground.

"Yeah," says Tufty. "I'd rather be savage than a pervert. You think I ain't seen your pictures and your dolls? You think we ain't all seen what you got in there? All of us in this whole allotment. We all know about you."

"You bastard!"

Mr. Devlin must have got up off the ground and charged at Tufty because all of a sudden both men slam into the wall of Mr. Devlin's shed. A flashlight drops to the ground. If Leon can get the light then he won't be so afraid to walk deeper into the allotment on his own. If he can get near the light, he will switch it off and hide with it until they have finished.

But they keep pushing and shoving each other and shouting.

"I seen you with that boy that comes in here. Making friends with him. Getting him to like you. You going to take his photo now? Is that it?"

"You shut your filthy mouth."

"I seen you giving him things. Presents. I seen him go inside."

"I've never—

"You got no wife. You got no children—"

"Wife?" screams Mr. Devlin. "My wife? How dare you?"

Leon stares into the darkness. He can see the shape of the two men standing like black scarecrows against the purple sky. He can hear them panting, feels the current between them that raises the hairs on his arm and fires the beats in his chest.

"Yeah," continues Tufty, "you got no woman but you got pictures of little boys all over the place, eh? Pictures not enough now? Is that it? You want a piece of the real thing?"

"You've got a filthy mouth, you black bastard."

The smack that Mr. Devlin gets doesn't stop him speaking.

"You're a dirty-minded fucker. I'll show you."

Leon leans his bike against Mr. Devlin's shed, crouches down, runs for a few steps, then goes slowly toward them. He drops down onto his belly. He crawls forward on his elbows like he's seen in the war films. Feels around for the flashlight. He grips something but it's soft and squishy. He gasps and pulls his hand back, wipes it on the grass. He feels around on the ground but can't find anything. He hunches down behind the water barrel. Suddenly, Mr. Devlin dashes into his shed.

"Come in here!" he shouts. "Come on! I dare you! I'll shut your mouth for you. Come on. Bring your filthy mind with you."

Tufty stands at the door of the shed. He shines the light full on and Leon can see clearly now. He can see Mr. Devlin through the window acting like he's gone mad. All his nice things are falling off the shelf and smashing onto the ground. He is staggering and bawling. Tufty takes a step back.

"You're crazy, man. I ain't got time for this."

"No, no, no. Not crazy. I'm a pervert. That's what you said. A pervert. I'll show you. Come on, come and see the monster."

Mr. Devlin begins throwing things down. Leon knows what he's looking for. He has it in his backpack.

"Where is he? Gabriel! Where is he? Where's he gone?"

Leon can hear all Mr. Devlin's favorite things breaking on the floor of his shed and him breaking as well.

"My baby, my son, where are you?"

"Fucking hell, man. Calm down," says Tufty. He steps into the shed and, as soon as he's gone, Leon runs. He can't see where he's going but he runs. He runs with the pack banging against his back, with the baby's wooden head inside, bouncing up and down. He falls and falls, and by the time he gets to the shed his back is wet with sweat.

It's dark in his halfway house. The air is too hot and too sticky to fit down Leon's throat. He throws the backpack on the floor and drops to his knees. He pulls his T-shirt up over his head. It's as sticky as tape on his skin. His scalp is itching, his back is itching, his feet in his sneakers are burning and damp, his chest is thumping so hard it might break open, his heart will jump out and he will be dead and then Maureen will look for him and be sorry and his mom will cry because she never loved him as much as she loved Jake and when he has a funeral everybody will say they are sorry for not being nice to him and he won't care because he will be dead.

He looks out of the dirty window toward Mr. Devlin's shed. His shouting is almost drowned by the sirens but Leon can still hear him and Leon wonders what Tufty is doing, if he's still trying to calm him down or if they are arguing or maybe Tufty has gone home. Something scuttles at his feet. A scratch. Leon notices how dark the shed is. Creatures and spiders might live in here, rats, black moths, mice, animals, people, ghosts. A rasp of wind hisses on the broken glass. Anyone could be in the shed with him and he wouldn't be able to see. They could grab him and attack him like in his nightmares. Kill him. Eat him. Tear him apart. Leon bursts back out of the shed and the door bangs shut behind him. Twice.

Everything goes quiet. Mr. Devlin and Tufty have suddenly gone quiet. They must have heard the door bang. If there is a monster in the shed, it's stopped moving. His money, his pack, his T-shirt, his address on Dovedale Road, he left them all inside with whatever made the scratching noise. Leon remembers when his dad was crying after the funeral, the look on his face. "I got no one, I got no one, I got no one." Leon feels sorry for his dad. He thought his dad was being a girl, crying and leaving the tears on his face for people to see. If only it was his dad making the noise in the shed. They could go and get Jake together. But his dad didn't like Jake even before he was born and if he wasn't always in prison then his mom wouldn't have decided to love Jake's dad instead and she wouldn't have had Jake and he wouldn't have said horrible things to her and made her cry and then everything would be like it was.

Fire engines and police cars are wailing in the blackness but Leon can hear something coming close, soft and careful. He can hear footsteps and whispering and the only thing he can do is to creep back inside the shed. Castro is dead, he heard Tufty say. But what if Castro has climbed out of his grave and it's him that's roaming around the allotments? He hears feet on the stones. Deep voices, hoarse and quick.

They're coming to get him. It's the police who took Castro away. Killed him. Kicked him to death. They've come back. They've come for him. Leon pulls the door open. Crawls in. Crouches down in a corner, his sticky back against the rough plank walls.

They're right outside. He can hear them breathing. Whispering. In the gloom, he can just see his backpack. He reaches his hand out. The door flies open.

37

It's Tufty and Mr. Devlin. They shine their flashlights inside, all over like searchlights, and then the beams land on him.

"Fucking hell!" says Tufty. "What you doing, Star?"

"Ah, him!" says Mr. Devlin.

Tufty holds him by the upper arm and pulls him up onto his feet.

"What you doing in here?"

Leon looks away from the harsh light. He can see that his pack has burst open and Mr. Devlin's baby's head has fallen out. It sits on the floor looking out at Mr. Devlin like it's alive.

Mr. Devlin picks it up, holds it against his heart.

"You? You took him," he says. "When did you take him? Why?"

Tufty is still holding Leon's arm.

"He's my son!" shouts Mr. Devlin. "You stole him. He's all I have."

"What you doing, Star? You don't do them things, you don't take other people's things, man."

Mr. Devlin has the head cradled in his arms like the rest of the baby is still attached.

"How would you like it if someone took something from you?" he says. "Something precious. One of your toys."

"Yeah," says Tufty. "Come on, tell the man you're sorry."

Leon looks at Tufty and Mr. Devlin. Their faces look strange in the flashlight beams. They are devils. They are social workers and doctors and Carol's boyfriends and his dad when he went to prison and the teachers at school that make him catch up and the owner of the candy shop and the man in the sports car and Tina and her boyfriend and Earring with his pen and fat policemen that trample on flowers and Crazy Rose and Sue's mouth full of cake and dead Castro. Every face he has ever seen starts crowding into the shed. He can hear them breathing, thinking about what they will do with him in the long term and the short term, making scratching sounds on paper and whispering about how to get rid of him so they can get a dog. Leon pulls away from Tufty.

He bends down, picks up his backpack, and feeds his arms through the straps. Tufty stands in the doorway.

"Come, Star. Tell the man you're sorry and I'll take you home."

"I'm not sorry," he says.

He tries to push past Tufty.

"What?" says Mr. Devlin. "What did you say? Do you realize what this means to me? My son is dead. Dead, do you hear me? He died when he was younger than you are now. How dare you say—"

"All right, all right," says Tufty. "Leave him. He don't look right. Leave him, come, let's go."

But Mr. Devlin grabs Leon's arm and pulls him backward.

"You're not going anywhere without giving me my apology."

"Leave him," says Tufty. "You can't see it's late? What's he doing out so late? Where's your clothes?"

But Mr. Devlin isn't listening.

"You need to have respect for other people's things. He is mine. Not yours."

"What you doing in here, Star?" says Tufty. "It's too late for you to be out. Too dangerous. Where's your top? Get dressed. I'll take you home."

Leon feels his teeth sharpening themselves against each other. He can hear the sawing in his temples, the grinding in his ears.

"I don't care," he says.

Both men speak together.

"What?"

"I don't care," repeats Leon.

"You can't say that," says Tufty.

"I don't care!" he screams. "No one cares!"

"All right . . ."

But Leon hasn't finished. He screws his fingers into tight fists and shoves his hand in the air like Black Power.

"No one cares about me. No one cares about my brother. I've got a baby as well. He's my baby. He's a real baby, not a wooden baby. But no one cares about that. I can't see him. I keep asking and asking but you only care about yourself. Everyone steals things from me."

Mr. Devlin shines his light up at the ceiling and the whole shed becomes bright. Leon knows they can see the tears on his face and he knows they will think he's behaving like a girl but they're wrong, as usual. He's like his dad and he will leave the tears where they are and he won't wipe them off even though they are itchy. Instead he slaps his chest with the palm of his hands.

"Why can't I have my things? Everyone else can have theirs. People tell lies to me all the time. They pretend to care but they don't."

They are staring at him, listening, dead still. He slips the backpack off and holds it in one hand. His other hand fishes around inside.

"Anyway, I don't care, because I can look after myself. And I can look after my brother. I've done it before. So I don't care if I can't go to the seaside."

Leon can feel himself growing stronger. He can see they believe him. They look at each other and then back at him. He is tall. He's strong and powerful, like Maureen said. And he's been making plans for a long, long time.

"And I've got lots of money and all of our food so I don't need your things and the head doesn't even look like Jake anyway."

Mr. Devlin opens his mouth but Leon slips the pruning knife out and slashes the air.

"No!" he shouts. "Don't say anything because I won't listen. No one listens to me so I won't listen to them."

It's about time everyone realizes who they are dealing with. It's nice to see that two grown-up men can be scared. The knife feels slick and heavy in his hand; he can see Mr. Devlin and Tufty stiffen because they're scared, they can see how big he is and they know he will stab them if they get in his way. Leon swings the knife from right to left and both of the men back off.

"Easy, no, man," says Tufty. "Easy, Star."

"I'm in charge now," says Leon. "And I don't have to listen. I don't have to take it easy."

He keeps stabbing the air between them until Tufty backs away from the door.

"Wait, Star! Come on. Talk to me, man."

Tufty is holding his hands up like he's being robbed but Mr. Devlin takes a few steps away. The noise of the police cars and fire engines is loud and constant. There is shouting as well, far away, like a soccer match or a party.

When Mr. Devlin speaks, he is quiet and slow.

"Leave him. The boy is right. He is in charge. He has the weapon."

Leon nods. He can feel the fear in the air, between him and the two men. Between him and the rest of the world.

"Yeah. I'm in charge."

"Yes," says Mr. Devlin. "You are in charge. We can see that."

Mr. Devlin and Tufty quickly look at each other. Mr. Devlin holds his hands out.

"What would you like to do now?" he says to Leon.

"I'm going to Dovedale Road to get my brother."

"I see," says Mr. Devlin. "Dovedale Road."

"Yeah," says Leon. "And then I'm going to find my mom because she needs him."

"Yes, I understand," says Mr. Devlin. "Your mother. I see. You've got her address?"

"Bristol. The Halfway House."

Tufty opens his mouth then shuts it again. Mr. Devlin nods.

"Right. Dovedale Road first and then to Bristol? That's a long way. Isn't it, Mr. Burrows?"

"Yeah, man. You need someone with you, Star."

They think he's stupid.

"I'm going now," Leon says.

Mr. Devlin backs away farther into the shed and pulls Tufty away from the door.

"Yes, of course," he says. "We won't stand in your way, will we?"

Tufty is frowning.

"But first," continues Mr. Devlin, "perhaps you should put your clothes on. Or maybe you would like something to eat. Or drink. Dovedale Road is a long way."

"No," says Leon. He points the knife at both of them and opens the door with his foot. Leon has seen this plenty of times on *The Dukes of Hazzard.* If you want to get away, you have to keep your weapon on the enemy at all times. They could rush you. They could have their own weapons hidden in their sock. They might have reinforcements. All the time, you hold the weapon up, strong in your hand. Keep eye contact. Be brave.

But they don't move. They stand together at the back of the shed. Leon's in control now. Nobody else.

The door is open. He steps out backward with his knife in the air. He watches them for a few seconds and then he runs. He hears them after him. He hears them scuffling behind him on the path, the flashlight beams bounding all over the place, so Leon sticks to the bushes that lead around the allotment. He crouches low like a soldier, stopping every so often. Crouch, stop. Crouch, stop. Whips of leaves and brambles attack him but he keeps going. Crouch, stop. He can hear them shouting at each other, chasing him, angry because of the stolen knife and the baby's head, because he wouldn't say sorry. Mr. Devlin doesn't like him anymore. Crouch, stop.

"Star! Come out. Come on. It's not safe."

Tufty knows he steals things and wants to take him back to Maureen and Sylvia but they don't want him, either. They want a new dog that's no trouble, a well-behaved little mutt. Crouch. Stop. Tufty and Mr. Devlin have run to the gate and are shining their lights everywhere and shouting at each other.

"Yo, Star!"

"What's his name?"

Tufty doesn't answer.

"Christ, you don't know his name?" says Mr. Devlin.

"Danny. No. Ian, no, Leo, something like that."

"Christ," says Mr. Devlin.

"You were the one sitting in the shed with the child. Don't say nothing to me about it. I just showed him a few things with some seeds."

"He liked you."

Mr. Devlin starts shouting. "Hello! Hello! Boy!"

"Don't say 'boy,'" says Tufty. "You don't call black people 'boy.' Never."

"What is he then? He is a boy. I'm just calling out what he is. You call people 'man,' don't you? I've heard you."

"'Boy' means something else."

"Mother of God, every child in my class was 'boy' when I wanted his attention. It means nothing."

"Yeah? That depends on who you're talking to."

"Brazilians. Boys from the slums of São Paulo. Brazilian boys in my class in my school that I ran with my Brazilian wife, you bloody fool. Black boys, brown boys, white boys. Just boys."

"All right, all right. We're wasting time."

Tufty starts walking away.

"Shine over there," shouts Mr. Devlin, "I'll go by the Atwals' and by the fence. Spread out, spread out. Look low, he will go low."

"If he's still here."

Leon stays hidden. The trees and bushes make inky shapes against the purple sky and every so often their leaves move in the wind, whispering, trying to tell him something, warn him, tell him what to do. Invisible things scuttle past his feet, stop, start again. Like Leon, they know how not to get caught. Leon smells bonfires and burning plastic. There must be fireworks somewhere. There's a streetlight just outside the gate and if he gets up too soon they'll see him. And anyway, before he does anything else he has to get his bike from where he left it near Mr. Devlin's shed. He doesn't want to walk all the way to Dovedale Road. He hears them coming. He cramps himself into a ball, down low behind a metal trough full of dirty water.

"He's gone home," says Mr. Devlin.

"Home?" says Tufty. "You didn't hear him say his mother is in Bristol?"

"And his brother. What did he mean about his brother?"

"I don't know."

"The child should be indoors."

"Look," says Tufty, "his bike is there by your shed. He ain't going without his bike."

"Maybe," says Mr. Devlin. "But he's desperate."

"Yeah, when you're desperate you do desperate things."

"Yes, all right, Mr. Burrows. I get your point."

"Them people on the street—"

Mr. Devlin growls like a dog.

"Enough of the street, the street. You people are so fucking stupid! You can't even organize yourselves."

"Who you calling stupid?"

"It's ridiculous what you're doing. You have no plan, no structure, no chain of command . . ."

All Leon has to do is wait. Eventually they'll start fighting and forget all about him. But then Tufty starts to laugh. It's a laugh like Sylvia's, with nothing funny in it, bitter and tired.

"I ain't fighting you, man." Leon hears Tufty taking deep breaths. "You're an old man and I'm better than this. I'm not a fighter. I don't hate people. I ain't fighting no more."

Mr. Devlin goes to say something but Tufty shouts at him.

"Go about your business, man!" he says. "Go on. Fix up the gate. I'll look for my friend. He'll come out for me. Go on. Go home."

Tufty walks away toward Leon's bike. Leon has missed his chance. He should have gone while they were still angry. He can just make out Tufty picking up the bike and wheeling it toward the gate. Mr. Devlin is breathing somewhere close, shining his light in long steady sweeps across the allotment. Leon has to run for it.

He scrambles up, darts out, and slinks along the hedge. He comes to the path, then it's open country. He must get his bike off Tufty and make a run for the gate. He still has the knife.

"Yo! Yo!" calls Tufty.

Leon runs and pulls the bike but Tufty grabs it back and Tufty is so strong that he wins.

"Yo, Star! Wait."

Leon runs straight past him, twisting and feinting so Tufty can't grab him. He hears Mr. Devlin running, getting closer.

"Stop him!" he shouts. "Get after him."

But Leon's gone. They're old. They can't catch him. He's free.

38

Inside Leon's body, everything is mixed up. He feels hungry but he also feels full. His blood is hot and bubbly, making him want to run all the time, but he's cold and so tired he could curl up on the sidewalk and go to sleep. He wants to fight. Men and older boys are running in the middle of the road, shouting at each other and not noticing him. He wants to fight them all. He wants them to stop and help him.

The smell of smoke is everywhere—seeping through his skin, in the fabric of his pants, on his scalp, his naked back, his hair—and if he was at home, Sylvia would tell him to get changed and have a bath. She would close the windows and light a cigarette, she would put the TV on and give him a bag of potato chips and a drink. Maureen would be worried about where the smoke came from and whose house was on fire but Sylvia wouldn't.

He runs into the next street. How far is Dovedale Road?

What bus is it? How much is it? He stops in front of a shop and takes his map out of his backpack. It's soaking wet and, as he pulls it, it rips in half. A bottle of soda has smashed in his pack. His map is ruined. His breath comes in short bursts in time with the thrumming of his heart, sudden and sharp. Behind him he hears an explosion and the noise hits him like a fist. He crouches down in case something lands on him from the sky and he scampers to the doorway of a shop with all its windows smashed in.

An angry ghost of black smoke rolls up the street. If Leon stays where he is, it will cover him over, eat him up. He feels the soda dripping out of his pack and running down the back of his legs. It makes him want to pee and then he's crying again.

"I don't know where I am," he says.

Run away from the ghost. Run all the way to Dovedale Road. Knock on the door where Jake lives. Ask them if he can stay. Maybe they do want another boy. No one's probably asked them. No more stealing. No more lying. No more creeping around, eavesdropping. The TV always on low. Promise.

He turns a corner and sees a car lying on its side. Fat arms of white fire curl out of the broken windows and wave at him. Something in the car is hissing like fat in a frying pan. Leon turns and runs back the other way. The next road is deserted. The streetlights are broken but the lights are on in every house and a woman stands on the corner covering her face and crying. Two men in turbans shout at him.

"Get off the street! Can't you see? Go home!"

"No! Come with us. Over here."

Leon takes a few steps toward them. "I'm lost," he says.

"Take him inside."

"Get him off the street."

Leon backs away.

"Dovedale Road!" he shouts.

"Don't run away," they say but Leon is too quick. He dashes down an alley, kicking bottles and bricks out of the way. He needs to get back to the allotment and get his bike. He can cycle all the way to Dovedale Road. He's strong. He can do it. The alley goes on and on forever and right at the end there is a bright light. He runs toward it, stumbling and banging against the brick wall. He can hear himself breathing and words keep coming out of his mouth even though there is no one to hear. He wants to stop talking to himself but he's too scared.

"I'm lost. I don't know where I am. Help me."

He bursts out of the entry into the middle of a wide road and the noise turns itself off like a tap.

The road and the pavements are covered in bricks and bottles and glass and bits of iron. In the middle of the road is a bike on its side. It could take him all the way to Dovedale Road. He takes two steps toward it.

"Down Babylon!"

Something whizzes over his head and when it smashes it explodes into a puddle of fire, the flames jumping high off the street. Leon turns and runs and then he sees them. Crowds and crowds of black men at the end of the street, surging forward and back like one wild lion about to pounce. Leon stares at them but they are looking past him to the other end of the road, where there's a wide wall of shields and baton, hundreds of policemen lined up across the street.

The words through the loudspeaker are angry.

"Clear the street. Disperse and clear the street."

Leon wipes his arm across his face. He doesn't want the policemen to see his tears. He goes to walk away when a brick lands near his feet. He turns to the crowd of men at the other end of the street. They begin shouting all together. Chanting with one voice.

"Justice! Justice! Justice!"

Someone else cuts in.

"Break down Babylon! Break down Sus!"

"Fucking pigs! Police brutality! Murderers!"

"Racists! Killers!"

The same policeman says it again. "Disperse and clear the street."

Leon cups his hands round his mouth. "Dovedale Road!"

His words are drowned. The voices of the black men rise and snarl together like a monster's roar that carries right over Leon's head, all the way over the glass and the bricks and the fire and the bits of metal, all the way over the shields, snapping and biting. No one is looking at Leon. No one is listening. No one ever listens. No one even knows he's there.

Leon takes his backpack off and puts it down by his feet. He opens the top and takes out Mr. Devlin's gun. The policemen have batons and shields. The angry men have bricks and swearing. Leon has a gun. He holds it out toward the police. He turns and points it at the black men.

Everything goes quiet. Leon stands tall and raises his head.

"Hey!" he shouts.

The loudspeaker screams.

"Put the weapon down!"

Leon turns back to the police and holds the gun up to eye level, looking down the barrel. Mr. Devlin has done a good job with this gun. The dark wood is oiled and shiny. It has a little trigger and a little sight on the end of the barrel.

"Dovedale Road!" he shouts. "Take me to Dovedale Road!"

The angry men start creeping forward behind Leon.

"He's got a fucking gun!"

"That kid's got a gun!"

"Get the fucking gun, man!"

As they get closer, Leon hears scuffling.

"Don't crowd him!"

"Get him!"

Then Leon hears one voice, clear and sweet over all the others.

"Yo, Star!"

39

Tufty! It's Tufty! Waving with both arms.

"Star!"

Leon raises the gun to wave and everyone drops to the ground. Some scatter off to the side, to the dark houses and shops with broken windows.

The police crouch down behind their shields.

Then Mr. Devlin runs out into the middle of the road. He's waving at the police and the crowd.

"It's wooden!" he shouts. "It's not real. It's wooden!"

He is turning round and round, waving and all the time coming closer and closer to Leon.

He holds his hand out for the gun.

"Good boy," he says. "Give me the gun. Give it to me. Put it down."

Leon backs away. He picks up his pack and backs away.

"Give me the gun. You don't understand. Give it to me."

He makes a quick and sudden move for Leon and grabs his arm. A bottle smashes at Leon's feet. Another bottle and brick fly over and something hits Mr. Devlin in the head. Leon sees him stagger.

"Pig!" shouts the crowd. "He's a pig!"

The bottles come hard and fast, smashing on the ground, shards of glass splintering everywhere. A stone hits Leon on his leg, something scratches past his back. He cries out.

"Run!" says Mr. Devlin, the blood on his forehead trickling down into his eye, then something hits him on his shoulder. He cries out and falls down.

"Run, boy!" he says and pushes Leon away.

Under his feet, Leon feels the thunder of the policemen's boots. They stamp toward him, crouching behind their shields, and all the angry men run forward, cheering and shouting. They are feet apart.

Tufty grabs Mr. Devlin by the arm.

"Get up, man!"

But Mr. Devlin is swaying and won't move.

"Help me, Star!" shouts Tufty. "We got to move. Quick!"

But they can't get Mr. Devlin up and there are people screaming, rushing past them from both sides. Tufty shields Mr. Devlin with his back but all Mr. Devlin does is moan and there's blood running off his face now, onto his green jacket.

"Help me!" shouts Tufty. "Get his arm."

Leon throws the gun down and grabs Mr. Devlin under his arm. He pulls and pulls but Mr. Devlin is very heavy and he isn't even helping. Tufty puts both arms round Mr. Devlin and hauls him to his feet.

"Get up, man!"

People everywhere are tripping, barging into them. Mr. Devlin falls again.

"Get up, Mr. Devlin!" Leon shouts. "You have to get up!"

He does try. Leon can see he's trying. He holds his hands out to Leon and Tufty but the blood is in his eyes.

"Come on!" says Leon and puts Mr. Devlin's arm over his shoulder. Tufty helps as well. Mr. Devlin scrambles up onto his feet and Leon takes his hand.

"This way," says Tufty, "over there."

"Walk, Mr. Devlin," says Leon.

Tufty steers them back toward the alley. They push and shove. Shields clash into arms and heads and chests. It sounds like a battle. Tufty and Leon and Mr. Devlin claw their way. Find a space at the edge. See the alley. Quick. Then suddenly Tufty goes down. He makes a terrible noise when he falls and when Leon turns around he sees a policeman with a baton in the air.

"You fucking coon!" he shouts.

He bends over Tufty and brings the baton down and down and down again on Tufty's back. Tufty writhes on the ground, his arms up over his face. The policeman beats Tufty so hard his helmet falls off and rolls away.

"Leave him!" shouts Leon. He pushes the policeman out of the way. "Leave him alone."

The policeman stumbles and nearly falls over and as he gets up he screams at Leon.

"You little black bastard!"

He raises his baton and flexes his arm. He's panting, his mouth open in a horrible shape. Leon stands still and looks up at him. There is no one else. Mr. Devlin is lying in the alleyway. Tufty is lying on the ground. He might be dead. This is the time when there is really no one to look after him. The policeman blinks and a thin line of spit falls from his bottom lip. Leon holds his arms open.

"We are not a warrior," he says. "We have dignity and worth."

The policeman's mouth falls, slack and loose, his baton still in the air, like he's raised his hand at school to answer a question. Leon nods.

"We've been growing things," he says. "Scarlet Emperors. That's what we do."

The policeman stares at him. At the other end of the road there are people screaming and swearing, bellowing at one another, roaring like the fires in the bins and in the cars and in the shops. There are fire engines and ambulances joining in. There are people running past and people lying on the ground. But right now, in this place, there is no one else.

It seems like Leon and the policeman look at each other for hours and hours and Leon knows the policeman's scared. It's in his eyes. The policeman wants to say "Can you help me?" so Leon says it for him.

He walks over to the policeman's helmet, picks it up, and holds it out. "Can you help me?"

The policeman drops his arm and the baton swings back and forth, then stops. He grabs the helmet and puts it on.

"Fuck off," he says. "Go on, fuck off home and take your dad."

The policeman turns then and runs back to the fighting crowd, his baton in the air. Leon has to make Tufty stand up.

"Come on, Tufty. Mr. Devlin needs us."

He pulls one of his arms and Tufty yells out. He pulls the other arm and turns Tufty over. He grabs Tufty's shirt and pulls and pulls, straining and keening until Tufty is sitting up.

"Get up, Tufty, get up!"

Tufty rolls onto his side, brings his knees up, and staggers to his feet.

He walks like he's drunk, holding Leon's shoulder, and they shuffle into the alley. He's not exactly crying but he's making the same sort of noises. They both pull Mr. Devlin up onto his feet.

A bottle smashes against the alley wall.

"Move," says Tufty. "Move."

They all squash into the alley. There's no air, only smoke, no light but—at the far end—gray instead of black. They stumble through, falling into one another. Leon feels his way brick by brick, scratches his elbows on the wall, feels it cold and weeping on his skin. His feet turn on the slippery stones. Mr. Devlin follows, bumping and shuffling, and Tufty leaning all the time on Leon's shoulder. They come out into the street, thick with silence; the burning car is smoking at one end. Mr. Devlin slumps against a low brick wall and, inside the house, a curtain moves.

Mr. Devlin's face is red with blood and Tufty has blood running from his scalp. One eye is half-closed. He holds his head in both hands and speaks through his fingers.

"Where are we? What street is this?"

Leon points at a street sign.

"Moreton Street."

"Moreton Street. Moreton Street," repeats Tufty. "We got to get off the street. Hurry."

They both help Mr. Devlin up onto his feet and pull him along. He's muttering and groaning like he did in his shed and Leon takes his arm.

"Shall we call an ambulance, Tufty?"

"No," says Mr. Devlin. "No. I'm all right."

Tufty squints at him through his good eye.

"Neither of us all right, man."

They walk and turn the corner, turn the corner again, and Leon knows where he is.

"That's College Road," he says.

Tufty grunts. He swaps the arm that's carrying Mr. Devlin and carries on.

"I live there," says Leon. He points down the hill where Sylvia lives. "There," he says. "Right there."

40

Leon knocks on the door. He tries to think how long he has been away but he doesn't know. It must be a very long time. The door opens. It's Sylvia.

"It's him! Mo! It's him. Mo!"

She stops suddenly and looks at Mr. Devlin and Tufty.

"Bloody hell, what's happened?"

She grabs Leon and holds his face, turns him round, checks him back and front.

"You hurt? Mo! Quick! Who's this?"

Sylvia takes hold of Mr. Devlin's arm. "You better come in."

"Sorry," he mutters.

"Careful, this way," says Sylvia, helping him inside.

Then Maureen comes. She's got her coat on and her purse in her hand. Her face is red and her lips are moving but there are no words. Leon stands next to Tufty because he doesn't know if she'll be angry that he left or angry that he's come back. So he stands next to Tufty and if she says anything he's going to ask Tufty if he can stay with him for one night until he can find Dovedale Road. He still has his backpack, wet and dirty, and his money, but he will need a new map. Maureen shakes her head, opens her mouth to say something, and then closes it again.

Tufty puts his hand to the back of his head and when he looks at his palm, it has blood on it. He groans and starts walking down the path.

"You need to keep your eye on your boy," he says.

"And you are?" shouts Maureen, shoving her purse in her pocket.

"He's Tufty Burrows," Leon says. "He's a gardener."

Maureen looks hard at Leon then beckons Tufty back.

"Oi! Wait! Where do you think you're going in that state? Come on. Get yourself inside. Let me have a look at that head. Where did you find him? No, don't tell me. I don't think I can bear it."

She keeps talking all the time while Tufty steps inside and she leads him to the kitchen.

"We've seen it all over the news. I've never seen the like. Terrible. A policeman's half-dead and someone's been beaten to death in a police cell. I don't know, I honestly don't."

She sits Tufty on a kitchen chair and wrings out a cloth.

"Civil war, it is. What happened? Were you involved? No, don't tell me."

She dabs the back of Tufty's head, all the time talking and not looking at Leon.

"I owe you my thanks, I know that much. You've brought him back and that's all that matters."

She says nothing to Leon. She's not telling him off. Not noticing him. Sylvia is looking after Mr. Devlin, talking and dabbing and worrying about stitches and doctors and the ER and getting the police involved.

"Don't," says Mr. Devlin, one of his eyes almost closed up. "I don't want the police. I saw what they did to him."

He turns his head to Tufty. "Thank you," he says.

Leon stays in the doorway. He slips his pack off and puts it on the floor. He knows Maureen has seen it.

"Can I go to the toilet, please?" he asks.

"I don't know," says Maureen. "I don't live here. You better ask Sylvia."

But Sylvia doesn't answer him. She's acting busy and bossy as usual and she keeps shaking her head and looking at Maureen and then looking at Mr. Devlin and filling a bowl with hot water and fussing a bit more.

Leon walks along the hallway to the bathroom. He washes his hands and looks at himself in the mirror. Where he was crying there are little tracks on his dirty face. He has a few leaves stuck in his hair and there are scratches on his back and arms where the brambles caught him. He's even got blood all over his chest, Tufty's or Mr. Devlin's. Maureen will have noticed but she hasn't said anything. He does a lovely long pee and then flushes the toilet. He closes the lid and sits down. One of his legs is moving and shaking all on its own and he can feel the tears again just behind his eyes, waiting to come out.

It's too dark to leave now. He might get hit by a rock or a policeman. It was very easy to get lost even with a map. His bike is at the allotment and he's too scared to go and get it. He walks back to the living room. Maureen is ushering Tufty onto the sofa.

"Sit, go on. Sit down. I'll make you a cup of tea. Go on, sit. You're in no fit state to be walking the streets. Go on, sit down. You're safe in here."

Tufty holds a cloth to his head and leans back.

Maureen stands over him. "Good, that's it. And you," she says finally to Leon, "you go and sit next to him. Have you had a pee? You'll need a sandwich before bed. Bet you're starving, aren't you?"

He can't see her face, because she's on her way to the kitchen, but her voice sounds shaky and thin.

"Yes," he says and suddenly she stamps back into the living room, stands in front of the television, and puts her hands on her hips.

"What the bloody hell are you playing at, Leon?"

They all go quiet. Sylvia has shut up and Tufty puts his head down.

"Do you know what I've been through tonight? Not knowing where you were? I've been trying the police fifty times but they're too busy. Apparently. Too busy to bother with a ten-year-old runaway. I haven't called Social Services because I don't want you ending up in a bloody home, do I? I don't want them coming in here and saying I can't look after you."

She wipes her face with a tea towel, her chest heaving and her breath ragged and torn.

"Where were you going and why? Why are you half-naked? What in the name of God has got into you? What's it all about, Leon?"

Sylvia walks out of the kitchen and puts her arms round Maureen.

"Mo, love. Calm down. You've just come out of the hospital, Mo. Calm down."

But Maureen wriggles away from her.

"I'm fine," she says. "I'm calm. I am. He's home now."

They both go into the kitchen. Tufty raises his eyebrows.

When Maureen comes back she has a huge plate of sandwiches that she puts on the coffee table, a can of Coke for Leon, and a cup of tea for Tufty.

"Sugar's there," she says.

She sits in Sylvia's chair and closes her eyes.

"You're back. That's enough for now."

Tufty nudges Leon and nods in Maureen's direction.

"Say sorry," he whispers.

Leon has a mouthful of cheese sandwich. He looks at Tufty

because he doesn't want to say sorry, and anyway, Tufty doesn't know about Maureen and Sylvia's plans.

Tufty nudges him again and frowns.

"Say it," he hisses.

"Sorry, Maureen," says Leon.

She half opens her eyes.

"Off to bed when you've had that. No, actually, get a wash, a good wash all over. You're sleeping in my room on the floor. The window's painted shut and I'll move my dressing table in front of the door. Think you can move that in the night, Leon?"

He shakes his head.

"Bloody right," she says and closes her eyes again.

A sharp sliver of sun cuts through the curtains and into Leon's eyes. He can see the pinkish back of his lids, dots of color and light like a kaleidoscope he once had. He can hear pots and pans clanging in the kitchen and the radio on with Sylvia's music. He hears Sylvia laugh. He remembers getting into the bath and hearing the grown-ups talking in the kitchen. He thought he could hear Tufty and Mr. Devlin and Sylvia and Maureen all laughing together but maybe they were arguing. He doesn't remember getting into bed. He didn't dream.

He opens his eyes and sees that he is on the floor on some cushions at the bottom of Maureen's double bed. Under the bed is dusty where Sylvia forgot to vacuum. He scrambles up, squeezes past the dressing table, and opens the door. He's starving.

41

Something's different about Maureen. She's not exactly in a bad mood but she's not talking a lot. She's not sick, because they're still living with Sylvia and she makes Maureen sit down all the time and eat salads. Maureen says that lettuce will kill you slowly instead of cakes that will kill you fast. She woke Leon up very early and told him to get dressed in his best clothes. She put rollers in her hair and made it very see-through and wide. She put on a fluffy cardigan with diamonds for buttons and a new pair of old ladies' sneakers with Velcro fasteners. Then she went quiet for the whole day and when she did speak she just said "Hmm" and "Maybe" or "Let's see how the day pans out."

But the day's been quite boring so far. First they had a very long train journey, which was just fields and fields for miles. Maureen said he could have a bar of chocolate from the cart and they played cards but she wasn't paying attention and Leon won easily. After a while they settled back in their seats and Leon must have slept until they got to Bristol.

At last the train stops and everyone gets off. Maureen actually takes his hand like he's a little boy but when they get out of the station she lets it go. They have to wait in line for a taxi and, when they get one, Maureen keeps looking at her map.

"Have to keep your eye on this lot," she says. "They'll take you around the long way if you let them."

They cross a bridge and then walk down some steps to a wide walkway overlooking a river. On the opposite bank, there's a massive battleship and Leon asks Maureen if they can go and have a look.

"Later," she says. That's her favorite word of the day.

She stops and looks up and down, left and right, and then turns around, then turns back.

"Is this the right place?" Maureen asks. She looks at her watch again. "Must be."

They sit on a bench by a concrete building so Maureen can catch her breath. She opens a Tupperware container of sandwiches.

"Here you go, ham and cheese."

Leon can see in her bag. She's bought chocolate and potato chips and two cans of Coke, so they are going to be here for some time. Maureen isn't eating anything. Says she's not hungry.

"Go and stand over there and have a look at the river. Go on. It's lovely."

She pushes him in his neck-back and Leon walks off. He leans on a low wall at the river's edge. Some of the gray-and-white seagulls bounce on the waves while others swoop up and away, losing themselves in camouflage against the low cloud. A scruffy barge, wide as a house, slugs through the water carrying hundreds of yellow containers stacked up like gigantic Legos. On another boat with lots of windows, people stand on the deck pointing at buildings and taking pictures, but compared to the battleship, everything else on the river looks like a toy. It has masts and flags, and huge guns, chimneys and chains, and two massive antennas sticking out of the smokestacks. Every sailor must have his own TV.

If he was a sailor, Leon would live on that battleship and sleep in a hammock suspended from the ceiling. He would have an anchor tattooed on his arm and wear a white vest tucked into his pants, and when the battleship went to war he would be in charge of loading the weapons. He saw it in a film. First of all the torpedo drops down from a rack, then you slide it along to the next person and he loads it into the firing cylinder. Then you have to trap it in so it doesn't come backward and kill you and then you have to press a button and count down from five. But there are two of you to do this, because it's important you don't make a mistake. Leon sees himself, sweaty, covered in black oil in the belly of the boat. Then you open the loading cylinder again and repeat this until the enemy submarine is destroyed. You know it's destroyed when the captain sees it on the radar or looks at it through the periscope. Leon closes one eye and brings the periscope down. He holds his fists either side of his head. He sees the grid of the sight and the blinking green smudge of light of the German U-boat. Then, *pow*, nothing. The green light disappears and up on the waterline metal debris bursts up into the air. Hoorah! In the engine room and in the torpedo room and in the control room and everywhere, all the sailors cheer and cheer and the other men slap Leon on the back because they are safe.

When he opens his eyes, Maureen's standing next to him.

"Someone here to see you, love."

She moves out of the way and Leon sees his mom sitting on a bench. He looks at Maureen and she licks her finger and wipes something off his face.

"She's waiting for you. Go on."

He runs. It takes him four seconds. He runs and stands in front of her.

"God," she says, "look at you."

Carol stubs her cigarette out and gets to her feet. "You're taller than me."

She measures them both, waving across the top of their heads.

"Like my dad. That's where you get it from."

She takes his hand and squeezes it but as soon as they sit down, she puts both hands flat on the bench next to her. She starts to stroke the wood with her yellow fingers, picking out splinters and smoothing them down again. Her arms are skinnier than before; so are her legs, her face, her ponytail. Wispy fronds of hair stand up all around her head like the seeds of a dandelion. And she has freckles, brown marks on her face he's never seen before.

"Are you all right, Mom?" he asks.

"Me? Great. Yeah. Course I am. Anyway, it's me that should be asking how you are."

"We're going on that battleship later."

"Good," she says. "How's school?"

"It's summer vacation."

"Did you have a nice birthday?"

"Yes."

"Yeah?"

"Yes."

"That's good. I remembered on the day, you know. Woke up and remembered straightaway. Told my friend, 'It's my son's birthday today,' and I got you something but I forgot to bring it. I'll have to put it in the mail."

Leon sees Maureen trying not to watch. Carol notices as well.

"Is she nice to you?"

"She went into the hospital but she's better now. We have to live with Sylvia, that's her sister, until she's back to how she was. Or even better."

"I never come here," Carol says. "Rivers make me think about dying. It's always cold if you live by the sea. Or by a river. Water makes you cold. Did you know that? A few degrees colder."

While Carol is talking, Leon takes her hand again. Sometimes, squeezing fingers is easier than talking.

"Leon," says his mom, "I want to tell you something."

He squeezes her hand but she doesn't squeeze back. Her voice becomes muffled and scratchy.

"I can't look after you properly, you know that, don't you?"

"Why not?"

"I don't know. I just can't."

"Why not?"

"I really don't know, Leon. Please. I just can't."

Carol has gotten smaller since he last saw her. No one is looking after her and he wonders why she doesn't come and live with him and Sylvia and Maureen. She could share his room and have loads of dinner and have some sleep and get better. Maureen could wash her clothes and show her how to look better. Maybe Sylvia would lend her some makeup. He knows he shouldn't say it but it just comes out.

"Me? With her?" She jerks her head back and pokes herself in the chest. "Me? Live with her?"

"And me," says Leon. "She wouldn't mind."

"Kids have foster parents, Leon, not adults. I don't need a foster family. Is that what you think, that I need to go into care or go into a hospital, is that what you think, that I'm sick or something or incapable, is that what people say about me?"

Her head is shaking and wobbly and her shoulders are jerking up and down.

"I mean we can live together. That's all. You and me."

Maureen walks over.

"Everything all right? You all right, Carol?"

Carol tucks her hands under her legs and rocks forward and back three times.

"I'm great," she says.

Maureen smiles and pats Carol on her back. Carol clears her throat.

"I was just telling him I can't look after him. I told him what we agreed. You get it, don't you, Leon? So, you're not to go running away, all right? Cuz you can't live with me but the lady says you can come and see me whenever you like. If you give me enough warning, I can meet you here another day. All right?"

Carol stands up and looks around quickly like she's lost.

"I've got to get back," she says.

She puts her hand out and Maureen shakes it.

"Thank you, Carol," she says. "It means a lot. I'll be in touch."

Carol bends down and kisses Leon on the cheek. She smells of cigarettes and the house they used to live in where Leon had to leave some of his toys. He's too old for them now but he still wants them, just to see if they are like he remembers.

He watches her walk away and he stays sitting down. He watches her pull her handbag onto her shoulder and he stays sitting down. All over the concrete walkway, there are white splotches of chewing gum stuck to the ground and Leon wonders if Maureen will let them have some on the way home, because she usually does when something important happens. He loses sight of his mother for a few seconds and he stays sitting down and then he runs and runs, grabs her from behind and holds onto her so she can't turn around, can't see him crying. She doesn't speak but she stops dead. She seems to go from hard to soft without moving a muscle. And then Leon asks her, finally.

"Do you know where he is, Mom?"

"No, love. I don't."

"Do you still love him?"

She says nothing but he feels a little gasp of air leave her body. She peels his arms from her waist and turns around.

"And you," she whispers. "I still love you."

She smiles then like she used to and scrabbles her fingers on his chest. She kisses him and walks backward for a few yards. She gives a little curtsy like he's a king and she's a servant. She turns and is gone.

After the battleship, Maureen buys two ice creams and they walk a long way through loads of people, get on a bus and off by the train station. They're much too early for their train so they have to wait on another bench until it comes. Eventually, they're sitting opposite each other in the carriage, a beige plastic table between them, jutting into Maureen's belly.

"Snack?" says Maureen, pulling out a bar of chocolate. She breaks off two small pieces and pushes the rest across the table. Leon can't believe how many treats she brought with her and how she isn't telling him off for eating them. He's had a toothache all day and the sweets make it worse but he still takes the chocolate. As it melts, he presses his tongue against the molar at the back and the pain becomes nice pain and slinks off to the back of his mind with all the things he doesn't want to remember.

"Something I've been meaning to tell you," says Maureen.

Leon looks out of the window. They're passing the backs of houses, graffiti on walls, skinny trees growing out of concrete, underwear and vests strung up in gardens, paddling pools, abandoned fridges, scrubland, old factories, houses again. He wonders what it would be like to live so close to a train station or a train track and, if he lived in one of those tall, narrow houses, whether or not he could run to the end of the garden, climb over the fence, and jump on to the train as it sped past, and he thinks again about running away, riding on the roofs of the carriages with his backpack.

"You listening?" she says.

Leon nods and Maureen leans forward.

"You are not going anywhere," she says and she says it slowly, like he's five years old.

"You're staying with me," she repeats, with her heavy chest flat on the table.

"At the seaside?"

"Leon," says Maureen with a little shake of her head, "I'll tell you what the danger is in hearing half a conversation."

She waits for him to say something so he says, "Yes."

"You're likely to jump to conclusions. Know what that means?"

"Being wrong."

"Exactly. I'm not going to the seaside. Sylvia's not going to the seaside. You're not going to the seaside. I'm not getting a bloody dog. Do you believe me?"

"Yes."

"So, for the tenth time, we are not going to the seaside. Except for a day trip maybe."

"When?"

"I don't know when."

She leans back in her seat and goes quiet. Leon sees right inside her head. He sees her thinking of what to say to him and it's going to be something bad, because she looks like she's going to cry again, and he's sick of ladies crying all the time. He only cries when things are bad but they cry all the time, sometimes for ages, and their lips go fat and their faces go blotchy. But this time, Maureen's tears don't come out. Instead she looks at him and winks.

"When I was your age, well, fifteen actually, I broke my arm and I had it in plaster for the longest time. It was summer vacation. We had the school playing fields at the bottom of our garden and I used to be a bit of a tomboy—yes, use your imagination, Leon. I would climb over the railings, kick the sand out of the box where they did the long jump, bend the branches off the trees, and try to break in. Couldn't wait to get out the place when it was open. I was always on my own, up to no good. Anyway, I broke my arm swinging from a tree, fell over, landed funny. God, it was bloody itchy in the heat. I used to get my mom's knitting needles and shove it down the gap and scratch it but I couldn't quite get the right spot. Know what I mean? I couldn't quite reach the right place and I would squirm and wriggle, trying to get a bit of relief. Sylvia used to have to help—sometimes she would knock on the plaster but that would hurt as well. Used to make me cry sometimes with the frustration of it and the pain and the way I was trapped in this bloody plaster of paris and I couldn't go out exploring and, oh, I know it seems like nothing to you but I was so unhappy. I hated that summer. Hated it."

"Yes," says Leon.

"What I'm trying to say is this, Leon. And that was a bad example but never mind. This isn't the whole of your life, love. This is a bit of your life. It all seems bloody awful, I know, with your mom and Jake and . . ."

She takes a tissue out of her handbag and puts it in his hand. She undoes a family bag of Mint Imperials and tips a handful on the table and they roll all over the place.

"The thing is this and you have to believe me. I've made arrangements with the Social. I've been working on this for weeks but I didn't want to tell you until it was official. It's taken forever to get it all organized. So, the point is, you'll be with me until you leave school and even after, if you like. I get you. You get me. That's the deal. But it's got strings attached. Do you know what that means?"

"Yes."

"What?"

"It's got to be tied up."

"No. Well, yes. It means that to tie the deal up, to make it a proper thing that you can't undo, you have to make a promise to me. And if you make the promise you can't go back on it. Two promises, actually, Leon."

"Yes."

"Wipe your face."

She sniffs and holds two fingers up but not the swearing ones.

"One," she says, "you have to tell me when something's wrong. Don't matter what it is and it don't matter if it's me that's done it. And I'm not saying I can fix it, because I can't fix everything. I'm not a magician, am I?"

"No."

"Second, don't run away."

"Yes."

"Sorry?"

"I won't."

"Good. That's a deal then."

"Yes."

"No more sweets for a week. Not for me and not for you. We've gone overboard today and I get weighed tomorrow."

She pinches the fat on the top of her arms.

"Shit."

42

On the day of the Royal Wedding, Mr. Devlin comes by really early in the morning. He rings the bell before Sylvia and Maureen are out of bed, so Leon has to run to the door.

"Good," he says, "someone's awake at least."

He walks in and puts the kettle on.

"Sylvia said come early," says Mr. Devlin and Leon runs and knocks on Sylvia's door, opens it an inch.

"Sylvia," he says, "he's here."

"Victor? Shit, shit, shit . . ." she hisses. "Ten minutes."

Leon runs back to the kitchen.

"So," Mr. Devlin says. "We've got a lot to do for your party."

"It's not my party," says Leon.

"It's not mine, either," he replies. "She is not my queen, he is not my prince. I don't believe in royal anything."

"Why not?"

"That's a long and complicated explanation and I haven't had my coffee yet."

Leon takes a mug out of the cupboard and shows Mr. Devlin where the coffee is. Sylvia always makes Mr. Devlin's coffee, so she won't mind. Leon takes a bowl for himself and sprinkles his cornflakes in.

"Is your queen in Ireland?" he asks.

Leon needs to be at the sugar stage before Sylvia comes into the kitchen and catches him. Mr. Devlin leans on the kitchen counter and folds his arms.

"There are no kings or queens, Leon. There are people. This marriage is a marriage between two people, a man and a woman, nothing more. Maybe they love each other, maybe they don't, but it is not a fairy tale. It is a wedding. And today we're making a wedding party, a celebration for people who believe in witches and wizards and princesses rescued from towers."

"Are you still coming?"

"Yes."

"Why?"

"Because I was invited," he says and nods at Sylvia, who is standing in the doorway pulling the belt on her dressing gown.

"Morning, Vic," she says. "Bit early, isn't it?"

Sylvia has creases on her face and she keeps fluffing up her hair at the sides. She looks like she's still asleep. Mr. Devlin stands up straight.

"I'm sorry, I thought I'd make an early start. I can come back later."

"Make me a coffee and I'll think about it."

She brushes past him and opens the back door. She lights a cigarette and blows the smoke up the garden path.

"Don't say anything," she shouts behind her. "I'm not having that conversation again. I have to have one first thing."

"The worst one is the one you can't do without," Mr. Devlin says.

"That apply to men?" she answers and he laughs.

Mr. Devlin is clean these days and he's found some other clothes. Leon has seen him washing his hands in the water barrel by his shed before he comes to see Sylvia.

While no one is looking, Leon sprinkles extra sugar on his cornflakes. Mr. Devlin won't notice anyway, because all he does these days is look at Sylvia, and she keeps saying what he thinks about things, like, "Victor thinks there'll be more riots," or, "Victor thinks Northern Ireland is merely a symptom of a greater disease." And Maureen always winks at Leon and raises her eyes to the ceiling. Sylvia saw a leather jacket on TV and she said she was going to buy it for Mr. Devlin so he didn't have to wear his army coat anymore but Leon thinks he will look silly in it, like he's borrowed it from Tufty.

Mr. Devlin finishes his coffee and puts the mug on the side.

"Right, me and Leon can start. Mr. Atwal is bringing the trestle tables in his van. I need the triangles from you and the flags on string."

Sylvia laughs.

"Triangles? Bunting, you bloody fool, bunting. How many times?"

"Ah, yes, bunting," he says but Leon knows he's teasing her.

Maureen shuffles into the kitchen in her new purple slippers.

"Well, they fit," she says, smoothing her dressing gown over her belly. "Thank you, Leon. Though how you managed to get the money and go to my favorite shop and get the right size, I don't know."

"I . . ."

"He did some clearing for me," says Mr. Devlin and winks. "Once we got the go-ahead from the committee, we had to get the place ready for the party so he helped me."

"Hmm," says Maureen as she shoos him out of the way and puts the kettle on. "Didn't realize that I was moving into a house of conspirators. Sylvia's decided to stop buying cake, biscuits, chocolate, and anything that tastes nice, thank you, Sylvia," she shouts. "Leon's never in the house and couldn't get the dirt from under his fingernails if he washed with carbolic soap, and as for you—"

"What about him?" says Sylvia, coming in from the garden.

"He's got you like a sixteen-year-old, that's what."

"Belt up, Mo. You're jealous."

They elbow each other and start sniggering like little girls but the kitchen's too small, so Leon goes and gets his backpack and puts it up by the front door. Then he goes into the lounge and presses the button on the television.

"No you don't, mister," shouts Maureen. "Not today."

From then on it's up to the allotment and job after job after job for Leon. No one seems to realize he can't be in two places at the same time. Hold this, carry that, wait here, duck under there, balance this on that, fetch me this, hold that straight, little to the left, higher, where's my this, have you got a that. It goes on all morning until the wedding itself. When everyone else disappears to watch it on television, Leon, Tufty, and Mr. Devlin decide to stay where they are. They sit on the folding chairs while Mr. Devlin's barbecue heats up and Tufty takes some cans of Coke out of his tub.

"May I ask if you remembered the right music, Mr. Burrows?" says Mr. Devlin. "Please have some regard for your neighbors. We don't all like African music."

"Reggae, man. Roots, rockers, dub."

"Precisely. We don't want that today. At least, the ladies won't want it. I don't mind."

"Yeah, right."

Leon likes it when they pretend to argue like they used to. He gets up and pokes the charcoal with the metal tongs.

"What do you think, Leon?"

"It's nearly ready."

"Good," says Mr. Devlin, "and don't forget to water your plants before the guests arrive. It's going to be hot."

Leon finishes his drink, takes his backpack, and walks over to his plot. It's taken weeks and weeks but finally some of his Scarlet Emperor beans are ready. They are so tall they hang in twisting plaits off the top of their wigwams, and tiny little bean pods are sprouting everywhere.

Leon fetches his watering can and fills it up. He waters his Scarlet Emperor plants until he's sure they have everything they need. He's always been good at looking after things. When Maureen comes he's going to pick all the best beans for her but he'll let the tiny little ones stay out in the sun for a bit longer. Tufty told him that he had to leave some of the beans on the vine to grow long and fat, then at the end of the summer he has to pick them, hang them up to dry in his shed, and put them in a jar for next year. Mr. Devlin said that next spring he can have half a plot instead of a quarter.

One of the young pods hangs low, right next to Leon's face. He pulls it off gently and breaks it open. Inside are five tiny black seeds, smaller than his little fingernail. He picks one out and holds it up to the sun. It's glistening and damp from its bean-pod bed and so light he can hardly feel it on his palm. It's as black as the middle bit of Jake's eyes, and just as sparkly. If Jake was here, Leon would let him hold the little seed for a moment but he would have to be careful in case he's still putting everything in his mouth.

Leon rolls the seed between his fingers and feels it yield under his skin. It's strange to think that this little black bean will grow up to be a big plant and that plant will have its own seeds to make another plant and another seed and this will go on, over and over again, for years, and he remembers what Maureen said about Jake. He hasn't left forever.

He unzips his pack and tips everything out, his gardening tools and his packets of seeds. He scratches out a straight line with his trowel and makes ten little holes. He picks up the packet of Take-A-Chance and tips the seeds into his hand. They are small and brown with wrinkled skin and nobody knows what's inside. He places them carefully in the soil and covers them over. He'll water them and look after them and hope for the best. There are lots more seeds to plant but he's got too much to do today, and anyway, he can hear Maureen calling. She'll want him to do another job or carry something or fetch her a chair.

"Leon!"

He turns and runs.

"Coming!"

ACKNOWLEDGMENTS

I've had lots of help along the way. You know who you are, hand-holders, tear-wipers, cooks, listeners and laughers, critics, advisors, strategists, dressers, nip-and-tuckers, trainers, architects, sages, and optimists as well as the lovely, quiet people of constant faith, always in the background with affection, tea, and biscuits. Thanks to you all: Caroline Smith, Anna Lawrence, Steph Vidal-Hall, Elisabeth Charis, Rhoda Greaves, Bart Bennett, Justin David, Nina Black, Esther Moir, Lezanne Clannachan, Matt Hodgkinson, Renni Browne, Leslie Goldberg, Julia Bell, Annie Murray, James Hawes, and all the dedicated writers of Oxford Narrative Group; also Julia de Waal, Edmund de Waal, and Alex Myers.

Thanks also to the scary talents at Leather Lane Writers for your support, your brains, and your dedication to the craft.

I'm indebted to Venetia Butterfield and the Viking team and to Millicent Bennett at Simon & Schuster US for incisive editorial brilliance. Special thanks and appreciation to Jo Unwin, my wise and clever agent, for being there and taking me forward.

Thanks to Marcus Gärtner at Rowohlt Verlag in Germany, Melissa van der Wagt at Uitgeverij Cargo in the Netherlands, and Deborah Druba at Editions Kero in France for all their energy and enthusiasm for Leon's story right from the beginning.

To my brothers, Conrad and Dean, and sisters, Kim, Tracey, and Karen—can't put it into words but probably don't have to. Always.

Thank you to John for his love and support. And, finally, to my beautiful children, Bethany and Luke, admiration, boundless love, and my profound gratitude for inspiring me to tell Leon's story.

ABOUT THE AUTHOR

Kit de Waal is published in various anthologies *(Fish Prize* 2011 & 2012, *The Sea in Birmingham* 2013, *Final Chapters* 2013, and *A Midlands Odyssey* 2015*)* and on *Radio 4 Readings.* She came second in the Costa Short Story Prize 2014 with "The Old Man & The Suit," second in the Bath Short Story Prize 2014 with 'The Beautiful Thing,' and second in the Bare Fiction Flash Fiction Prize. She won the Readers' Prize at the Leeds Literary Prize 2014, and the Bridport Prize for Flash Fiction in 2014 and again in 2015. She lives in Leamington Spa, England with her two children. *My Name Is Leon* is her first novel.